# my valentine in verona

TESS RINI

ISBN: 979-8-9904586-3-5 (e-book)

ISBN: 979-8-9904586-4-2 (paperback)

Tessrini.com

Publisher: One Punch Productions, LLC

Cover design and interior formatting by *Hannah Linder Designs*

# FRIENDS OF THE RINALDI FAMILY

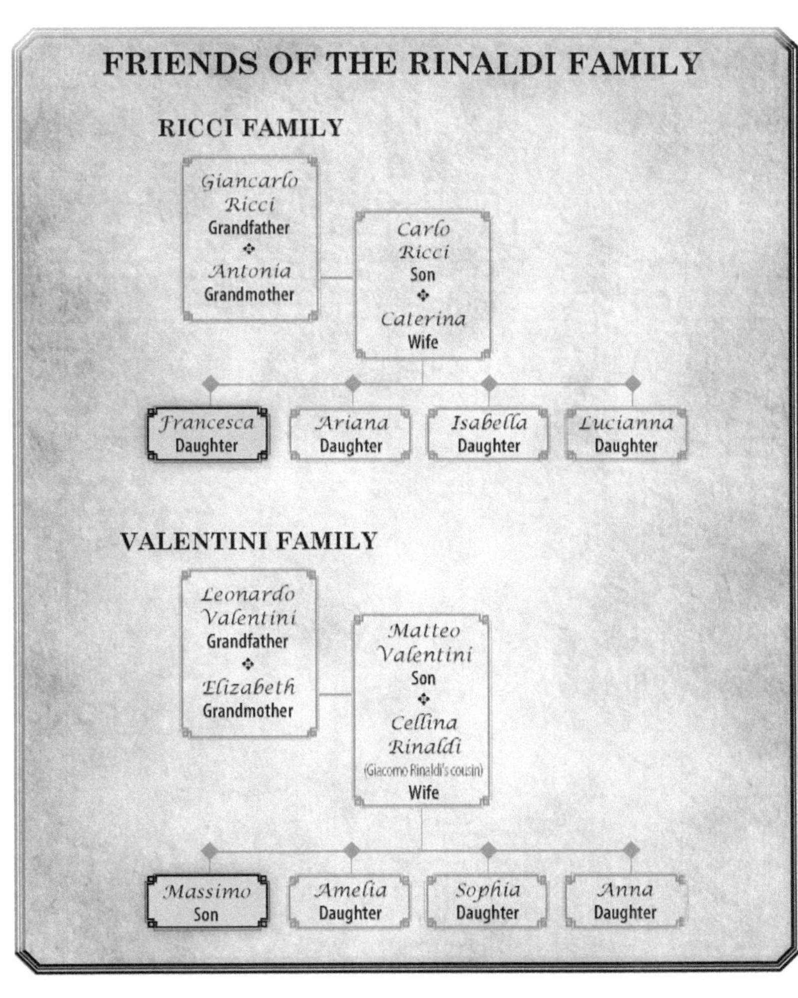

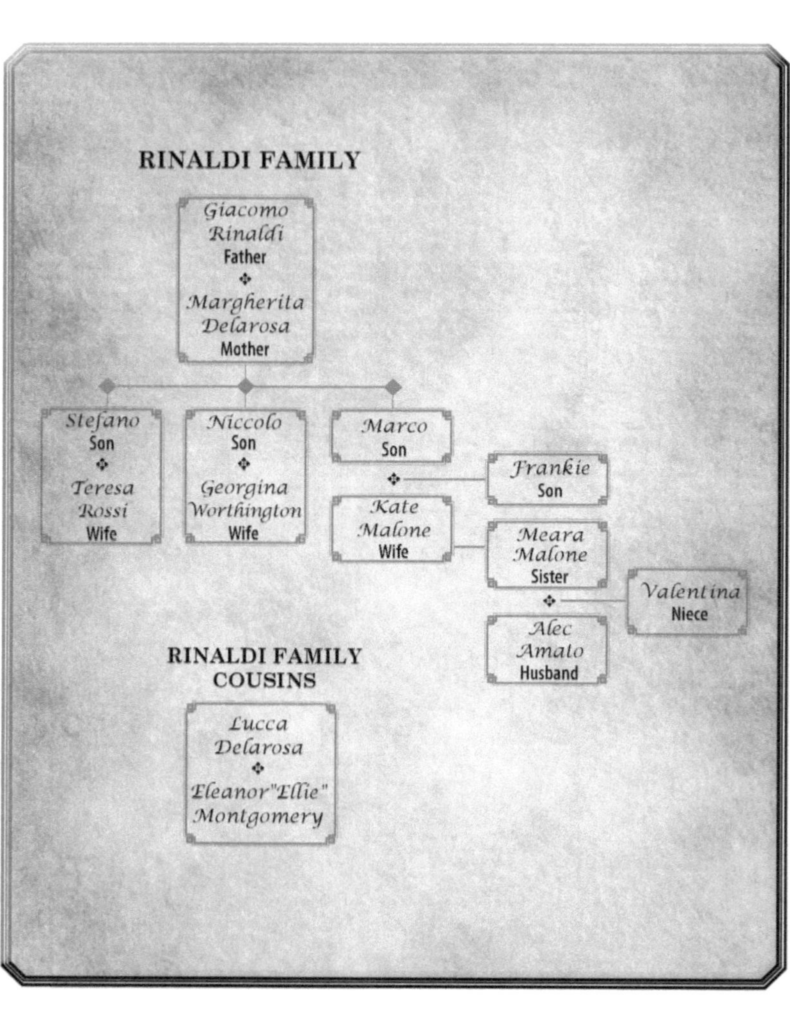

RINALDI FAMILY
Giacomo Rinaldi
Father
Margherita Delarosa
Mother
Stefano
Son
Teresa Rossi
Wife
Niccolo
Son
Georgina Worthington
Wife
Marco
Son
Kate Malone
Wife
Frankie
Son
Meara Malone
Sister
Alec Amato
Husband
Valentina
Niece
RINALDI FAMILY COUSINS
Lucca Delarosa
Eleanor "Ellie" Montgomery

Where we travel in *My Valentine in Verona* (with Rome as a reference!)

*one*

Francesca Ricci swung her long legs out of the luxury black SUV and stood in the circular drive. She gazed upward at her childhood home, its intricate stonework and twin turrets silhouetted against the Verona hills. The villa stood majestically, overlooking the famed Adige River with its varied bridges criss-crossing it.

She took a deep breath and smiled at the chauffeur, thanking him in a quiet voice. It was a pleasant treat that her friend and boss Marco Rinaldi had kindly arranged for her travel home. She was flown by helicopter from the Amalfi Coast to Verona, where a driver had been waiting. It was only a short drive, and she hadn't had time to even think about her arrival. Behind her, the driver was busy getting her luggage from the vehicle. Smoothing her hands over her chic blue dress, she carefully stepped up to the door in her usual spikey heels. Before she could even grasp the old-fashioned door knocker, the massive mahogany door was swept open.

"*Signorina* Francesca! You are a sight for sore eyes!"

Francesca grinned and accepted the kiss on each cheek and long hug from Graham, the family's trusted friend and butler of sorts. He had been with their family as long as she could remember. Standing a little hunched now, his hair had almost disappeared except for tufts of white in the back. He still wore his trademark gray suit with a striped old-fashioned waistcoat. His wide smile was welcoming under his thick white mustache.

"I waited to welcome you," Graham said, his eyes twinkling.

Francesca turned to kindly ask the chauffeur to carry her luggage inside, since Graham would try and undoubtedly strain his already weak back. She stepped inside the impressive entryway with two elegant marble staircases, one on each side, which traveled up to the second level. But that's where the simplicity ended. The entryway was a collection of eclectic furniture, both antique and modern, painted in different hues that somehow all came together in what visitors often deemed as a "comfortable home." She took a deep breath and smiled.

"It's unusually quiet in here," Francesca commented. "Where is everyone?"

"They have all gone to church. It's Sunday," he reminded her. "Therefore, the staff have the day off. Your parents and sisters have been invited out for luncheon. They probably will not return until later this afternoon. They were unsure of your arrival time."

The chauffeur put down the last of her cases, and she thanked him profusely, opening her purse, wanting to give him a tip.

He held up his hands, smiling. "No, no, *signorina. Signore* Marco would be very upset. *Per favore*, it is my pleasure." He inclined his head and departed with a smile.

Francesca turned back to Graham, who placed his bowler hat square on his head. "I am sorry, *Signorina* Francesca. I already made plans with Miriam, or I would have stayed for the afternoon." He looked uncertain. "Perhaps I should cancel."

Francesca rushed to reassure him. Graham and his longtime friend Miriam had a standing Sunday lunch date. It would be awkward to tell him the truth, which was that she had intentionally not communicated with her parents about when she was to arrive. In fact, she had not spoken with them since their summons home.

"Of course not, Graham! I'll be fine on my own. In fact, it will be nice to have the place all to myself before everyone gets home. Please go enjoy yourself and give my best to Miriam."

She saw Graham to the door, and he walked dignified down the drive toward his small Fiat. Closing the heavy door, she sighed. Kicking off her high heels, she grabbed one of her suitcases and began the ascent to her room. Of course, her room had to be on the third floor of the house.

Dragging the suitcase up another smaller flight of stairs, she finally arrived at the circular room located in one of the turrets. Still painted a light lavender, the room looked just like it had when she was sixteen years old with its canopy bed and matching vanity. How she had loved it here, sitting on the chintz-covered window seat and watching the city of Verona at her feet. Walking over to the window now, she smiled a little. Though she was not pleased about involuntarily returning home, she felt a little calmer in this beloved little corner of her youth.

Stepping away from the window, she frowned. She was no longer a lovesick teenager dreaming of her handsome prince. It was time to face reality and her parents and grandparents. At least she had several hours of peace to look forward to before she would need to inform them of her intention of not staying long.

In her closet, hung the clothes she had purposely left behind. Grabbing a T-shirt that advertised her once favorite pop star and a pair of faded Levis, she quickly changed. Might as well get comfortable and have some lunch. She swept her waist-length, straight blonde hair into a high ponytail and took her contacts out of her dry eyes. Putting on a pair of stylish tortoiseshell glasses, she felt much more comfortable.

Thirty minutes later, Francesca, sat back in a kitchen chair.

After raiding the refrigerator and grilling herself a *caprese panino*, with ripe tomatoes and soft fresh mozzarella cheese, she was now full and already a little bored. Suddenly, an idea came to her. She would cook dinner for the family! Sunday nights were always a family dinner, but with the staff gone, the family usually foraged through the refrigerator, often making a frittata filled with a variety of ingredients or ate a cold dinner of Italian meats or cheese. They had indulged in some wild creations over the years. Tonight, they could have a proper dinner.

Cutting vegetables and adding them to a pot, Francesca began assembling everything for a *pasta fagioli*. It was a favorite, with its fresh vegetables, tomato sauce, and beans. She loved it with enormous amounts of parmesan cheese and some good crusty bread. With that image, she put together a dough to rise. Tonight promised to be a battlefield. Maybe she could weaken her parent's fortitude with some delicious food.

After setting the cast iron Dutch oven to simmer, she added ingredients to a mixer for her signature chocolate cake. Pouring that into two round pans, she deftly shook them so the batter was even and then placed them in the large modern oven. Straightening, she adjusted the pink apron she had donned before cooking.

Cleaning up the kitchen took some time, as she was not an organized cook. She wiped down the antique wooden island that stood in the center of the modern kitchen and took a deep breath. The combination of the soup and cake smelled like home to her. If only she was home under different circumstances!

Stirring the *pasta fagioli*, she smiled a little. If her friends on the Amalfi Coast could see her now. Over the years, she had intentionally presented a polished and confident image to them. Marco and his wife, Kate, who had now become a friend of hers as well, would be flabbergasted that she could even crack an egg, let alone make a meal.

The door knocker's banging echoed through the kitchen, and

she frowned. Who could be at the front door? Her stomach twisted with unease. Wait. Maybe it was Armando. The foreman sometimes liked to stop by after church. As she entered the entryway, the person outside was now impatiently banging the knocker. It was Armando alright. He was always an enthusiastic knocker. Whipping the door open, she opened her mouth to greet him, only to close it quickly in surprise.

Standing there was an extremely handsome man, wearing a gray suit and conservative burgundy tie. Though he was dressed formally, his brown wavy hair was a little unruly, and a small shadow of a beard graced his strong jawline. His deep brown eyes humorously twinkled, surveying her from head to foot. Remembering the pink apron, she instantly wanted to whip it off, but quickly remembered what she wore underneath it wasn't much better. The man looked slightly familiar, but she immediately dismissed that thought.

"*Posso aiutarti*?" she asked in Italian, speaking purposely with a clipped tone.

"*Inglese*?" he asked gently. "My Italian is a little rusty."

She gave a cool nod. "Can I help you?"

"I believe you can," he said, his smile growing slowly, his eyes still dancing with humor. "I am here to see you, Princess Francesca."

Frowning darkly, she straightened her posture in what she hoped was a dignified manner despite the apron. She cooly surveyed him. "While my name is Francesca, I am not a princess."

"But you are," he said softly.

Her frown grew. "Yes, technically. But we no longer use titles in Italy. I am not addressed as such...by *anyone*," she said with emphasis.

He nodded, confidently leaning up against the doorjamb, as if he had all the time in the world.

"You seem to know who I am, but I am sorry I do not know

you." Suddenly, she became suspicious, and placed her hand on the doorknob in case she needed to close it quickly. Perhaps he was there for some nefarious reason. She should have been more careful before opening the door!

"Who are you?" she asked sharply.

His eyes searched her face, as if memorizing it. His gaze was almost mocking. When he spoke, his voice was succinct.

"Your fiancé."

*two*

"You are definitely *not* my fiancé," Francesca said matter-of-factly. "I have been betrothed to Mario Bianchini—well, I mean, my grandparents promised—not me. It's not a real betrothal..." she stammered, feeling her face flush.

This stranger continued regarding her. Finally, he spoke. "Mario is my cousin," he said, raising an eyebrow. "And how do you say 'he's flown the coop' in Italian?"

Francesca opened her mouth, unsure how to answer. She was completely thrown off balance. Suddenly, her nose twitched. "*Mia la torta!*" she exclaimed. Forgetting the tall, immensely attractive stranger in the quest to rescue her cake, she took off running toward the kitchen.

Taking the round pans from the oven and placing them on the waiting racks on the island—the man having followed her—she blew a couple of strands from her hot face and waited for her glasses to de-mist. Taking off an oven glove, she patted the cakes gently with her long fingers.

"Did they burn?" he asked from the doorway.

"No, thankfully. They'll be dry, though. They're over-baked," she explained without looking up. Her nerves were shooting

7

through her. This was the old Francesca, the one she had worked so hard to overcome. Why could he not have arrived when she was dressed in her armor—wearing fine sophisticated clothes, her makeup and hair perfectly styled? Finally, she glanced up and met his eyes and her heartbeat faster at his intent gaze.

"Who are you really?" she asked, her voice sounding higher pitched than normal. She cleared her throat. "And I did not give you permission to enter our home."

"Please excuse me. I can go back to the doorstep if you prefer. I thought we should discuss this inside."

At her silent shake of her head, he continued. "I should have introduced myself earlier." He moved away from the doorway and came closer to her in the kitchen, his eyes never leaving hers. "Massimo Valentini," he said, reaching a hand out to shake hers. "But you can call me Max."

She had started to extend her hand but now backed away, her eyes growing wide. "But that can't be true."

He smiled a little. "I assure you, I am not lying."

Shaking her head, she looked at him uncertainly. "I do not doubt who you are. It's just that you are a Valentini. My parents...mostly my grandparents...despise anything to do with the Valentini Family. They would never want me tied to anything to do with your family."

"I understand," he said quietly. "But it is complicated and I wish to explain it to you and see if we can come to . . . some kind of agreement. You see, my flighty cousin has gone off to marry this week's love of his life. They should be arriving in America about now. And with him goes his promise to marry you. And there is more if you will listen."

FRANCESCA POURED the tea with a steady hand that betrayed how she really felt. Max was sitting at the kitchen's rustic farmhouse table, drawing a well-tailored pant leg over another. He looked comfortable, like he sat there every day of his life, gently sipping tea.

Trying to regain her composure, she flung her apron off and shook her hair out of the ponytail. His eyes widened, but he didn't comment on the sheer amount of it.

She flung it behind her back with a forced, fake confidence and sat down across from him, her brown eyes staring at him. Racking her brains, she tried to think of where to even start, but she couldn't formulate words. Her mind was a turbulent train of thought in front of this stranger who somehow knew her identity. It was only two weeks ago her parents had called her while she was at her good friend, Nico Rinaldi's wedding. She had known the Rinaldi brothers, Marco, Stefano and Nico for a long time now. Marco, the oldest and now CEO of the family's vast dynasty, had initially hired her to run a small shop in Positano. That was before he had ascended to lead Oro Industries on the death of his *Zio* Angelo. Prior to that, he had overseen all the small local businesses his uncle had invested in during a time when Positano did not attract the tourism it now did. Initially, Francesca had a small crush on the handsome billionaire, but he had always been the consummate gentleman around her and they had instead become good friends. He had even introduced her to his mother, Margherita, who insisted Francesca was now adopted family and should call her "Rita."

Eventually, through Marco, she met Stefano, a much leaner, serious version of his older brother. Ironically, Stefano had married Kate's best friend Teresa. Though he still worked for Oro, he was also now traveling the country filming a television series produced by their movie star cousin, Lucca. The youngest Rinaldi was Niccolo, who was the sweet brother she had always yearned for. Nico, who was a well-known expert on agricultural and sustainable farming, had recently married a woman he first fell in love as a teenager. It was at Nico and Georgina's wedding that she had received the phone call from her parents.

Growing up with three sisters, Francesca had been surrounded by female energy. Her sisters, Arianna, Isabella, and Luciana, differed vastly from her, both in looks and personality. Francesca, the oldest, was the only blonde. Her sisters were all brunettes. With the exception of Isabella, who was on the quieter side, they all tended to be loud and gregarious. Francesca also outshot them all in height. As she continued to grow taller, she tried to shrink herself down, but her mother had constantly been there to rap her on the spine and tell her to stand up straight. Now she liked her powerful height.

As the oldest daughter, Francesca believed she should be confident and self-possessed. Instead, she was painfully shy, happier to spend her days reading and dreaming than having conversations. As the eldest daughter of the House of Ricci, she was extended the title of princess, but as she had told Max, that was something from days gone past.

Her family descended from a branch of Italy's royal family. They had lost their fashion business in Milan in a fierce battle with Leonardo and Elisabetta Valentini. And though she was very young at the time, Francesca remembered the stress on her parents, Carlo and Caterina. They had relocated to Verona with her paternal grandparents, to manage a small vineyard. That small vineyard had grown over the years, with her grandfather buying more and more property in the Veneto region, as well as Lombardy to the west and Emilia-Romangna to the south. Meanwhile, Carlo had studied under some of Italy's finest winemakers and had honed his own skills. Now, decades later, their father's winemaking skills were renowned and Ricci wines were sold globally, especially their prosecco and soave wine.

Francesca, who had no interest in winemaking at all, had left five years earlier, right after university at the age of twenty-two. She had traveled south, longing to be near a coastline. Settling in

Positano, she soon met Marco and was pleased when he hired her to manage a small shop. As she stepped into the role, she continued to transform into a much more sophisticated version of herself. The new Francesca wore designer clothes and carefully applied makeup. Francesca perfected a cool exterior. And though she made friends cautiously, she now boasted many. Often she felt guilty for not sharing much with them. She remained guarded about her personal life. Few knew anything about her family and remarkably, didn't ask many questions.

It was only after her upsetting call from her parents at Nico and Georgie's wedding that the truth emerged. While she was happy for Nico and Georgie, people likely noticed her pained expression at the reception. Marco's wife Kate certainly did, and she stared at her suspiciously before whispering something in her husband's ear. Dear Katie must have known Francesca was ready to lose it. Marco had solemnly asked her to dance, leading her over to a corner of the immense dance floor. It was there at his gentle probing that she told him her parents wanted her to return home. It had been difficult explaining without telling him her entire life story. Marco had asked no questions but offered to help her with transportation. He told her he would leave her position open for a while should she choose to move back. Francesca's assistant, Allegra would temporarily stand in for her.

Francesca had kicked herself for even answering her phone at the reception. Her parents rarely contacted her, trusting to wait for her faithful call every Sunday evening. When she saw her father's name flash on her phone, her mind went to the worst. Was someone ill? Instead, her father had calmly told her it was time for her to return to Verona and begin the next phase in her life. She understood this all probably originated with her grandparents, and her father was forced to appease them. It was frustrating to know her parents and grandparents focused on her taking her place in society, which also undoubtedly meant marriage. While her parents would never insist she marry someone, she didn't love or even entertain the ancient betrothal promise, she knew they wanted to see her at the very least represent their family. It had been her grandparents and Mario's grandparents that had claimed them betrothed as children. They were part of Italy's old guard, and her grandparents had sought who they thought would be an appropriate husband for her. She and Mario had often laughed about it, never taking it seriously.

Good-looking but always a flirt, Mario had stolen her heart very early on. He obviously never felt any attraction to her. As teens, they relaxed in the fields beyond their vineyards while he talked and she listened. Tall and gangly, with enormous glasses and braids, she felt honored to be his friend. He would wax on about his current infatuations, and she would hang on his every word. She watched the girls at school throw themselves at him, and he was seemingly in his element as they did so. It wasn't all for naught; he often thanked Francesca with a hearty slap on the back, saying she was the best. The best what? Listener, she supposed. When he left for university and they had kept in touch for a time, but again, only as friends. He seemed to seek her advice about the most recent girl of the week. And while deep down she knew he was self-absorbed and pompous, she still thought of him as the friendly boy who laid in the grass with her at least giving her attention. Even if it was all about him.

As she got older, her glasses were replaced by contacts. She had her hair styled and watched videos online on how to put it in a tight chignon or pulling pieces of it back on the crown of her head. Practicing that faithfully, she also bought expensive makeup and taught herself how to best apply it, wondering what Mario would have to say now if he saw her. But he didn't return. Instead, he went to work in Milan's financial district, which his grandparents boasted about.

Despite her glow-up, Francesca was mortified at the thought of Mario ever feeling forced to marry her. It was an archaic custom that no one ever practiced anymore. These were modern times and it was with her parent's full blessing that she had left to find her way in life.

Her younger sisters didn't have to face reality yet. In fact, they were thriving. Arianna was working as a junior architect in Milan, Isabella was finishing university and the baby of the family at twelve, Luciana was still attending school.

Admittedly, Francesca had been shocked when she received a call from Mario one day. For a moment, she had shrunk back into her former self, shy and insecure. But then, realizing he couldn't see her, she relaxed, and they spent an hour talking. Of course, he did the talking and she listened, but it still had been nice. It was he who had brought up the decades old betrothal and she had laughed and assured him it was family folklore. He seemed uncertain about it, insisting his grandparents still hung on to the fact that once each of them got over sowing their wild oats, they would return to Verona and marry.

They had agreed to not rock the boat and instead pretend that was their intention. Mario's grandparents were getting older and the idea of their grandson marrying into the House of Ricci brought them happiness. Francesca and Mario agreed it wouldn't hurt to continue the pretense. After all, they hadn't seen each other in years. What would a little more time hurt?

"If I'm not mistaken, that's the oven timer."

Francesca jumped and felt herself turning pink, hearing the incessant buzzing coming from the kitchen timer. She ran to the oven, taking out the loaf she had put in when she had taken the cake out. Turning around, she met Max's intent gaze. She had almost forgotten he was there.

"What were you deep in thought about, Princess?"

"I told you. Lay off the princess thing! I'm not really one. Only in name. How...how did you know who I was? I could have been the cook!"

He smiled gently. "I'd have known you anywhere. Mario's description was spot on."

She frowned slightly. "I don't usually look like this."

"Of course not. I don't imagine you are wearing an apron all day."

"No, it's not that," she began uneasily. "I actually usually look quite different."

He raised his eyebrows. "That's a shame because I like the way you look."

Francesca felt flustered. "Uh, thank you. I mean, I don't know what..." Stopping, she took a deep breath and got to the point. "Why are you here? Were you serious before? And how could you be? Mario was not a Valentini."

He nodded and put down his cup, leaning forward attentively.

"So many questions," he said and smiled briefly before continuing. "You are correct. Our grandmothers are sisters. His grandmother married a Bianchini and mine, the evil Valentini. We are the black sheep, of course, and I'm sure the Bianchini family would never have wanted you to know about that detestable branch of the family that has long been cut off. The sisters—our grandmothers—have not spoken in decades."

She glanced at him suspiciously, but he continued. "Mario and I met at a university in the States. Though we were never close, we kept our meeting a secret. We became reacquainted in Milan. He confided in me his grandparents' edict to marry their best friends' granddaughter. But then last week he suddenly called me to tell me he was eloping with his fiancée."

"And you just showed up here in his place? Like you're just going to swap?" she asked incredulously. She stared at him with narrowed eyes. "The strange thing is you do look vaguely familiar."

"I can promise you we have not met. But I have an idea, and I hope you'll listen."

Shaking her head, she stared at him astounded. "If my family even knew I was talking to you right now, they would throw you out of the house. Do you know how deep the wounds are? What your family did to mine? I've heard about the old feud all my life!"

He leaned forward and his hand grasped one of hers that was lying on the table. She started to withdraw it, but he held firmly on to it and she ignored the tingling that shot up her spine. His eyes searched hers and she almost forgot who he was for a minute. "What if we were to try to heal those old wounds and also build something spectacular?"

She raised an eyebrow, feeling interested despite her reservations. "What do you have in mind?"

MAX SAT BACK, still grasping her warm hand. He ran his thumb over her long fingers, intentionally trying to throw her off balance. He was delighted to find her at home by herself, dressed casually and in the middle of baking. If her family had been home, his plan would have been to say he had a message from Mario and possibly arrange to meet with her in town.

Fate had intervened, and not only was she alone but also seemed to be feeling vulnerable at being caught unaware. She was a far cry from the chic and confident woman he had seen at Marco's wedding. Francesca had been correct about him being familiar and at some point, he would admit the truth to her. He had almost worked up the nerve to approach her when Marco Rinaldi had casually dropped her name. That had the effect of cold water rushing over him as he knew the negative reaction would be similar to her current feelings.

"You need to get on with it," she said sharply. "My family is going to be home soon, and you will need to leave before they do."

He let go of her hand reluctantly. "What happened between our families was more than twenty years ago," he began.

"Oh, believe me, my grandparents remember it like it was yesterday," she interrupted sharply. "Your family stole our family crest! It was the one thing that was ours. The one thing we can't replace or use. It means everything to my grandfather. What's a royal family without a crest?"

He stared at her, a small frown on his face. "The story that was told to me was that our grandfathers agreed to go into business together, joining their fashion houses so many decades ago. They used the House of Ricci's crest as their logo, but then they had some dispute and your grandfather wanted out."

She stood and crossed her arms. "The story I heard was that your grandfather swindled my grandfather. They had a falling out, and my grandfather no longer trusted him. And for good reason! He had no idea that the crest was tied up as part of the business for 100 years. He only found out when he tried to bottle his own wine and put the crest on it, only to have the House of Valentini sue him!"

Max's eyes widened. "I never heard the part about the wine, but yes, the terms were clear in merger papers your grandfather signed. He saw them for himself. My grandfather put in most of the money—your grandfather put in the crest which had its own value. But, if you know the terms, then you know my family hasn't been able to use it since. The terms state it can't be used unless your grandfather or the heir to his estate gives permission or is part of the business."

"I know what the crest means to us, but why do you care?"

He shook his head. "Think of all the name brands and their logos. My grandfather's company has been without that logo now for two decades. Of course, they produced a new one, but the vintage clothes with the crest go for thousands online. I assume I can trust you to tell you that my grandfather's business is not doing well. It's upsetting to see. We can talk more about it, but that's it in a nutshell. I just want to help him. I haven't been the most attentive grandson," he finished quietly.

"I understand you wanting to help," Francesca said quietly. "I think it's bothered my nonno more than he conveys. Losing the business and the crest has eaten away at him. I know it depresses him still. But do you think anything would change if somehow they were able to end the feud?"

Max raised an eyebrow. "You can imagine the publicity and the hype that would come with the announcement that our two Houses were once again one."

She sat down tentatively and stared at him. "But how do we do that? You're not suggesting marriage for real?"

"No, of course not. I thought we could *suggest* that we have been dating. An engagement would be hinted at. Our families would be forced to reunite for our sakes. Eventually, we could push them toward an agreement."

"I don't know about your nonno, but mine is as stubborn as they come. I don't think it's that easy," Francesca said and gave a small laugh. "It would be like pushing a giant boulder up a hill. Right after he disowned me, of course."

"What about your parents? How would they feel?"

She shrugged. "My parents are much more modern, though I have to say they would be excited at the thought of me even dating someone. After it happened, my father wanted to leave Milan. We moved to Verona, and Papa found success with his wine. He's happier in the long run. But the feud remained as evidenced by how many times over the years these old tales have been repeated. Papa will do whatever Nonno wants."

They both stared off into the distance. Finally, she spoke. "It would have to be slow. Like first, they'd have to get to know you and come to like you."

He turned to meet her gaze. "But once they hear who I am…"

"Perhaps we don't have to tell them for the time being."

"You mean lie?"

She flushed a little. "Well, it doesn't sound great if you put it like that, but just sort of fudge the truth. What's your full name?"

He tried to keep his expression neutral but decided to answer honestly. "Massimo Leonardo Rinaldi Valentini."

Francesca shot out of her chair and stood frowning at him. "That's it! Rinaldi! You were at Marco and Katie's wedding! I saw you there. You kept staring at me!"

He stood slowly and approached her, looking earnest. "Yes, I'm sorry. I should have told you sooner, but I was afraid of your reaction. I didn't dare approach you at the wedding. You would have kicked me to the curb!"

"I don't understand. Kicked you to the curb? What does that mean? And why did you ask me to speak English if you are Italian?"

"I was raised in the States. While I spent some summers here as a child, I didn't move back until recently. My Italian is improving but I'm still more comfortable speaking English. I am learning, though."

"Why did you move back?"

He shrugged. "It's a long story. Someday I may bore you with it. But for now, I am trying to make up for lost time. Marco is another cousin—on my mother's side of the family. He urged me to come speak to you when I told him the story. He told me you would at least hear me out."

"Marco knows? About the betrothal stuff and everything?" she exploded.

Max slowly nodded.

She shook her head. "He never said anything to me."

Max smiled gently. "He knew if you wanted the story told, you would tell him yourself. Marco is the sole of discretion. I can promise you, he will not discuss this with anyone."

"I know he won't. Still, I hope he knows that I didn't intentionally lie to him. I just...people treat you differently when they know about the whole royal bloodline and all that."

He nodded seriously. "I completely understand."

Francesca stared at him. "What do we do when it's over? I mean, if we accomplish this."

For the first time, Max's expression grew serious. "We part. Simple, amicable. I can assure you this will not be a permanent thing," he said coolly.

"But what will our grandparents think then?"

He shrugged. "They'll be so busy with their business they won't care. Especially if we portray it as a mutual and amicable decision."

Francesca bit her lip in thought. She should send him away and think about this. Her family was going to come through that door in a minute.

Almost as if he read her thoughts, he put his hands on her shoulders and met her gaze directly. "I hate to rush you, but either we try or I leave. You said your family was about to return. What is your answer, Francesca?"

Taking a deep breath, her gaze met his. "I'm in," she said quietly. "So, what's next?"

He grinned invitingly at her. "We date!"

# *three*

Francesca opened her mouth to ask Max another question about this plan. This was so sudden and ludicrous. They needed more time to strategize. He should probably leave, and they could meet later and formulate a better timeline. Before she could speak, the front door slammed, and her sisters chattered in the entry hall. Max stepped away from her, his eyes twinkling with humor. She looked at him in horror. They weren't ready for this yet!

"Frannie, please tell me you made your chocolate cake!" Luciana shouted as she ran into the kitchen. Leaping into Francesca's arms, she hugged her tightly. "I missed you."

"I missed you too, Luci," Francesca said, returning the hug. The rest of her family soon followed, excitedly greeting her with hugs and kisses. It took longer than she expected, but suddenly they all turned and realized they had a guest, who was now lazily sprawled against the side of the refrigerator, trying to stay out of the way. If it wasn't so awkward, Francesca would have burst out laughing at their astonished faces.

"Uh, Massimo...Rinaldi, I'd like to present my parents, Carlo and Caterina Ricci and my sisters, Arianna, Isabella and

Luciana," Francesca said in English. Before they could even react, Francesca interjected, "He is a cousin of Marco's."

Her parents, who had advanced forward to greet him, stopped dead in their tracks and turned to glance at her, their eyes wide. Her mother recovered first, approaching Max to kiss him on each cheek.

"*Buonasera*," Caterina said, breaking into rapid Italian.

Francesca interrupted. "Mamma, while Max is Italian, he wasn't raised here. Let's just speak English for now."

Her mother nodded like she understood, but she likely had a million questions.

Carlo was next, moving forward to shake the younger man's hand. "We welcome you into our home," he said formally.

"Are you her boyfriend, and are you staying for dinner?" Luci asked excitedly.

"Luci!" Francesca said, flushing. Arianna clapped a hand over Luci's mouth, obviously trying not to laugh.

"Sorry about that. She doesn't get out often," Arianna said, holding the struggling young girl.

Max's rich laughter seemed to bounce off the walls of the kitchen. "Those are perfectly legit questions, Luci," he said reassuringly, as he strolled toward Francesca, putting an arm around her. "It is so nice to finally meet you all. Francesca speaks of you often, don't you, darling? And yes, Luci, I am her boyfriend. And I will stay for dinner if that is an invitation."

Francesca's mother put a hand to her chest, her quick gaze sliding over Francesca and returning to Max's handsome face. Any moment, she was going to swoon like a Victorian mama. "Of course, Massimo, you are very welcome," she said and beamed up at him.

"Please call me Max."

Arianna had finally let go of Luci, who now came forward to closely assess Max. She looked over at Francesca with admiring eyes.

"No wonder you made the chocolate cake," she whispered loudly, followed by the family's nervous laughter.

FRANCESCA CHANGED into black jeans and a chocolate brown cashmere sweater that matched her eyes. Having popped her contacts in, she sat at her vanity to apply some makeup. She had left Max downstairs with her parents and sisters, and God only knows what was happening or what he was saying. They hadn't had any time to discuss a back story or details about their brand new phony relationship.

Her bedroom door opened slightly, and Arianna peeked in before sliding in and closing it. "I slipped away to come see you. Frannie! Why didn't you tell me? He's absolutely hot! Where on earth did you meet him?"

Francesca glanced briefly at her sister before continuing to apply mascara. "I didn't want to jinx it," she fibbed. She bit her lip. Should she tell her? She and Arianna were close, and she hated lying to her. Still, it was already a tangled web, and that would force her sister to get swept up in this complicated plot. She still wasn't even sure it was going to work.

"We met at Marco's wedding," she said, hedging a little. That was the truth in a way. Whatever was he saying downstairs?

"Well, that's what Max said before I came up. But that was ages ago. You never said a word!"

Francesca stared at her face in the mirror before brushing her hair one last time. She was leaving it long, hanging like a curtain down her back.

"Ari, it's complicated. It's been only recently that we . . . got together," she trailed off, not wanting to lie further. Still, it was true, wasn't it? Very recently.

"He's so sweet and polite. He has Mamma eating out of his

hand already, and Papa offered to show him the vineyard, so he must like him, too."

Francesca frowned into the mirror a little.

"Frannie, don't just sit there frowning at yourself. You look amazing in that sweater."

Francesca pulled it down a little self-consciously. "It feels a little tight."

"That's what makes it look so good," Arianna teased. "And those jeans look great on you. Oh, why can't I have long legs like you? What DNA did you get that the rest of us did not?"

Francesca grinned, standing up and staring at her beautiful petite sister, who was lounging on the bed. "You know, we have some ancestors from the Dolomites. I come from that hearty stock where the rest of you are stereotypical petite Italians," she teased. "Come on, I better get downstairs before the interrogation starts."

Arianna laughed. "Oh, it's already started. I left Luci down there!"

MAX WOULD HAVE BURST out laughing if Francesca hadn't looked so terrified. She walked into the room, gorgeous and fresh, and he couldn't take his eyes off her. The living room was cluttered with colorful but comfortable furniture, framed photos of the family, and a mixture of décor that was oddly cohesive. He sat on a small sofa with Luci sitting next to him, intent on grilling him on his ambition in life. Francesca's parents were sitting opposite on another larger sofa, staring at him, and Isabella had gone to the piano in the corner and was playing softly. The entire scene presented a cozy family happy in each other's company.

Standing, he approached her, searching her eyes. He felt the entire family's gaze on them and though he suddenly desperately wanted to kiss her, he was not going to have their first kiss be in front all of them. Instead, he leaned down and his lips grazed her cheek.

"There you are, looking beautiful as always," he said. Putting an arm around her shoulders, he gently led her back toward a vacant sofa. "Luci, if you don't mind, I'm going to move over here so I can sit next to Francesca," he said with a gleam in his eyes.

Arianna plopped down next to Luci. "That's English for 'take a hike,'" Arianna said, nudging her younger sister.

Luci rolled her eyes. "I hate being the youngest. You all bully me!" she said indignantly.

"Try being the oldest and forced to put up with all of you," Francesca quipped back.

"Girls, girls," her mother admonished gently. "Remember, we have a guest," she said, smiling widely at him. "Max, dear, you were just telling us about what you do."

FRANCESCA SAT NEXT to Max's warm body and was almost startled when his hand clasped hers, bringing it to his lap. Her family's faces held slight movements without changing expressions, the slight lift of eyebrows, the lights in their eyes. Max's fingers stroking her palm was distracting and she almost shivered at his touch. She didn't even know him. Why did a small touch affect her so much?

"I worked on Wall Street in New York for a few years," Max was saying. "One day I realized it was becoming a grind, and it was only after I came to visit my family in Milan that I realized how much I loved it here. I joined the family company, and I'm really enjoying it. It was an easy decision to stay."

"What's the business?" Carlo asked sharply.

Francesca tried to dig her nails into his hand, but he showed no reaction. They hadn't discussed this. If he said the fashion business, her father would certainly hone in on the subject like a heat-seeking missile.

"Didn't Francesca tell you? Oro Industries is the largest exporter of lemon and olive oil products."

Carlo sat back and smiled. "Well, of course. Yes, with your cousin. Good, good. Nice to work with family."

Francesca's heart dropped. Yet another lie. They were already in so deep. She needed to talk to him before this got any worse!

"I have to go add the pasta to my soup," she remarked. Putting her hand on his arm, she gave him a speaking look. "Max, please come help me, and then we can all eat."

Luci stood. "I'll help, Frannie."

Francesca pulled Max behind her. "That's okay, Luci. Max wants to help."

She smiled at her family as they headed out the door. They were almost to the doorway when her mother said in a loud stage whisper, "Isn't that sweet? They obviously want to be alone."

Francesca sighed and continued walking quickly into the kitchen. As soon as they arrived, she shut both the doors to the kitchen and turned abruptly, staring at him with a severe frown.

"What was that all about?" She hissed. "Now you work for Oro? We are already telling lie upon lie!"

Max regarded her with raised eyebrows. "I hate to remind you, uh, *Frannie*, but you were the one who suggested we lie."

Francesca glared at him. "Don't call me Frannie. Only my family calls me that. And I hate to remind you," she said sarcastically, "But I only wanted one fib. Now they are mounting up!"

He smiled, gently picking up a piece of her long hair, running it through his fingers. "Sorry, but this distracts me. I just had to touch it. It feels like silk, just like I thought it would."

Francesca grabbed her hair and stepped back. "Would you focus?"

"What were we talking about?"

She rolled her eyes. "The lies. Now they think you work at Oro."

"I *do* work at Oro."

"But I thought you were here working with your grandfather, and that's why you thought of this entire scheme."

"No, no. When I initially came, I spent a few months trying to help him. He didn't want me to, but I finally was able to look at his books and, to be honest, I didn't like what I saw. After all these years, my grandparents should be at the height of their fashion career or else retired. Instead, they are running a fledgling business."

"What about your papa? Why doesn't he run it?"

"My father is no longer with us," he answered quietly. "I realigned the financials and gave Nonno the best advice I could. That's when he told me about the feud. It all sounds so archaic."

"I'm sorry about your papa," she said softly. He inclined his head but stayed silent. Francesca walked over to the stove, remembering their excuse for being in there. She went to the refrigerator and took out the fresh pasta that their cook always kept there and added it to her soup. Stirring it quickly, she turned off the burner. Only then did she turn around and look at him.

"Well, it may sound like an ancient feud, but it's not. It's like it happened yesterday," Francesca said sadly. "So, then you went to work for Oro?"

He nodded. "Yes, I had dinner with Marco, after not seeing each other for a while. He filled me in on his brothers seeking a smaller role in the business, and he suddenly asked me if I was interested. I'm working as his Chief Financial Officer now."

Francesca smiled a little. "I'm so happy," she said. At the startled look on his face, she rushed to explain. "I mean, he had terrible luck before. His uncle's business partner, Sal, was committing all kinds of crimes, and Marco finally figured it out."

Her face heated with embarrassment as soon as the words were out of her mouth. How embarrassing. She averted her gaze. "You probably know that if you're doing the financials."

Max nodded and gave her a small smile, as if he understood her discomfort. "We are still unraveling some of his misdeeds. I'm glad he's sitting in a prison cell!"

"He belongs there!" Francesca agreed, her gaze meeting his briefly. She quickly glanced at the counter and began stacking bowls nervously. Everything was happening so fast.

He gently stilled her hands so she was forced to glance up at him. "So, do you feel better? Technically, I said I first saw you at Marco's wedding. And I work for Oro. That's all true."

She sighed. "I know, but we're still misrepresenting things."

His eyes searched her face. "It's for a good cause in the end," he said quietly. Grabbing her arms gently, he leaned closer. "Trust me?"

"I don't even know you!"

He grinned. "But Pretend Francesca does."

"Pretend Francesca is very confused," she admitted. "Reality Francesca met you what...four hours ago? And suddenly my life is turned upside down!

He chuckled. "You like things nice and orderly, don't you?"

She tried to shrug his arms away, but he held on. "Well, yes, don't you? If you work with numbers and all, you must like things organized."

"Numbers make sense to me," he admitted. "Sometimes when life gets crazy, math is the only thing that you can rely on."

She laughed a little. "You do math to relax?"

He smiled, bringing her even closer. "Sometimes."

"What else do you do to relax?"

His lips were coming closer as if to answer her and she shook her head. "You can't kiss me!"

"Isn't that what your family thinks we are doing in here?"

"Well, yes, of course. But we just met."

His lips came closer. They were a breath away from hers. Her heart was racing, and hopefully, he couldn't feel it. She readied herself, but he moved slightly, his lips barely touching her cheek.

"That may be so, but destiny pushed us together long ago," he said softly.

"I don't believe in destiny," she remarked shortly, pulling back.

"You will," he responded confidently.

Now it was her turn to look searchingly at him. Just exactly what did he mean?

Suddenly, the door flew open so hard it banged into the wall.

"Are you guys done kissing in here? Because I need some pasta before I pass out from hunger!" Luci bellowed.

*four*

"Do you mind if I help myself to some more soup?" Max asked, turning to smile at Francesca. "This is so delicious."

"Frannie makes the best *pasta fagioli* you'll ever taste," Carlo boasted. "We love when she's home just for that alone!"

Francesca flushed. "I'll get it for you," she mumbled as she took Max's bowl over to the sideboard where she had left the soup tureen. She filled it and carefully set it down in front of him before sitting down.

"Thanks," he said, smiling at her. Leaning over, he brushed her hair back from her face gently, staring into her dark brown eyes, which were now shooting daggers at him.

"Have some more bread, too, Max," Caterina said, sliding the basket toward him. "Frannie is a wonderful cook. My mother-in-law taught her. I'm frightfully bad at it. We are fortunate to have a regular live-in cook."

"What is your favorite dish that Francesca makes?" Arianna asked out of the blue, her face registering suspicion. He glanced at Francesca and could see slight surprise cross her face.

"Well, she doesn't cook for me that often," he answered smoothly. "I prefer to take her out for a romantic dinner."

Arianna leaned forward. "But of course, she's cooked for you. What do you like the best?"

"I couldn't possibly choose," he remarked firmly. "Tell me, Arianna, I know you are a junior architect. What is the name of your firm? I'm sure Francesca told me, but I forgot."

Arianna tossed her curly brown hair behind her shoulder and immediately launched into her new life in Milan. Francesca relaxed a little next to him, and he put his arm around her gently, confident he had deflected more questions.

Eventually, with dinner devoured, the chocolate cake was brought out with much fanfare and everyone pronounced it *deliziosa*. The family sat relaxing, catching up with each other, giving Max a respite. Thank goodness Marco had given him a thorough sketch of the family.

It had been hard to focus on everyone's questions during dinner while also being hyper aware of the woman next to him. Francesca was a mixed bag of contradictions. When he had first noticed her at the wedding, she was so cool and collected. While he was attracted to her physically, he had wondered if she had a softer side. Now with her family, he saw that side as she finally relaxed as well. In fact, during dinner, she laughed so much that she had to dab at the corner of her eyes with her napkin. This time she was almost snorting, as Arianna teased her about a former classmate who she had just run into in Milan.

"Frannie, you have to remember him!" Arianna protested. "He followed you everywhere, even trying to bribe you with food!"

Francesca kept laughing. "I was seven years old! And the food was his half-eaten lunch," she said with a shudder. "His mother packed him the same *mortadella panino* every day! And I hate *mortadella*!"

"Do I have competition?" Max asked with a short laugh. "Is

this former classmate still interested?" He had meant to be funny but was confused when his joke landed flat. Serious and uneasy faces all stared back.

Caterina was the first to recover. "Mario," she whispered loudly to Arianna, who was seated next to her. "We forgot about Mario!"

"Mamma, you don't have to worry about Mario," Francesca said loud enough for everyone to hear. "He found someone he truly loves and is eloping with her right now."

She gave Max an uneasy glance, and he guessed what she was probably thinking. This was not the opening to explain he was related to Mario or else her family would ask more questions, and his real identity would come to light. He grabbed her hand quickly.

"Francesca has explained it all to me," he said confidently. "Though she tried to convince me the betrothal was made a long time ago, I am relieved he has moved on."

"We like you better anyway," Luci stated. "Mario is a bore. He only cares about himself!"

"Luci!" Caterina exclaimed. "*Per favore*, please excuse my youngest. She speaks . . . how do you say? Without a filter! For that, Luci, you may help me clear the table." Glancing at Max and Francesca, she smiled.

"Frannie, why don't you take Max for a walk around the garden? Max, are you staying the night or heading back to Milan?"

He stood and helped Francesca slide her chair back. "I am staying in a hotel in Verona for a few nights," he answered. "I have some business here, and then I am returning to Milan. But I promise that you'll see a lot of me!"

Caterina smiled, a light in her eyes. "Well, isn't that nice? The girls are all home this week for the Italian holiday. We hope you will dine with us again."

"Thank you, I will enjoy that." He threw an arm around

Francesca before she could protest. "Show me the garden, darling."

As they exited the dining room, Max glanced back to see the family's stares.

Luci was busy piling up the plates and sighed loudly. "They just want to go outside and kiss some more!"

"YOU'RE LAYING it on too thick!" Francesca exclaimed, tossing her blonde hair over her shoulder. "They just met you, and you're 'darling this and darling that.'"

They walked through the garden, down stone steps and stopped to stare out at the city of Verona which lay before them. Dusk was settling in, and the lights were flickering on in the lampposts that lined the riverwalk.

He grinned at her. "I think if I just glanced at you, it would be too much. Your family seems very aware of every move I make. It's like you've never brought a man home before!"

Francesca shifted uncomfortably, staring at the view. "Well, I haven't," she finally admitted.

He looked thunderstruck. "Not even just a casual acquaintance or a date?"

"No."

"What about Mario?" he asked.

"We haven't seen each other for several years. And I never considered him a date or anything like that," she explained.

He turned his back to the city, resting on the stone balustrade and stared at her. "Want to tell me why you never brought anyone home?"

"Because there's never been anyone. I mean, anyone I wanted to introduce to my family."

Shaking his head slightly, he continued to survey her. "Are you regretting that you introduced me?"

She finally turned to stare at him for a minute. "Not quite. I guess it's just that we have to slow it down a little! They'll have us married by the end of the week! We're supposed to let this play out, remember?"

"You are right," he said softly. Picking up a strand of hair as he had done in the kitchen, he ran it through his fingers absentmindedly. "I promise I'll be a complete gentleman in the coming days."

"Yes, what was that in there? How long are you here for?"

He shrugged. "It's true, I'm here on business. But with the banking holiday, everything is closed for the next two days. I came early hoping to see you, and then I can get some business done."

"How will we do this when you leave?"

He smirked a little. "Missing me already, princess?"

She rolled her eyes, and he laughed, putting the strand of hair gently back in place. "We'll have to make it work with me in Milan. You can come visit me, and I'll come here. What do you think your grandparents will say when they find out you are dating me and Mario is a loss?"

"To be honest, I'm not sure. But we have some time to figure it out. They are cruising in Greece with their friends for the next few weeks. They go this time every year."

"What about Mario's grandparents?"

"They are with them as well," Francesca said. "That will be tricky. We can probably avoid them for a bit. Will they know who you are?"

Max shrugged. "I don't think so. They've never met me. Remember, my branch of the family was cut off. And there's certainly enough Rinaldis. But we should try to avoid that as long as possible."

Francesca nodded. "How do we even begin softening our grandfathers' feud?"

Max smiled. "We get our families to like the idea of us being a couple. There will be an initial shock, but maybe with our help, we can broker the deal."

"I hope you're right," Francesca said, glancing at him. His face was so close to hers. She suddenly had the oddest urge to lean over and kiss him. Drawing back sharply, she looked at him with widened eyes.

"Uh, we should go in now, and you should say goodnight."

"What if we say goodnight right here?" he asked softly. "I can assure you there are spies right now watching us. Luci's face is probably pressed right up to one of those dozens of windows at the back of the house. They all expect us to say goodnight in a more romantic way."

He turned quickly and put his arms around her. "I'll keep trying my Italian on you so you can help me improve," he said huskily. "*Buona notte, cara.* That means goodnight, dear one, right?"

"*Vero,*" she whispered. "Correct."

His lips slowly lowered toward hers. She could feel his breath. "*Posso baciarti?*"

She only had time for a brief nod before his lips were on hers. He gave her a sweet kiss before drawing back. It was difficult to see his expression in the dark. "Did I say that right?"

Francesca's heart hammered, and she couldn't think. "Did you say what right?" she whispered.

He smiled slightly. "Can I kiss you?"

"Yes," she answered, leaning up for another kiss.

She heard his grumble of laughter. "I meant did I say, 'can I kiss you' correctly? But if you want me to kiss you again, I will." He swooped and kissed her, this time longer and more thoroughly, drawing back and then returning, his hand gently caressing her cheek. Finally, he lifted his head.

The world spun, disorienting her. This morning, she didn't even know this stranger and now she was outside kissing him like her life depended on it. She pulled back, putting a hand to her flushed cheek.

"I'll see you inside," Max said, pulling her back up the wide stone steps.

As they passed a lamppost, he looked completely unaffected. Had he not felt anything? Perhaps there was no chemistry for him. For some reason, the thought made her heart sink. As they arrived at the side door, he turned toward her and smiled. "Until tomorrow," he said.

"Tomorrow?" she squeaked.

"Will you show me Verona tomorrow.? Your Verona? Not something from a guidebook."

She smiled shyly. "Yes. Of course. What time?"

He grinned. "I'll pick you up at ten."

# *five*

"This is our first stop," Francesca said, turning to smile at Max as she led him into the small café. She grinned watching him edge into the narrow space between the one row of tables and the counter. The walls were filled with tea, coffee pots and kitschy items to buy. But before them on the counter was a vast array of *cornettos,* Italian croissants.

"The coffee here is amazing," Francesca said. "Do you want a cappuccino or something else?"

Max was busy looking at everything, obviously distracted. "Max, over here." She snapped her fingers. "Cappuccino?" she asked again. At his nod, she ordered two cappuccinos and a chocolate *cornetto* and a plain *cornetto.*

While Max paid, she carried their large cups to a small table. Max carried the *cornettos* and eased into a small wooden chair. Francesca hid her smile at its creaking. Hopefully, it wouldn't break. Glancing down at the big white cups, she tried not to roll her eyes. The barista had made a milky white heart on top of their foamy cappuccinos. The two young baristas were giggling and making eyes at Max.

He was particularly handsome today in his dark wash jeans and crisp blue button-down shirt. He had an even darker stubble alongside his jaw and today, he had smiled when he saw her. Her heart fluttered. When he had picked her up in the blue Alfa Romeo, she had hopped in eagerly. When he protested that he was going to get out and come to the door, she assured him it wasn't necessary. She was ready. The truth was, she didn't want him spending even more time with her family. The two of them needed time to discuss this ludicrous plan she had agreed to.

Last night she had tossed and turned, thinking of all the ways this was going to end badly. Not that she wanted to admit it, but his kisses had greatly stirred her. How could he have this effect on her? She barely knew him. Eventually, she got up early, finally dressing in her favorite pair of jeans and a simple light blue sweater. She could have put on one of her chic dresses or suits, but she'd look ridiculous walking around Verona dressed like that. Still, when she was dressed up, it was easier to keep her detached demeanor. Her one concession had been her high-heeled boots. They made her feel confident.

Straightening her shoulders now, she took a quick sip of her cappuccino to get rid of the heart. Max did the same and groaned in appreciation.

Looking up, she gave him a smile. "You have a little foam on your lip," she said, reaching out and then quickly withdrawing her hand. Instead, she pointed to his upper lip. He grinned before wiping his mouth with a napkin.

"This is the best cappuccino I have ever had in my life," he remarked.

She nodded. "See, I told you! It's an important first stop. You have to set the tone for the day. I had them drizzle chocolate on top for you. And you can have the *cornetto al cioccolato.*"

He chuckled. "How did you know?"

Shrugging, she reached for the plain one. "I saw you dig into my cake last night."

He sighed. "I love sweets. And that cake was fantastic."

She shook her head. "If I was on one of those baking shows, I would have gotten eliminated and sent home in the first round. I usually am a better baker."

Grinning, he took another bite of his *cornetto*. "I distracted you, though. So maybe the judges would have given you a pass."

They sipped their cappuccinos for a minute, each deep in thought. At the same moment, they both spoke.

"You go first," Francesca said graciously.

He was looking at her intently. "I was just wondering if this morning you regretted our arrangement."

Francesca's face grew hot . "It was a rash decision yesterday," she admitted. "My parents and sisters are already big fans of yours. I'm not sure we are going to achieve anything but disaster."

She avoided telling him how after she had gone inside, they all clamored for more information about him. Not wanting to make stuff up, she had pleaded fatigue from her long day and promised to catch them up. Her parents had wanted to ensure she wasn't heartbroken over Mario's betrayal. Telling them that Max was a far better choice than Mario had rolled off her tongue. The strange thing was she already felt that, even after only knowing Max for several hours. She was also relieved in a way for the distraction. Her parents hadn't even addressed their summons for her return or what that actually meant. That conversation would be coming soon, though.

"I know it's a little crazy, but we have to try this scheme," Max said. "The worst that can happen is our grandfathers remain in a feud."

"I can think of a dozen other things just as bad," Francesca remarked dryly.

He leaned over and grabbed her hand, and a tingle went through her. He smiled. "Let's just focus right now on getting to know each other and spending the day together."

"We need to. My family asked a million questions about you, and I deflected them because I wasn't sure how to answer without more fibs. I hardly know anything about you."

Smiling gently at her, he finally took his hand away and drained the rest of his cappuccino. "Then let's take care of that today. By dinner, you'll know all there is to know. I'm not that complicated. But let's get out of here and get started with our day."

Francesca nodded, and he gently guided her out of the warm little shop. She waved and called "*Ciao*" toward the baristas and counter staff. Emerging onto the cobblestone streets, she automatically turned right toward the Piazza Dell Erbe.

"For me, Verona always conjured up Shakespeare and all the Romeo and Juliette stuff," Max remarked. "I suppose that's why all the tourists still come."

Francesca nodded, expertly moving through the crowd easily. "They do, but we're going to avoid that today. Juliet's balcony isn't even authentic, so we're definitely not going there."

He laughed, and she loved the sound of it. "Please don't ruin that love story," he said.

She stopped walking to stare at him. "You do know how it ends, right?" She giggled. "What I was trying to say is they erected a balcony here that isn't the real balcony of the family that resided there. Today, I'm showing you the real Verona."

Max grabbed her hand as they walked through the busy piazza, where vendors were selling leather, T-shirts and other tourist trinkets. When Francesca lifted their hands in question, he shrugged. "You don't want me to get lost, do you?" he asked with a pitiful look. She laughed ruefully and kept walking, pointing out the medieval buildings.

"We are a UNESCO World Heritage Site," she explained. "That means our cultural and historical sites are protected. So Verona is stuck in time. But I kind of like her that way," she admitted. "This *piazza* was a Roman forum at one time. Hard to believe, right?" Francesca waved over the bustling kiosks built for tourists. "The good news is the city is pretty compact. We probably can see everything in one day!"

Max only smiled, looking up at the architecture. "What's that tower? I saw it from my hotel room."

She nodded. "That's the Torre dei Lamberti. It was built in the Twelfth Century. We can climb it later if you want."

They continued strolling past the crowds toward the banks of the Adige River. Crossing Ponte Pietra, Francesca explained it was one of the most photographed bridges, but she had other favorites. "You can take some photos of it when we get up this hill. I thought we'd start with taking the Castel San Pietro Funicular, so you can see all of Verona," she said, getting in line for tickets to the popular cable car ride.

Max glanced up at it as they waited. "I bet you liked riding this as a kid."

She shook her head. "It wasn't around until I was a teenager. It was built before World War II, but then it was shut down and never re-opened. Finally, it got modernized and now it's great for tourism."

"I thought you were going to show me your Verona," Max remarked, staring at her.

"Oh, I will. But I want you to see the view. It's one of my favorite places. Then we can keep going."

Now at the front of the line, they crowded into a cable car to quickly ride up the hill. Emerging at the top at Castel San Pietro, they walked over to the edge to see the panoramic view of Verona. The river below them curved through Verona with its historic bridges, each one different. Max took out his phone to take a few photos. "Selfie?" he asked with a smile. She leaned in and they took several from different angles.

They turned to look at the stunning view. "Isn't it breathtaking?" Francesca asked.

"Absolutely," he said, his gaze on her face. For some reason, his focus unnerved her. He seemed to sense her uneasiness. "Let's go sit down on that bench for a few minutes."

They walked to a stone bench and continued to look out at the view. Finally, he turned to her, his eyes alight with curiosity. "Right, let's take a few minutes to get to know each other. Tell me all about Princess Francesca Antonia Ricci."

She narrowed her eyes. "How do you know my middle name?"

He leaned back, giving her a sly grin. "I did my research. Google's a powerful thing."

She raised an eyebrow, sizing him up. "If I tell you my life story, does that mean I get yours in return?"

"Of course," he said with a straight face. "That way, when your family interrogates you, you'll have the complete dossier."

She laughed. "They grilled me about you all night until I finally went to bed!"

He gave her a crooked grin. "It's only to be expected, but let's focus on you. What was it like growing up in this magical city? Were there dragons? Fairy godmothers? Please say there were."

She giggled. "No, sorry, not quite. But it was lovely. We really didn't even think about it. It's just home," she said with a sweeping hand.

"What were you like as a kid? Were you as precocious as Luci?"

Francesca smiled a little and looked down at her hands in her lap, biting her lip. "Not really," she admitted slowly. "I was really shy. Very much an introvert. When I was small, I would climb a tree and read a book for hours. There *were* dragons in those books," she added.

He laughed. "You could read about all those adventures without falling out of the tree? You must have been talented."

She laughed, too. "Well, I wouldn't go that far. I was just trying to hide, and the world in my books was so much easier."

He stroked some of the hair that had fallen in front of her face, gently pushing it behind her ear. "You must have driven the boys crazy when you got older, especially in school—whatever the version of high school is here."

Looking at him, she quickly averted her gaze and took a breath. "Actually, not quite," she said, trying to sound casual. "It was a long time ago."

"Did I say something wrong?" he asked.

She shook her head. "No, not at all. It was, you know...childhood. I was awkward. Let's just leave it at that."

"What were your favorite things to do besides reading?" he persisted.

"I liked to cook with Nonna and we all worked in the vineyard from time to time," she said. "I was always a home person."

"Homebody," he corrected gently with a smile.

"Yes, that's it."

"So there were never special events or things you went to as part of a royal family?"

She shook her head. "No, not really. I think my grandparents were more in the social scene when they lived in Milan. A couple times a year they go with my parents for an annual grand ball or when some dignitary is visiting. But I never wanted to go." She shuddered. "It's not really my thing."

"You're different than I imagined," he remarked casually, laying an arm across her shoulders gently.

"In a bad way?" she asked cautiously.

"No, never that," he said in a soothing voice. "You're more authentic and family-oriented. I guess I just assumed you were more of a socialite. But Marco told me you would surprise me."

She smiled a little. "Marco was my first friend in Positano. He had faith in me and eventually made me a manager. I love the entire Rinaldi family."

"The entire family?" he asked softly.

Rolling her eyes, she stood quickly, trying not to show him how embarrassed she was. "Come on. We have a lot of Verona to see."

MAX GRABBED Francesca's hand companionably. She seemed used to it now and didn't tug away. He was happy he'd gotten a small amount of personal information from her. She was a bit of a chameleon. Her complexity made him eager to find out more, but he needed to be patient. It was obvious she remained guarded with people she didn't know well.

They walked through the Teatro Romano that Francesca told him dated back to the First Century BC. Listening to her rattle on the dates and figures of the theatre made him smile, and he tried to listen but he was distracted by the animation in her voice and hands, that were constantly pointing observations out to him.

"Was this in one of your books that you read in the tree?" he teased.

"Don't laugh at me! I learned a lot up that tree," she protested before smiling and then giving him an uncertain look. "Am I boring you?"

"Not in the least," he responded. As they continued walking, he gave her a reassuring smile. "But are you getting hungry? There's something about all this history that has made me starved."

Smiling, she nodded and they walked silently back toward the center of town. Turning to him, she indicated a *trattoria*. "I have just the place if you're okay with an antipasto. They specialize in great boards here."

He nodded, his eyes dancing. "Here's where I am all in on trust."

As they entered the darkened entrance, an older man hurried

over. "Francesca!" He spoke in rapid Italian, and though Max understood some of it, he didn't quite catch it all. Francesca was smiling and accepting the exuberant hugs from the owner.

"Max, I would like to introduce you to Gianni. He is an old friend of the family."

The older man scrutinized Max as he greeted him. They were about to be shown a table when a man about Max's age appeared. Tall and handsome, the man strolled toward him, and Francesca stiffened beside him. Was this an old beau?

"Francesca," the man said, before kissing Francesca on both cheeks. He held on to her a little too long, lingering on each cheek. Max flexed his fingers that suddenly itched to pry him off her.

Francesca was flushing and pulled away on her own accord. "Enzo, I didn't know you were in town."

"For the holiday," Enzo said, smiling at Francesca. He put a hand on her shoulder. "And you? Are you home for a brief time? Perhaps we can meet for dinner."

"Max Rinaldi," Max said, sticking out his hand. Enzo finally took his focus off Francesca to size him up. "Enzo Bocci," he said dismissively.

"Francesca . . ." Enzo began.

Max decided to take matters into his own hands. Putting a possessive arm around Francesca's shoulders, he turned to Enzo. "I'm sure Francesca would love to, er . . . catch up with you, but I'm afraid we have limited time together as it is," Max said firmly, purposely keeping his eyes on Francesca's face. "My fiancée and I want to spend every second together. Isn't that right, my love?"

Francesca's face had gone from pink to pallor, but she soon recovered and smiled at him tentatively. "Yes, of course we do."

Enzo looked from one to the other. "*Mi dispiace.* I wasn't aware of your engagement."

Max tightened his arm around her and gave him a cool smile.

"If you'll excuse us, Francesca and I have been walking all morning. She has promised me a delicious lunch."

Francesca smiled weakly at Enzo before going to the table that Gianni had indicated. Max held her chair out for her, already trying to determine how he was going to explain to her their sudden engagement.

*six*

Francesca frowned at the menu before them, only to glance up and see Max's intent gaze on her.

He smiled gently. "You're upset at me."

Her frown deepened. "What do you think? You just got us engaged in front of the whole town, and my family doesn't even know yet!"

Max's eyebrows went up. "You're upset because your family is the last to know about your fake engagement?"

"Shhh," Francesca admonished him. "You know what I mean!"

They were interrupted by the server who set a bottle of prosecco down before pouring them two glasses. "Gianni sent this over with his compliments." The server smiled as he nestled the bottle into a wine cooler and departed discreetly.

Francesca rolled her eyes. "See! It's already starting! Everyone will know by sundown."

Max reached over and grabbed her hand. "I am sorry. Really. You are right. It's just that guy seemed so pompous and you . . . I don't know, looked uncomfortable. It just came out. Is he a former boyfriend?"

Francesca's eyes widened. "Enzo? Oh my God, no. We went to school together, but he rarely even looked at me."

"I'm not sure why he didn't then," Max drawled. "But he was looking at you today. And he was touching you as well."

Francesca stared at him and sighed. There was something about Max that made her feel like she could confide in him. "If you want to know the truth, I had a crush on him for a short time," she began slowly. "Then he suddenly acted like he liked me, and I was over the moon. It was later I learned it was all part of a bet to see if I would . . . you know." She lowered her voice and bit her lip. "The boys called me the ice queen. The ice queen," she reiterated. "Apparently, they all thought that I was not only awkward but also some kind of twisted conquest to be had."

Max's gaze darkened. "Then I'm not sorry I said that! What a jerk. I knew I wanted to punch him!"

Francesca laughed a little, suddenly feeling lighter. "I'm not sure why I even told you. It was a long time ago. Truly. I'm sure he's a very nice person now."

"I doubt it," Max murmured. "Leopards don't change their spots."

Francesca opened her mouth to argue when the server appeared.

"Why don't you just order for us?" Max asked, setting his menu aside. "You know better than me what's good."

Francesca smiled at him. She didn't know many men who would let her take charge, even if it was just a meal. She ordered her favorite, a large antipasto, and then after the server left, she turned her attention back to Max. "So, we now have a bigger problem," she said, shooting him a nervous look. "What's your grand plan now?"

He sat back, crossing his legs and regarding her. "The same as before only, I guess things have sped up."

"We'll have to go home and break the news," Francesca said uncertainly. "My family is going to ask so many questions."

Max grinned. "Well, Luci will, that's for sure."

"Luci *and* my mother." Francesca agreed and laughed.

Max straightened and picked up the prosecco out of the wine cooler and studied the label. "This is your family's prosecco."

Francesca nodded proudly. "Gianni wouldn't serve us anything else."

Max picked up his glass. "I can't wait to try it. Let's have a toast."

"To what?" she inquired. "Our fake engagement?"

He smiled a little. "How about to a nice day together? I can't wait to learn more."

"About Verona? Oh, yes, there's lots more."

"I actually meant about you," he said quietly.

Francesca's heart gave a little flip. She ignored it. "Here's to a nice day," she said, clinking her glass with his.

"I'M STUFFED," Max remarked with a groan. They strolled through the piazza following lunch. He couldn't believe the immense board that arrived filled with various cheeses, meats, breads, fried eggplant, olives and other fried and pickled vegetables. "I'm going to have to run extra long tomorrow."

"Oh, do you like to run? So do I!" Francesca said and grinned at him.

Max nodded. "I do. It's when I think the best."

"Other than when you're doing math," she said wryly.

He caught her hand and swung it. "Yes, other than that. What's next, fabulous tour guide?"

She grinned engagingly at him. "Want to see some old stuff?"

He laughed. "Isn't everything here old?"

"That was a trick question," she said with a giggle. "To see if you remembered my facts earlier about preservation. Come on."

The rest of the afternoon spent seeing more historical sites. They wandered through the Arena di Verona. Francesca took her role as tour guide seriously, explaining all the details about it, reminiscing about all the performances she had gone to there with her parents, including operas and concerts. Max enjoyed watching her cheerful expression as she told him about it.

Wandering the streets of Verona with Francesca had far exceeded his expectations. Max admired how she pointed out the smallest detail and recited encyclopedic knowledge to him in an interesting and humorous way.

When they got to the Piazza dei Signori, they sat on a nearby bench, overlooking a statue of the poet, Dante, who once lived in Verona. Surrounded by Renaissance buildings, Max asked more questions just to hear Francesca's musical voice explain about them.

He was listening but also contemplating how she was an oxymoron to what he thought he knew about her. It sounded like she had grown up introverted and had a tough time in school. He had wanted to punch that arrogant Enzo, and now he knew why. Max prided himself on having great instincts about people, and that's why he was so surprised by Francesca. He had assumed she differed vastly from who she was.

He hated to admit that when he arrived at her doorstep yesterday, it was to convince her to enter into some form of a relationship for the sole purpose of getting his grandfather's business back in the black. When Mario had informed him of his plans to marry, Max had put the idea together quickly, not even thinking about Francesca or her feelings. His only thought was settling this ridiculous feud and providing for his grandparent's future. Sure, he hadn't ignored the fact that she was a beautiful woman with a fancy pedigree. The royal bloodline part made him uncomfortable, despite assurances that no one paid attention to that sort of thing. But it would only be for a short time and it was hardly selfless, as he imagined a few weeks in her company not being a hardship. Now the guilt was edging in as he realized his thoughts had been more mercenary than he acknowledged. The Francesca he was beginning to get to know was extremely sweet and almost naïve. He hadn't expected that. It made Max feel a little disingenuous. Disgustedly, he realized he was more like the detestable Enzo than he wanted to admit.

"You're not listening to me!" she suddenly exclaimed. Looking uncomfortable, she averted her gaze. "I've probably been boring you."

"Not at all," Max rushed to reassure her. "I was just thinking that I don't understand how you keep all these facts in your head."

She gave a nervous giggle and finally turned to look at him. "Well, to be honest, I was once a tour guide. It was for a short while before I went to university."

"Really? But you told me you were an introvert."

Francesca nodded. "I was! My parents urged me to find a job where I could come out of my shell. I found that if I focused on all the facts and figures about things, I was less nervous. It actually helped me overcome it a little. Just like in my current job. If I focus on the sales aspect of it, it's almost like playing a role."

"Surely, you don't have to work," Max noted.

Francesca shrugged. "What else would I do? Garden parties? Luncheons? Charities? Besides, my parents have always had a strong work ethic. And believe me, if nothing else, I'd be working in the vineyard. I'd much rather do anything else!"

"So, what did you study at university?"

Francesca looked uncomfortable. "Actually, business management and sales."

Turning toward him, she raised her eyebrows. "We seem to have spent the day talking about me. And yet, I still know very little about you. You better tell me more or else my family is going to be suspicious."

Max smiled. "They'll wonder if you know your fake fiancé at all!"

She elbowed him. "I'll buy you a gelato if you give me your life story."

"How can you eat again?" he asked with a laugh.

"Gelato goes down easily. It doesn't really count," Francesca protested. She pointed to a *gelateria* on the corner. "Come on, let's go *at least look*. Then we need to spend some time on you."

She pulled him to a standing position, and surprisingly she didn't drop his hand until they entered the small shop. The smell of waffle cones greeted him, and he smiled at Francesca's enthusiasm. She was like a small child, eyeing all the flavors.

"Order for me again," he told her.

Her eyes widened as if he had just told her to do something extraordinary. "Really?"

A few minutes later, he wasn't surprised when he was handed a cone with dark chocolate gelato. She eagerly bit into something pink.

Returning to the same bench they had just vacated, he watched her enjoying her cone. She stopped eating for a minute to look at him nervously. "Do you not like it? I figured dark chocolate chunk was what you would like."

He shook his head and smiled. "No, it's wonderful, thank you. What did you get?"

"*Fragola*," she said with a smile. "Strawberry."

Grinning, he took a bite and almost moaned. "This is amazing."

"Told you," she said smugly.

They sat eating their cones, silent for a time. Finally, Francesca took a sigh, glanced at the rest of her cone disappointedly and got up to throw it in a nearby trash can. "My eyes are smaller than my stomach," she said.

Max laughed. "Your eyes were *bigger* than your stomach," he corrected with a grin.

She rolled her eyes but laughed. "Whatever. Let's focus on improving *your* Italian instead of my English. Or better yet, how about you tell me everything about yourself?"

Max continued eating, intentionally delaying his answer. "What would you like to know?"

"Start at the beginning," she said, her eyebrows raised expectantly.

He sighed deeply and dramatically. "I was afraid you were going to say that."

"Why?"

He leaned in, lowering his voice dramatically. "Because the beginning involves a lot of awkward phases. Braces, undoubtedly some questionable haircuts, and a minor obsession with medieval battle reenactments."

She snorted. "Reenactments?"

"Oh yeah," he said with mock seriousness. "I was a knight, defender of all maidens, in our living room at least. My mom even made me a tin foil sword."

Her laughter erupted, and he grinned. "You sure you're ready for this?"

"I was born ready," she insisted, humor in her eyes. "Though I don't know if I can handle the image of a knight in braces."

"Well, prepare yourself," he said with a wink. "It gets worse. There's video evidence. If you're nice to me, I may show you some one day."

FRANCESCA WAITED while Max threw away the remnants of his cone and wiped his hands. He sat back down and turned to her, smiling a little.

"Your story?" she prodded.

He grimaced. "Okay, well, the sword part is true. Even the awkward years and definitely the haircuts. But that's as close as I got to a fairytale."

"Where did you grow up?"

"A long way from here," he remarked thoughtfully. "I was born in Italy, actually near Milan. My mother was a Rinaldi, and she met my father in Milan. They were very much in love and had me. At some point, my father admitted to her he was very disenchanted with working in the fashion industry. I never knew what had occurred, but he was restless. He and my mother decided to move to the States. My mother had a friend from university that was from the Pacific Northwest and they ended up traveling there to see her and liking it. They stayed, and I grew up outside of Seattle. Do you know where that is?"

Francesca smiled. "The Space Needle! We studied it in school. Do you wear flannel?" she asked excitedly.

Max laughed. "Well, yes. I'm not sure I've ever been asked that before!"

"I know. But Arianna and I were addicted to this television show. It was about a hospital in Seattle. People were always wearing flannel. Of course, that's what stuck out to me. But also the scenery. It looked beautiful there, with the water and mountains and all."

He nodded. "It is very nice, though rainy. It's a million miles from here. I think our oldest man-made landmark is 100 years old. Nothing from the renaissance era," he said with a wry smile.

At her silence, he continued. "My sisters were actually born in the States."

"You have sisters, too? So that's why you were so comfortable last night!"

"I was comfortable? I was sweating bullets with Luci's interrogation!"

They both laughed, and he continued. "I have three, just like you. Amelia, Sophia and Anna."

Francesca's eyes widened. "They all end in A! Just like my sisters!"

Max reached up and rubbed his chin. "That *is* odd, isn't it? How come I'm the outlier? Mine ends with an o."

She elbowed him. "You're a boy, that's why! So what did your father end up doing?"

A shadow crossed Max's face. "Eventually, my father went back to school. He decided he wanted to be a doctor. He was in the midst of his internship. But then... well, he was killed. He was driving home and he lost control of the car. I was ten years old, and I remember that day like it was yesterday."

Francesca's heart almost broke for him. She wanted to hug him but settled for awkwardly rubbing his arm. "Max, I am so sorry. You don't have to tell me anymore if you don't want to," she said quietly, eager to take the saddened expression off his face.

"No, it's important that you know," he answered, putting a hand over hers and stroking it absentmindedly.

"My mother's parents had passed by then and so there she was, alone with four little kids. My father's parents pressured her to return to Italy. I'm not sure why, but she didn't want to. I think she knew they would want all of us raised in the House of Valentini and be embraced by our culture. They love all that old Italian society stuff."

Francesca nodded. "All the stuff I spent my life avoiding."

He smiled gently. "Exactly. My mother agreed to send us during summers and when we were on holiday, but she wanted us raised in America. That had been what she and my father planned. My mother had a sizeable inheritance from her parents. We never wanted for anything material. And my mother did everything she could to ensure we still had a wonderful childhood. She was very strong, yet she must have been lonely now that I think about it."

"Where is she now?"

Max was looking off into the distance. Had he heard her? But then he spoke. "She remarried finally a few years ago. She lives with her new husband, Henry, right on Puget Sound. It's lovely there. We are all happy for her. Henry is a nice man. Very solid."

"And your sisters?"

"Amelia stayed in Seattle and is a nurse. Sophia lives in Boston and is a physical therapist," he explained. "And Anna is finishing up an internship in Washington, D.C., working for a senator."

"So you kind of mirrored your father," Francesca remarked thoughtfully. "He lived in Italy and chose to move to America, and you're doing the opposite."

Max turned to look at her. "I never thought of it like that. But, yes, I guess I am."

"Is it hard having a leg in two places?"

Max stared at her before chuckling. "A foot in each country," he said.

She rolled her eyes. "You know what I mean."

He nodded, his eyes still humorous. "It is. I am Italian and I love it here, but I'm also that guy who wears flannel, as you pointed out, who likes burgers, beer, and a good football game. Football meaning the kind with the brown oblong ball, not what Italians call soccer."

"I'm glad you clarified. Soccer or *calcio* is very important to us, especially now to Marco and his brothers. Have you seen their family friend, Alfonso play? He's advancing in the professional leagues. Any minute he's going to get picked up in an A league. We are all excited for him."

Max grinned. "Marco and I went to a match. I agree, he's quite good."

Francesca sat back, still smiling, remembering her friend Alfonso. Suddenly, she was homesick for the Amalfi Coast. She had built a little life for herself there. Now she missed Marco and

Kate, as well as the rest of the Rinaldi brothers and their new wives.

"Is something the matter?" Max asked.

Francesca forced herself to give him a bright smile. "No, I was just busy thinking about everyone back at home. I mean my adopted home. I miss them."

He squeezed her hand. "Speaking of home, we probably better get back to the car, and I'll take you home."

"You're staying for dinner, right? We'll have some explaining to do," Francesca said anxiously.

"That we do," agreed Max softly.

## seven

"Where's the ring?" Luci asked suspiciously, glancing at Francesca's hand. "You ask a girl to marry you and you don't give her a ring?"

This time it was the usual quiet Isabella that nudged her sister. "Luci, stop it! You're embarrassing him."

Max laughed. "Luci's right. To be honest, I thought Francesca would like to select her ring with me. We decided to shop for it together tomorrow."

All three of Francesca's sisters nodded vigorously. "It's so much better than having to wear some ugly ring that the guy chooses," Luci blurted out. "And pretend you like it."

The family all laughed, but Arianna rushed to explain. "Not that we don't think you have good taste, Max. You obviously do."

He grinned at all of them, putting an arm around Francesca to pull her close. He turned to gaze at her profile. "I believe I do."

The questions began again, and Francesca held up a hand. "See, I told you they would be rabid," she said, smiling up at Max.

When they had returned to Francesca's home, the family had pounced, just as she had predicted. Word had indeed spread quickly. He stared at her shining eyes and almost caught his breath. It was as if their engagement was actually real. Yet, for some reason, he almost didn't mind. He knew it wouldn't last, but it would be alright to pretend for a little while.

Francesca apologized. "I'm sorry we didn't tell you first. We were going to, but things just got away from us."

Max could see her heightened color and knew she was probably feeling bad that her parents had been told by someone other than her. He broke in. "I am the one who should apologize. As Francesca said, I was too nervous to wait. I was going to ask her tonight and then you all would have had a front-row seat."

Caterina stepped forward and put a hand on either side of his face. "Max, there is no need to apologize. If that busybody Salvatora Bocci had not come by, you would have been the first to tell us. Of course, she heard it from her husband, Gianni. That does not matter now. We are thrilled for you and Frannie."

Carlo, who had been silently appraising him, came forward. Grabbing Max by either shoulder, he kissed him on each cheek enthusiastically. Gazing at Max emotionally, he finally said, "It will be nice to have another man amongst all of these females."

Francesca laughed. "Papa, you love being around all these women!" He nodded emotionally. Turning to her, he tightly embraced her and this time, he had tears in his eyes. "It's hard to believe my little *topolina* will finally marry."

"*Topolina*?" Max whispered. "I don't know that one."

Francesca rolled her eyes. "Little mouse," she muttered.

"Better than me," Luci grumbled. "He calls me his '*pulcino.*' Little chick," she clarified.

"As long as he doesn't come up with a nickname for me," Max said, grinning.

"What's your full name?" Arianna asked. "He may be able to glean something from that."

Francesca was probably panicking.

"Oh no, I'm not revealing too much yet," he said. "You all will soon have too much material."

They were saved by the dinner gong and Caterina herded the family toward the dining room. "What does he mean by material?" Luci whispered loudly.

Max turned to Francesca, who was still rooted to the spot. Glancing back, he was relieved everyone was departing the room. Moving closer to her, his eyes searched her face. "It's going to be okay," he felt compelled to say, wanting to reassure her. She looked up at him and suddenly smiled confidently.

"I think so, too," she said. And for the first time, she leaned up and met his lips with hers, giving him a sweet kiss.

FRANCESCA SMILED as the family chattered and laughed. They were all taking a walk after an extended dinner. Their cook, Prudentia had come out and almost hauled Max out of his chair with her enthusiasm. The family had laughed as the diminutive, but strong, older women praised him in Italian, waving her hands and making it clear that she expected babies any minute. Next was Graham, who greeted Max warmly, which differed from his customary stiff welcome. Max had gone into the kitchen after dinner and met most of the staff, charming the housekeepers. He helped Graham with the heavy chair he had been trying to move into the kitchen. Max had done it quickly and efficiently and then went back to engage him in conversation. Francesca smiled a little, and her heart gave a small tumble at Max's thoughtfulness and his insight on how not to embarrass the obviously aging man.

Now her father was eager to show Max more of the property, including their vineyard, and they all strolled outside. At some point, he would probably insist on showing him some additional land as well as their winemaking facilities. Francesca had seen that look in his eye. He loved to talk about his business.

With Max occupied talking with her family, she had time to mentally kick herself. What in the world had made her kiss Max like that? It had been overwhelming emotions when they walked in, and their family immediately launched on them, talking excitedly about their betrothal. Perhaps it was the way that Max had simply stepped in and commanded the room, charmingly apologizing. He was so smooth about everything and yet, he had looked at her almost as if he actually cared for her. But Max had firmly told her this would end.

It was a surprise when she felt a hand grab her elbow and looked over to see Arianna slide next to her. "Frannie, we do like Max," she said quietly. "But you never said anything. I didn't know you were serious."

Francesca tried to prevent a guilty look from crossing her face. She went for honestly. "I had no idea it was all going to happen today," she told her earnestly.

Arianna surveyed her. "Well, Papa and Mamma already adore him. And he's got Luci eating out of his hand. And look, he's even managed to get Issy to talk."

Francesca's heart gave a small lurch. Isabella, the only other sister deemed an introvert held her feelings in check. When it was just family, Isabella was comfortable and talkative. But around outsiders, she instantly retreated, which broke Francesca's heart. She saw so much of herself in Isabella. She had hoped that when her younger sister went to university, she would open up, but so far, she had seemed to stay in her shell.

But Isabella was talking now, even smiling a little as she looked up at Max as they walked toward the vineyard. She was using her hands to describe something, and Max was intently listening. Francesca was in awe of his power to draw out Isabella, and at the same time, it made her heart burst with pride that he would make the effort.

"I've never seen Issy talk to a man she wasn't related to," Arianna remarked. "He's pretty cool."

Francesca could only nod and smile. "He is."

It was almost as if he knew he was the subject of conversation. Max turned his head and met her gaze. He gave her a slow, knowing grin. It was a look just for her, and Francesca could only blink before nodding awkwardly in response. He was so good at all this. Was he too smooth? This was all an act, right? Deep within her, a gnawing feeling rose. She tamped it down before she could analyze the feeling because she knew already what it was. She almost wanted this all to be real.

<h1 style="text-align:center">*eight*</h1>

"Max, what are you thinking?" Francesca hissed. "That is way too expensive! They won't let you return it!"

Max gave her a smile, humor dancing in his eyes. He moved his face closer to hers. "Do you like it?"

Francesca looked down at the square amethyst ring, haloed in diamonds. Its vintage setting in rose gold was just what she would have chosen. It looked like it was meant to be on her finger.

"It's beautiful," she acknowledged quietly. "But I can't let you buy it. This is a ruse! Remember? We are getting in deeper and deeper!"

Max put an easy arm around her and kissed her forehead gently. Turning to the jewelry store owner, who had been hovering nearby, he handed him his credit card and began the process of buying the ring.

Francesca bit her lip, watching him. He had picked her up just as he had done the day before, and they had gone to her favorite café for cappuccinos and *cornettos*. This time, Max walked in confidently and ordered in Italian. "I have to practice," he informed her with a wink. She rolled her eyes at the giggles of the girls behind the counter. Over breakfast, she tried to convince him that they should put off the ring purchase. "We'll say we didn't see anything we liked," she told him. "That we are going to look in Milan or something. They know how picky I am, and they'll believe it."

Max listened and nodded but then purposely steered her toward an exclusive jewelry store in the center of town. When they entered, he had transformed into the confident groom to be, asking for certain rings to come out of the case, shaking his head at the smaller ones. It only took two minutes for the jewelry proprietor to come to the realization that Max meant business, which translated to a high sale.

That's when the real process had begun. The other two saleswomen had been summoned and, one by one, they brought rings from deep in the back. Max asked her if she liked diamonds and she replied honestly that of course, she did. But he had zeroed in on the simple amethyst studs in her ears, which had been a gift from her grandparents on her twenty-first birthday.

His observation, "You like amethysts," had sent the shop assistants running.

"They are my birthstone. I love them," she replied.

"February birthday?" he asked. "What day?"

"February sixteenth," she responded, still looking at the displays before them. Glancing up, she saw he was smiling down at her.

"Just a couple days after Valentine's Day," he said softly.

She nodded. "Well, yes, but it's not as big of a holiday here. How did you know my birthday was in February?"

He smiled a little. "My mother's birthday is also in February and you will not believe this, but she also has an amethyst engagement ring. Well, at least the one my father gave her."

"What a coincidence," Francesca commented, averting her gaze from his intent one. The entire experience was proving to be overwhelming. She was grateful when the saleswomen returned with the proprietor and showed her a small tray with rings containing exquisite amethysts, which were a deep purple. She had spotted the ideal ring in the center. It fit perfectly. Now glancing at the gorgeous ring, she had to admit it looked beautiful on her hand.

"Ready to leave?" Max inquired, carrying a small glossy shopping bag.

"What's in the bag?" Francesca asked.

"They gave me the box if you wanted to keep it."

The proprietor was now racing around to hold the door open for them, so Francesca waited until they were outside. She stopped walking and looked up at him, her eyebrows raised.

"Of course, I do," Francesca said. "It will help when you re-sell it. Keep the receipt as well."

"Francesca, I am not going to sell your ring. When this ends —and it will end—you'll keep it," he said firmly. "Call it a memento of our time together. Or sell it. I don't care." He looked around. "Where to now?"

Francesca's mind was whirling. He so nonchalantly spoke of their ending. She had to remember that. This was all a game. Not a game, she corrected herself. It was for a good cause. To see her grandparents reunited with their crest and to re-enter the production of their well-known clothing line would be her reward. It was never about her and Max.

She paused and looked at his expectant face. "Well, if you really want to see Giulietta's balcony, we can go."

"The line isn't as long today," Francesca remarked. They entered the courtyard with the statue of Juliet. Visitors lined up to take part in the ritual of rubbing her right breast for luck in love. "Don't even think about it," Francesca said, rolling her eyes at Max's smirk.

"The house was once owned by a family named Cappello," Francesca whispered, as they quietly broke away from the tour.

"That was in the thirteenth century. The balcony wasn't added until the twentieth century," she said scornfully.

"Way to ruin it for me," he said, putting a casual arm around her. "Are those the letters to Juliet over there in that area? I saw a movie about it one time."

"Oh, that's a great movie!" Francesca said, smiling at him. "The custom kind of got out of hand. No matter what they try, people keep doing it."

As they walked out, Francesca looked up at him. "Well, now you've seen it. See what feuds can do?"

"Yes, in Shakespeare's imagination," Max replied. "This is real life, not a tragic play."

Francesca just raised her eyebrows. "You sure about that?"

"Very sure. Thanks for indulging me," Max said as they weaved their way through the crowd. "So, how about lunch?"

"Sure, there's a place I love nearby," she said.

"Not the one from yesterday where that arrogant jerk was," Max snarled, pausing to give her a look.

Francesca averted her gaze, secretly pleased that Max continued to be outraged in her defense. Still, it was a chapter of her life she'd rather forget.

She laughed a little. "No, not that one. Another nice place. But, you know, Enzo wasn't *that* bad," she said, walking ahead. "He was just doing what everyone else did back then."

"You got teased by more than just him?" Max asked gently, making her instantly regret bringing it up.

"Oh, Max, no one wants to revisit their teenage years! Yes, I got teased. Mostly about the whole 'princess' thing. People said I thought I was better than everyone. The truth was, I was awkward and introverted. But I'm over it. Obviously."

"Obviously," he echoed, though his tone was thoughtful. "But those things shape us. They either make us better, or they bury little insecurities that pop up at the weirdest times."

Francesca shot him a sharp glance, then gestured toward a

small pizzeria. "Get ready for the best pizza," she said as they waited for a table outside.

Once they ordered, she eyed him curiously. "So, don't tell me you were teased in high school. You look like you were the popular kid. Good-looking, athletic . . ."

He wiggled his eyebrows. "You think I'm good-looking?"

She snorted. "I'm sure you figured that out by looking in the mirror."

Max took a long sip of his beer, staring off into the distance, suddenly serious. "I guess I was popular. And yeah, I was athletic, too. I played baseball."

"Why baseball?" she asked, puzzled. "Not your American football?"

He grinned. "Football is too rough! I never had the appetite for it. Baseball's the quintessential American sport. Besides, my father bought me a mitt when we first arrived in America. When he had time, we played catch. So I pursued it. I was an Italian trying to fit in. I did everything I could to do so. That meant lots of fast food, sports, hanging out with the guys. But I always felt a little different," he added quietly.

Francesca felt a pang and wanted to reach for his hand but kept hers firmly in her lap. "I'm sorry, Max."

He smiled a little at her expression. "It's okay. That's just how it was. Summers in Italy were a crash course in the culture. But the language? I struggled. Ten months in America, two or so months here. I never quite fit in here either."

He suddenly smiled wryly. "How did we go from pizza to such deep conversations on a sunny afternoon?"

Francesca raised an eyebrow but returned his smile. "This is the kind of deep stuff we should've covered *before* getting engaged!"

"I suppose," he teased.

Before he could say more, their pizzas arrived, and Max's face lit up. "These look incredible!"

"Told you! Pietro is a genius. I'll take you to meet him later. He never comes out front. He likes to stay in the kitchen."

Max bit into a burrata and sausage piece and immediately groaned. "Oh my God, I've died and gone to pizza heaven."

"Almost," Francesca said, taking a big bite of her own.

"By the way," Max said, wiping his hands, "What was the deal last night? You kept running into the kitchen during dinner. Was your cook having some kind of crisis?"

Francesca laughed, chewing thoughtfully. "Well, Prudentia… isn't the best cook. She's good with ingredients but not with timing. If she's cooking more than one dish at a time, something's getting burned."

Max blinked. "You have a cook who can't cook?"

Francesca giggled. "It sounds worse when you say it like that."

"So, you just pop into the kitchen and rescue the meal?"

She nodded. "Pretty much."

"And what happens when you're not home? What does your family do?"

"They eat out a lot," she admitted, laughing.

Max shook his head. "And what about your butler? I was a little worried about him. He should taker it easier, maybe retire."

"Graham. Oh, he's great. He's not really a butler, though he likes to think he is. He loved *Downton Abbey*. But he does all the odds and ends around the house. My dad's offered him a pension, but he refuses to leave. He loves us too much."

"So, your butler won't retire, and your cook can't cook."

"They're our friends, and we love them!" Francesca protested, laughing harder.

Max grinned, wiping his hands. "And the man sitting at the end of the kitchen table? Who was he? The one who barely acknowledged me?"

"That's Fernando. He's the head gardener."

"Loves plants, hates people?"

"Sort of," she said with a chuckle. "He'll warm up to you eventually."

Max shook his head, still laughing.

Francesca rushed to explain. "My parents just collect people," she said with a shrug. "If someone needs a home or they come upon someone, we just absorb them. Believe me, we have quite an entourage when you add in all the other positions either in the villa or at the vineyard."

"Do you collect people, too?" he asked softly.

"Well, I've collected one fiancé in the last twenty-four hours," she answered dryly.

"Any regrets?" Max asked, his eyes meeting hers.

She shook her head, smiling, but didn't trust herself to speak.

Max reached across the table and took her hand. "We'll figure this out. Just remember that it's for a good cause."

He raised his beer. "To resolving feuds."

Francesca clinked her glass against his. "Resolving feuds." But deep down, she knew it was not that simple.

*nine*

"This bridge is made for you," Max commented, as he held up his phone to take another photo of her standing on the *Ponte di Castelvecchio*. "It almost looks like a castle the way it arches and with the battlements."

She raised an eyebrow and he laughed. "I know. Battlements isn't a word you use all the time." At her continued questioning look, he held up his hands. "Okay, okay. Arianna told me about the bridge last night in great detail, by the way." He walked toward her, smiling. "A princess on her castle bridge."

Francesca shot him a speaking look. "Please, stop. You're the one with the tin foil sword!"

He gave her a crooked smile. "You are right about that. I may regret telling you that! I'm sorry. I didn't mean to tease. I actually meant that you look beautiful on this bridge with the river and the hills behind you."

Francesca stared at him and then turned to view the river flowing below them. She had rebelliously tried to look as plain as she could for some reason that day. Scraping her hair back in a French braid, she had worn a black sweater and jeans and stubbornly put her glasses on her nose. She had even forgone makeup. Tossing her braid behind her shoulder, she had run down the stairs to meet him in the grand hallway.

Lying awake most of the night, she had thought about how fast things were moving with Max. He had made it clear from the beginning that this was not a permanent arrangement, and it was concerning that her family was already falling in love with him. In fact, her heart was a little more than taken with him. He was handsome, charming, and yet, there was a part he kept closed off. Yesterday's lunch was the most she had gotten out of him. She longed to ask more questions about his time in New York and truly what brought him to Italy. But this was a business arrangement, after all. She needed to relax and remember that.

Turning to him politely, she rattled off the facts about the bridge. "Did Arianna tell you it was built in the fourteenth century by the ruling noble at the time? It was intended to be an escape route in case Verona came under attack. It was rebuilt after it was destroyed, but they tried to keep it the same."

"I'll have to remember the escape route part," Max murmured.

Francesca turned to coolly assess him. "Escape from me?"

He laughed. "Just a bad joke. When your grandparents find out who I am, I better have a plan. When are they expected back?"

"In a few weeks, I believe," she said. "Max, maybe we ought to quit now. I . . . I don't know. It just feels awkward. You're leaving tomorrow and then what?"

Taking her arm, they began to stroll. "I was going to talk about that over dinner tonight with you. What do you say we go out alone tonight to discuss our future?"

"But we have no future," Francesca stated calmly.

"I mean our phony future," he teased. "Come on, let's go see something else. You were talking about a garden last night."

"The Giardina Guisti," she said softly.

"Let's go there and grab some lunch. All this medieval architecture is making me hungry again."

FRANCESCA STOOD before her closet and grabbed a somber black dress that covered her completely and fell to her knees, when Arianna walked in.

"Frannie, you aren't thinking of wearing that tonight?" she shrieked. "That's your funeral dress."

Isabella emerged behind her, entering the room and sitting quietly down on a bed. "I like Max, Frannie. Wear something that makes you look hot."

Francesca turned to meet her sisters' gazes. She shrugged. "I don't know if Max really notices what I wear," she admitted.

Isabella frowned at her. "He notices everything. He talked to me like . . . like I have important things to say. And he pointed out things at the vineyard and asked questions. He asks a lot of questions," she informed them matter-of-factly.

Francesca walked back into her closet. "I didn't bring everything with me. Most of my sophisticated clothes are still in my flat in Positano. I'm not even sure what to wear."

Arianna appeared in the closet, glancing around. Smiling, she pulled out a short red dress. "How about this?" she said triumphantly. "This will blow his socks off. But I'm sure you've done that already!"

"That's too . . . too much for Verona," Francesca argued. "I can wear it in a bigger city. But here, I'd look out of place."

Arianna put it reluctantly back with a frown. "I can't believe I have to choose something for you to wear. You're the one that walks into a store and grabs three things, and they all look perfect on whoever you're selecting them for."

Francesca laughed. "That's because it's not me! I'm good at dressing you or my friends. I never know what to wear."

Isabella walked into the closet and joined in the search, sliding hangers back thoughtfully. "I've got it," she said quietly. Holding a short wine-colored dress that dipped in the front and flared at the hips. "Look, it's beautiful. It's elegant and sophisticated without being flashy," she said.

"It's kind of low cut," Francesca said, biting her lip.

"That's what makes it perfect," Arianna said with a smirk.

MAX FROWNED at the *ristorante's* menu. He had to focus on that rather than look at Francesca across from him. If he did, his gaze might accidentally fall to her cleavage, and he would look like some lecher. When she had descended the stairs, his gaze traveled from her long legs upward and then eventually to her beautiful face. She looked so gorgeous he had cleared his throat awkwardly, suddenly completely out of his depth.

Over the last several days, he had seen Francesca in everything from an apron to ultra-casual, like earlier that day. In fact, she had looked amazing standing on the bridge. With her hair pulled back, her neck looked long and elegant. He resisted the urge to take her in his arms and run his lips along its length. Instead, he kept himself busy taking photos. With no makeup on, she looked fresh and lovely. And he adored her in glasses. They made him want to take them off and kiss her without restraint.

Now she looked every inch like a chic and elegant woman who was completely out of his league. He had dated a lot of beautiful women in his time, but Francesca was something beyond. He loved how she could easily move from casual to elegant without looking like she was trying.

He took a deep breath. This was more difficult than he imagined. It was about way more than her looks. When he had concocted this plan, he knew it would involve spending time with her. But he had assumed she would be self-absorbed and probably spoiled. Instead, he found her sweet, funny, and just completely loveable. With a sinking heart, he knew he had to do a better job of keeping her at arm's length. There was no way this relationship could continue after they achieved their goal. They were only together for a make-believe story involving a princess. He smiled wryly.

"What are you smiling at?" Francesca asked softly, leaning forward.

Good God, when she moved like that, it revealed even more. He cleared his throat anxiously. "I was relieved I could read the menu. Having you interpret everything for me is a little embarrassing."

Francesca took a sip of her wine. "You shouldn't be embarrassed. You weren't raised here," she said nonchalantly.

"Are you always so matter of fact?" he asked.

She grinned. "It's one of my finer qualities." Her hand twisted her wine glass around nervously. "So, in keeping with that, we were going to discuss the future. That is, our future," she finished.

He grinned at her and was about to speak when the server appeared. They both gave their orders, and he leaned back in his chair, watching the way the candlelight danced over her hair. Tonight, she wore it behind her head in some fancy bun. It made him want to take the pins out and watch it topple down.

"Max?" she prompted. "The future?"

"Well, I leave tomorrow as you know." he said. "I was wondering if you would like to come to Milan in a few days and see me there?"

She looked lost in thought. "I suppose I could. Arianna is going back to work. I could go with her and stay with her for a couple of days."

He arched an eyebrow. "Won't she think that's weird? I would assume she would think that you would stay with me."

Francesca was turning pink. "But that's…"

"We *are* engaged."

He wanted to laugh at her discomfort but took pity on her. "My flat has two bedrooms," he said. "We can explore the city a little. I have been busy working. I haven't had a chance to see much."

"Won't you have to work?"

"Well, if you come up Friday, we can have the weekend," he said. "And then maybe stay for a few days after that unless you'd be bored."

She smiled a little before taking a sip of wine. "To be honest, it will be nice to get out of town. My parents dropped a bomb on me last night," she said with a wince.

He raised his eyebrows and waited for her to continue. "They want me to go to the annual royal gala in a few weeks," she said. "That was the reason I'm even here. They summoned me home to begin to…establish myself in society, I guess you would say. It's not really them. It all stems from my grandparents, who put pressure on them. We were supposed to have this big discussion about it the night you showed up on our doorstep. So I guess you can say they have been distracted," she said dryly. "

"How did it go last night?" Max asked.

"They meant business. My father isn't often stern, but he was last night. He told me I would need to make a few appearances so people know who I am. Get involved in a few charities and things like that. I didn't want to tell them that I intend to go back to Positano. Of course, I think they secretly hope that now I'm engaged that also means I'll move back."

"Yes, for now having you here is ideal for our plan," he acknowledged quietly. "Is that what you want? To move back to Positano?" he asked quietly.

"I was happy there," she said with a shrug.

"Managing a shop?"

"What's wrong with that?" she said defensively. "I had a great time managing the shop with my friend Allegra. I enjoyed the Amalfi Coast."

"Nothing is wrong with it," Max said, softening his tone. "If that's what you want. But I know how smart you are, Francesca. Even in this short time, I can tell that you could be more than that if you wanted. But you hold yourself back."

She grimaced. "Now you are starting to sound like my parents. They don't care as much about the society stuff as they do about me being the most I can be."

"I'm sorry," he said, smiling at her gently. "We can talk more about it some other time. Far be it for me to pressure you as well. Tell me about this gala," he said, trying to change the subject.

"It's very formal. It's all about old Italy," she said nervously. "My worst nightmare."

"My grandparents haven't mentioned it to me," he said thoughtfully. "I wonder if they go."

"Probably," she shrugged. "I know my grandparents do. They'll be back by then."

"So that means I should go, too. It will be like our coming-out party," he remarked.

She looked startled. "I don't know, Max. This makes me so nervous. I guess you're right. I hadn't gotten past the idea that I need to persuade a designer to make me a gown in just a few weeks." Her eyes grew. "Our grandparents will be in the same room with us."

"By then, they'll know who I am." He smiled and reached over to pick up the wine bottle and refill her glass. "We better lay the foundation before then," he said. "Big time."

"What does that mean? Big time?"

"It means we spend some time in Milan planning just how we are going to do this," he said. "Are you good at poker?"

She shook her head. "I don't even know how to play."

"Then I'm going to have to teach you," Max said. "It's all about the bluffing."

*ten*

"Of course I understand, Frannie. You need to be with Max. Mamma and Papa have been hovering around the two of you in Verona. You need some alone time," Arianna said, sipping her prosecco.

She spoke in hushed tones as they waited in the gilded lobby of a famous Italian designer. Francesca had been startled when she called the designer, and she agreed to see her that very Friday. Francesca had nervously told her upfront that she would need a gown in a short amount of time. The designer had appeared nonplused by it.

"Thanks, Ari. Max said he only had to work today, and then he's off for a few days after the weekend. Thanks for taking the day off to come with me today. I can't believe they agreed to see me on such short notice."

Arianna rolled her eyes. "Frannie, you have a title. And now that you are engaged to a handsome man from two prominent families. You will be the most photographed woman at the gala. This designer is not stupid."

Francesca winced. "I know, but still." Suddenly she sat up straight. "Wait! How did you know Max is from two prominent families?" Leaning forward, she whispered, "Do you know who he is?"

Arianna's laughter rang out.

"Shh, you are making too much noise," Francesca admonished her.

Arianna glanced around at the quiet waiting room. "Who is going to care? Honestly, Frannie, how do you think I know? My sister suddenly brings home this hot man without saying one word. It took me awhile, but reverse image search is my friend. There he was in all his glory from his days on Wall Street. Massimo Rinaldi *Valentini.*"

Francesca winced and then looked down. "Are you mad at me?"

Arianna looked surprised. "Why would I be?"

"He's a Valentini," hissed Francesca. "The feud, remember? Nonno and Nonna will be livid."

"Is that why you didn't tell me before? Or is that why you're faking this engagement?" Arianna asked.

Francesca stood abruptly and stared down at her sister, her face stunned. Arianna stared back smugly, sitting back on the light pink couch.

"Princess Francesca," said a voice behind her.

Francesca turned abruptly to see a tall woman in a couture dress. "The designer will see you now."

"Saved by a designer," Arianna said, putting her glass down on the ornate coffee table. "Yet again."

"SO YOU THINK it will be okay?" Francesca asked Arianna, as she sipped her lemonade. The two sat at a table at a *trattoria* near the designer's studio.

"Yes, for the hundredth time," Arianna said, looking at the menu. "More than okay. What are you having?"

"How can you eat at a time like this?" Francesca asked.

Arianna lowered the menu. "What is wrong with you? I can always eat. Besides, it's hardly an emergency."

"Stop looking at the menu and tell me how you knew Max and I . . . well how you knew . . ."

"That you were lying?" Arianna said, raising an eyebrow. She turned and smiled sweetly at the server who appeared. Ordering both their lunches, she sipped her drink confidently and then popped an olive in her mouth from the little tray on the table.

"Frannie, it was so obvious. I've known you since birth. You looked shell-shocked every time you saw him. Like you were just seeing him for the first time. I'm very good at reading people," she said smugly.

Francesca looking at her questioningly. "I've never known you to be so observant," she remarked slowly.

"Well, I am," Arianna said.

At Francesca's look, she burst out laughing. "Alright, you got me. I called Allegra. I asked her about Max and, of course, she had no idea who I was even talking about. I figured if your best friend didn't even know, then the whole thing was a sham. That's why I went online. I just can't figure out what you're playing at."

Francesca laughed despite herself. She should probably text Allegra. As lunch appeared, she found it a relief to pour out the entire story. Finally sitting back, she took another bite of her crispy chicken Milanese and the fresh tomatoes and burrata. "By the way, this is amazing."

"You probably cook it better," Arianna remarked.

"If that's the case, then I'm looking forward to it," said a male voice and both girls startled and looked up to see Max smiling down at them. Sitting down in the chair closest to Francesca, he smiled at them before grabbing Francesca's hand and giving it a squeeze. "I got your urgent text, darling."

Francesca snatched her hand back. "Well then, you know that Ari knows. You can drop the act," she retorted.

He raised his eyebrows but then turned his attention back to Arianna. "So we have a little spy in the family," he drawled. "Online research, private detective? Rifle through my wallet? Which was it?" he asked calmly.

Arianna giggled. "I don't care if this engagement is fake, and I don't care you're a Valentini. I like you Max."

He grinned. "Likewise."

He was interrupted by the sever who had scurried over. She was looking at him so dreamily that he had to repeat his order. Turning back to the women, he frowned. "Did I not say it correctly? She seemed confused."

Francesca rolled her eyes at Arianna. "Oh, she wasn't confused."

He shrugged, clearly not understanding and then leaned back. "How did it go with the designer? Did you get a beautiful gown?"

"I don't know," Francesca said, biting her lip. "It may turn out hideous, and I'll have to push the ball."

Max looked confused. "You mean punt?"

"What's punt?"

"Never mind. I'll explain that later to you," he said and laughed. "You mean you don't know what it looks like?"

"The designer, Giancinta, wanted to make me something special. She sketched it out and we looked at fabrics, but in the end, she told me to leave it up to her. So basically they just took my measurements, and I'll come back in a week or so and she'll have something for me to at least try on."

"That will work out well," Max said.

"Why? Francesca asked. They were interrupted by the server who placed a plate of *penne all' arrabbiata* and a draft beer. He smiled and thanked her before turning back and picking up a fork.

Francesca frowned a little. Why did he have to be so darn charming to everyone and oblivious all at the same time? Patiently, she waited for him to swallow.

"Because then you can come up to Milan, and we can spend more time together," he stated.

"But is that necessary? If Ari already figured it out, the rest of my family may as well."

Arianna rolled her eyes and reached across the table to take a bite of Francesca's chicken. "They do not have my superior detective skills," she said. "Besides, they're all so starry-eyed at Max they aren't even thinking about asking questions."

Max shook his head, almost in embarrassment and took another bite. Francesca looked at his bent head. His stubble across his jaw was more prominent today. He suddenly looked up and met her gaze.

"Sorry," he said, wiping his mouth. "I was starved. I got to work really early this morning so I could take the rest of the afternoon off. What time did you arrive? I wish you would have let me send a driver," he said with a frown.

Francesca grinned. "That wasn't necessary. Lorenzo brought me."

"Who is Lorenzo?" Max asked sharply.

"Our chauffeur," Francesca replied. "Only I drove."

Max laughed. "Let me guess, your driver doesn't know how to drive."

"Oh, he knows how," Francesca said. "Only he used to be a race car driver. I told him to take a nap, and I would drive. I wanted to get here in one piece."

"I like the way Lorenzo drives," Arianna protested. "You get places quicker," she told Max confidently.

Max shook his head and laughed. "Speaking of getting places, how about we go pick up your luggage at Arianna's and take it back to my flat? And then we can relax."

"I can just stay with Ari now," Francesca said, waving her hand. "Now that she knows everything."

"Oh, no you don't," Arianna said, glancing at her watch. "I'm going out tonight. I don't need a big sister around."

"You have a date?" Francesca asked suspiciously. "You didn't tell me before."

"When did I have the chance?" Arianna asked and shrugged. "Besides, I like my space after living with all of you. Go to Max's and *relax*," she said, drawing out the last word and raised her eyebrows at Francesca. "Who knows what will happen?"

# eleven

"*Grazie*," Francesca said, accepting the tall glass of water from Max. She sunk into his soft leather couch and glanced around. "Your flat is lovely, and you can't beat the view. It's only a few blocks away from the Duomo."

She expected him to sit across from her but was startled when he sat down next to her, turning so he could gaze at her. "It's fine for now. But it's kind of sterile. I haven't really had a chance to make it be a home."

Francesca glanced around. He was right about that. Other than the leather furniture and a few tables and lamps, the walls were bare. After retrieving her suitcase, they had only walked a few blocks to Max's modern building, where he had the penthouse. At his urging to make herself comfortable, she had done so, settling into the luxurious second bedroom. She had grabbed a pair of soft yoga pants and a sweatshirt from her bag and donned them. Sweeping her hair into a ponytail, she emerged from the bedroom and went to look at the view.

Max was dressed in worn jeans and a long-sleeved polo shirt. He looked down and shrugged. "Guess we both had the same idea," he said with a grin. "We should go out and take a look around the city."

Francesca leaned her head back with a sigh. "It feels kind of amazing just to do absolutely nothing. I had to get up very early this morning for the appointment, and I can't remember the last time I was able to just sit and breathe."

Max leaned back too, rotating his neck a bit. "I couldn't agree more. But I wanted to take you out and have some fun in the city."

Francesca shrugged. "We can go out tomorrow. What if I cook for you instead?"

He shook his head. "Nope. That's not relaxing."

"For you, maybe. Cooking's my therapy!" she protested.

"Yeah, but tonight, we can just be couch potatoes. We'll order something in, binge a series, and find out just how comfortable this couch is."

"Couch potato?"

He chuckled, grabbing the remote and handing it to her. "You'll get it later. In the meantime, I'm bestowing all remote privileges upon you."

"Oh, Max," she said, her eyes twinkling, "you're just too selfless."

"Utterly noble," he agreed with a smirk.

"ALRIGHT, I'm revoking your remote privileges," Max grumbled. He reached his hand into the bowl that separated him from Francesca and took another handful of popcorn.

"What's wrong with this pick?" Francesca asked.

"You're diabolical," Max complained. "Do you know how many people this guy has slashed in the last ten minutes?" He shuddered. "I thought we were going to watch something pleasant, like you know, a nice rom com."

She looked at him, her eyebrows raised. "You thought I'd pick a *film da ragazze*," she said.

"Yep. I know that one. Translation is 'chick flick.'"

She made a face. "You told me I could choose what I wanted. And I like thrillers."

"I'm not going to be able to sleep tonight," he commented, throwing popcorn up in the air and catching it in his mouth.

"You're not going to be able to sleep tonight because you ate that whole bowl of popcorn," she told him and grinned. "Wasn't the Thai food enough?"

He shook his head. "I always need popcorn for a movie. And if I occupy myself with catching it, I don't have to see anyone else murdered in cold blood!"

As he gazed at her smiling face, he intentionally moved the popcorn bowl to the table. He had kept it there on purpose, but now he wanted to be close to her. Before he could think too hard, he moved toward her and put his arm around her. Her eyes widened, but after a minute, she relaxed her head onto his chest. He dropped a light kiss on her fragrant hair. She smelled like lavender and something else. He took an appreciative sniff and pulled her a little tighter.

"Max, no one is here. You don't have to touch me," she said softly.

"Always practical," he said. "But we do need to practice a little."

She broke away a little and turned to look at him. Seeing the vulnerable look on her face stirred him. He wanted to be honest with her. "Francesca, what if we...what if we think about turning this into something?"

"For real?" she whispered.

"Yes." He swallowed hard. "Not the whole engagement stuff. Just us. You and me. What if we spent the next few days getting to know each other? No hidden motives. No strategic plans."

"I'd like that," she said quietly.

"Can I kiss you?"
She smiled. "I'd like that."

# twelve

"It took six hundred years to build," Francesca said, her eyes wide, glancing up at the ornate ceiling of Milan's Duomo. "It's the fifth largest cathedral in the world. It's not only the house of God, it was the House of the Milanese—the people of Milan who helped build it."

"I should have known you would know all the facts about it," Max drawled, his eyebrows up. "Another book read in a tree?"

She giggled. "Don't be silly. I have come here since I was a small child. Nonna told me about it since I was a little girl. And really, the truth is, Ari is obsessed with this place. She gives me an architectural lecture every time I visit."

Max put a casual arm around her as they continued to stroll in the back of the cathedral. "Wait, stop here," Francesca said excitedly. "See that stained glass? It's a sundial! See how it lines up with the symbol for Libra on the floor? It knows what time of year it is."

Max glanced down at the zodiac symbols and the intricate marble. He smiled gently. "What other facts do you have in your head?" He stared gently down at her thoughtful face. He loved hearing her musical voice presenting facts and figures so earnestly.

"Well, it can hold forty thousand people," she said. "And there's something like 3,400 statues."

They walked over and sat in a pew while the tour groups and people wandered through. Francesca stared forward. "And up there over the altar is supposedly a nail from the cross of Jesus' crucifixion," she told him, pointing upward. "Every Easter, the archbishop goes up there on a lift and brings it down for the people to see. It's a mob scene in here."

"I bet," Max remarked. He glanced upward. "I like all the stained glass the best."

Francesca nodded. "It tells the story of the Bible. It was meant for those who can't read."

Max smiled at her enthusiasm. It felt good to focus on her. Their day had been busy, starting with a morning run. Francesca's long legs had easily kept up with his stride. He had run longer than intended, not realizing that ultimately, he was trying to work off some energy. She didn't seem to mind and kept up with him.

After showering and getting ready for the day, they had grabbed a quick breakfast and jumped on one of the trams that zigzagged all over the city. They had scrambled out every now and then to see some sights. He had told her that morning he had barely left the central area near his office or apartment. Each time he did, he admitted he got lost with the diagonal streets near the Duomo.

She had laughed and teased him, and he was happier than he had been in a long time. He had kept the day purposely light, and yet they had talked all day, enjoying themselves. Last night he had regretfully walked her to her room. At her door, he had the urge to give her a kiss that would knock any other kiss she had ever received right out of her head. Putting a hand on either side of her face, he simply kissed the heck out of her. She had slumped a little against the doorway, and he had to take an arm to support her. Smiling now a little, remembering it, he hoped that was a good sign that she felt the kiss down to her toes. He certainly had. In fact, it had kept him up most of the night. What was he doing? What had started out as a lark was growing more serious. And yet, he looked forward to being with her, laughing with her and learning how that beautiful brain ticked. Last night, he'd been impulsive to ask her if she wanted to turn this into something real. He had enough on his plate with his strained relationship with his grandparents, their preoccupation with their failing business, and him taking on the responsibility at Oro Industries.

She stared at him.

"I'm sorry. What were you saying?"

She raised her eyebrows but repeated her question. "Do you want to go to the top? There's an elevator and not that many stairs if your legs are sore from our run. It's a magnificent view of Milan."

Her upturned face was so beautiful, he couldn't resist. He leaned over and brushed his lips against hers gently. "No, thank you. I already have a magnificent view."

FRANCESCA SMILED AT HER MENU. She wore the red dress Arianna had previously wanted her to don in Verona. Purposely, she kept it hidden under her coat until they reached the exclusive *ristorante* Max had insisted on dining at. His sharp intake of breath was audible as he helped her remove her chocolate brown cashmere coat. It was all she could do to hide her smile and sit down. Not only did the dress show front cleavage, it also had thin straps that crisscrossed in the back, dipping shockingly low. She had twisted her hair up in an intricate style and put on a little extra makeup. For some reason, she had wanted to wow Max. He had treated her like a friend all day, purposely keeping his touch light. Even the kiss he had given her in the Duomo had been chaste. She frowned because, to be fair, they *were* in a church.

Her cheeks heated at the memory of last night's kiss. For whatever reason, he must have decided to make an impression on her. And he had. She almost slumped to the ground when they finished. She was hopeful he didn't realize how much it affected her. Walking into her bedroom in a trance after telling him goodnight, she sat on the edge of the luxurious bed for a long time, staring at nothing. What was she doing? This was supposed to all be for show, and yet she had agreed to pursue the chemistry between them.

All day she had poked and prodded, but Max had not really confided much more about himself. Instead, they had talked more about the city and its offerings. Tonight, she wanted to morph into the Francesca that made men stutter. Long ago, she had embraced that image, smugly aware they would never know the real her. Admittedly, it was her armor as well as a little vanity. Today, the wary feeling washing over her was vulnerability. It was time to suit up and protect her heart.

Max ordered prosecco, and she lowered her menu, giving him a questioning look. "What are we celebrating?"

He grinned at her. "I have a surprise."

She slid her menu away and stared at him. "Do tell."

He shook his head. "Not so fast. Let's eat first, and then we'll talk. Tell me what I should have."

She smiled and picked up the menu again. "I don't really know what you like . . ."

"I like tall blondes in red dresses," he said quietly. She met his intent look and tried to ignore the sudden racing of her heart.

"You look stunning, Francesca," he said, reaching over and grabbing her hand. "But you always do. It's just tonight you remind me of when I first saw you and I couldn't keep my eyes off you."

"Marco's wedding?" she asked. "I had on a similar dress, only it was blue."

He nodded, his expression serious. "It drove me crazy most of the night. I wanted to dance with you so badly."

She watched the muscle in his cheek twitch. He looked so handsome in his dark suit. "Do you want to dance with me now?" she asked softly, indicating the small dance floor where couples were swaying to an Italian ballad.

"If we go out there and I wrap my arms around that beautiful silky back of yours, we may never make it to dinner," he said huskily.

Francesca slid her hand out of his grasp and leaned back. "Max, we need to talk. All day, you seemed distant. It's like you don't want to discuss anything that matters. And then tonight you're…well you're being more intimate, I guess. Is it because of how I look?"

He blinked, opening his eyes wide. "What are you talking about? You looked beautiful today. I just said that you always do. It doesn't matter what you're wearing. And in the end, looks aren't that important. You know that."

"I'm sorry. Thank you for saying that. Sometimes old insecurities come out. But why were you being so aloof today?"

He looked chagrined. "To be honest, I never meant there to be anything real between us. But it's happening, and it's happening fast. I guess you can say I'm trying to slow this engagement down."

Laughing a little, she nodded. "I understand. But you're sending a lot of mixed signals."

"I am. I agree," he said, shaking his head. "You're not something I planned on. I'm trying to figure this out, and you may have to be patient with me. Can we just get to know one another and see where this goes?"

"I'd like that," she whispered.

"So would I," he said and smiled at her, his eyes glinting in the candlelight. Picking up his menu, he glanced over it. "And in the spirit of that, I'll tell you what I don't like. Starting with mushrooms. I intentionally learned the word *funghi* early on!"

MAX LEANED BACK and smiled at Francesca. "I don't think I'll ever eat again.

"Didn't you like it?" she said with a smirk, eyeing his empty plate.

"It was challenging, but I overcame it."

She raised her eyebrows, her eyes twinkling. "I'm glad you managed to get through it."

"You did an amazing job," he said, reaching for her hand. "You're hired."

Color crept into her face. Throwing her off her game was so fun. She carried herself with elegance tonight, dressed up in sky-high heels, wearing a chic red dress that accentuated everything. It was amazing he could even swallow. They had declined dessert and instead enjoyed sipping the rest of their prosecco.

"So, what's my surprise?" Francesca asked, her expression guarded.

Max reached into his pocket and pulled out his phone. Quickly opening an app, he pushed it toward her.

Francesca picked it up and studied it for a minute, her eyes growing wide.

"It's *calcio* tickets for tomorrow?"

He nodded. "I thought you would like to attend your friend Alfonzo's first match!"

"What? Are you kidding me? Of course I would. But when did this happen? No one has texted me or called me!"

"Katie was about to, but I told Marco to hold off. I wanted to surprise you."

"That's so exciting!" Francesca exclaimed. "I can't believe you did this for me."

"It's too late to get a box," Max said. "I got the best tickets I could closest to the pitch. We didn't want to bother Alfonso right now. It will be great to go to another soccer match. This time at San Siro. I'm eager to see the stadium."

"*Calcio*," Francesca corrected.

Max smiled. "*Calcio*. And I have more surprises, but you'll have to wait for those."

Francesca looked wary. "Max, there's something you need to know about me. I'm not a huge fan of surprises."

"Even good ones?"

She shrugged. "I guess I'm a bit of a control snob."

He laughed. "Control freak?"

"Yes, that's it. I like to know what's ahead of me."

"Okay then, I'll tell you. Marco and Katie are coming. I'm not sure who else in the family. But definitely them. I thought we could go out with them after the match and celebrate."

She smiled. "I'm glad you told me. See, now I can look forward to it rather than be nervous about the unknown."

He returned her smile. "I'll remember that."

thirteen

"Alè!" Francesca yelled at the top of her lungs, jumping with the rest of the crowd. Beside her, Max grinned down at her. She gave him a questioning expression. "What?"

"You're just, uh…louder than I expected," he said, his eyes filled with humor.

"This is important!"

He smiled gently, throwing an arm around her. He bent and gave her a kiss on the cheek. "I understand."

She smiled up at him, and they eventually sat down. Kate gave Marco a knowing smile. Unease slipped through Francesca. It was one thing when it was only her and Max. But now in front of Marco and Kate, as well as Marco's brother Stefano and his wife, Teresa, it was taking it to another level. She was thankful that Marco's cousin Lucca and his wife, Ellie, and Kate's sister, Meara, and her husband, Alec, were not in attendance. That would be four more pairs of eyes watching them more closely than the *calcio* match.

Katie must have sensed her uneasiness. She grinned at Francesca. "I love your jersey," she commented.

Francesca smiled down at the team jersey. Max had surprised

her with it over *cornettos* and cappuccino that morning. She had told him enthusiastically that gift surprises were totally acceptable in her mind.

"We'll have to go shopping afterward," Kate said, and Francesca agreed. She turned her attention back to the pitch. Max's seats were in a fabulous location. Alfonso had run past and saluted them. Francesca had become oddly sentimental. When she first moved to Positano, Alfonso had been an older teenager. Marco had asked her to watch over him a little, as he was like a young brother to him. Marco had explained when he was sowing his wild oats, his *Zio* Angelo had sent him to live with Alfonso and his parents. The small family had provided some stability and foundation for Marco that had deeply affected him.

"I should have known with Francesca here, you would want to shop," Marco said dryly.

"You like to shop?" Max asked Francesca innocently.

Marco turned and gave him a leveled look, but there was humor in his eyes. "Stand clear. You haven't seen anything like it."

"IT FEELS GOOD TO SIT DOWN," Marco commented several hours later, as he sat back in the *ristorante* they had chosen for dinner.

Katie rolled her eyes. "You guys were sitting down outside on the bench the entire time we were shopping. And we weren't even that long."

"I've never seen anything like it," Max said, shaking his head at Marco. "You were right. So much shopping and in such a short time."

Francesca frowned at Max. "Don't encourage him. He loves to tease me about leading Katie astray."

"Francesca is the best shopper I know," Kate said loyally. "She walks in, and it's like she sees a spotlight over what is perfect for me. The skies open and the angels sing," she joked. "So, of course, I'm going to shop with her whenever I can."

Francesca smiled and clinked her glass with Kate. It felt good to be with her friends after being separated this past month. The last few hours had been so much fun. After the *calcio* match, they had waited to see Alfonso for just a few brief minutes. He had enthusiastically thanked them all for coming and then run off to go celebrate their victory with his new team.

The women had then gone into the gift shop at the stadium to load up on jerseys, hats, and scarves for the future. They bought something for the entire family, knowing they would all be attending matches in the future to support Alfonso. Emerging with several bags, they had headed to the Galleria Vittorio Emanuele II, since it was an exquisite shopping mall and near the *ristorante*.

"I haven't bought clothes for a long time," Teresa said now, glancing at Stefano.

"Well, an entire month or so. However long it's been since Francesca left!" Stefano said, reaching for a piece of herb *focaccia*. "At least I could get a last-minute reservation here. It's been on my list for some time."

It was Teresa's turn to roll her eyes. "I cannot believe there is a restaurant yet where we haven't eaten. This menu is probably filled with all kinds of ghastly things. Maybe I'll be in luck, and it will have something like mac and cheese."

Stefano looked lovingly at his wife. "If not, I'll make you some when we get home, *cara*."

Francesca caught Max's gaze and smiled knowingly. She had given him a small debrief that morning about her friends. Though he was related to Stefano also, he hadn't spent as much time around him. And Max explained he barely knew Teresa, since he was in America visiting his mother at Christmas when

Stefano and Teresa were wed. Francesca told him how funny the couple was with Teresa's penchant for junk food and Stefano's love of fine dining.

"Stefano, I heard you were going to do another season of your show?" Francesca asked.

He grimaced a little. "Lucca and I agreed on at least two seasons, which is difficult because I'm also trying to build my new pasta company. But I guess I'm committed. But only if Teresa is my producer."

Teresa put an arm around him. "Of course I will be. I helped make you a star," she said, batting her eyelashes.

"Speaking of star, can you believe how well Alfonso played?" Marco asked. The men began a detailed discussion of the match.

Kate glanced at them, and with a glimmer in her eyes, she turned to Francesca. "Your ring is really beautiful," she said, picking up Francesca's hand to get a closer look. "Amethyst? Your birthstone. It suits you." Putting Francesca's hand back down, she sat back and stared speculatively at her. "So just how long have you known Max?"

"Oh, for a while. He saw me at your wedding," Francesca said, trying to keep her expression neutral. It was true, but she felt like a heel misleading her friend. She and Max had talked about it the night before and agreed they would carry on their pretense in front of the group. Francesca had felt conflicted about it but told Max in the end she couldn't believe one of them would inadvertently blurt it out at the wrong time. Her money was on Teresa, who had few filters. And if they knew, then the rest would know. In the end, Max had agreed. "Let's just take it one step at a time," he said.

"Max asked about Francesca that very night," Marco said, apparently overhearing Kate's comment and turning toward her, smiling. "He couldn't take his eyes off of her."

Heat crept into her face as Max grabbed her hand, playing

the perfect fiancé. "He's right. And I haven't been able to ever since," he said quietly.

Teresa leaned forward with her chin in her hands. "He's so romantic," she said. Turning to Stefano, she gave him a little rap on his arm. "You never say things like that to me."

Stefano laughed and grabbed her hand to kiss. "But I make you meatball sandwiches at odd hours of the night. Which would you rather have?"

Teresa laughed and leaned into him. "You know which one."

Kate grinned at them but turned her attention back toward Francesca. "And you're full of surprises, Francesca. Or is that your highness?"

Francesca frowned darkly at Marco. "I see some people cannot keep even a small secret," she commented.

Marco bellowed with laughter. "She's my wife. Have you met her? Katie is worse than any private detective. She would eventually have gotten it out of me."

Francesca made a face but smiled at Kate. "Well, yes, I am, but only technically. It's different from other royal families. Here, it means nothing at all. It's just old traditions from an ancient time."

Teresa leaned forward, her eyes wide. "Do you have a tiara?"

Francesca giggled. "No! It's not like that! I mean, yes, my Nonna has one that's been handed down through the family. But we don't wear it or anything. The titles mean nothing. No one pays attention at all."

"They'll pay attention at the royal gala in a month," Katie said.

"How do you know about that?" Francesca asked.

Kate smiled at her husband. "Because my husband and I will be attending. The Angelo Foundation is being honored at it for its work to bring healthcare to women."

Francesca's eyes widened. "I had no idea! I didn't even know

I was going until a few days ago. That will be amazing to have you there. What are you wearing?"

"I'm not sure yet," Kate said, and shrugged. "We don't have time to shop this trip. I want to get home for Frankie," she said, referring to their toddler. "I don't like leaving him for more than a day or so. He's actually with Rita right now."

"I've taken care of it," Marco said, leaning over to smile at his wife. "I've asked several designers to ship gowns to Mamma's. I thought you could try on dresses best there. We'll all be there for Mamma's birthday in ten days or so."

"Wait, Margherita's birthday is coming up? Can I invite myself?" Francesca said.

Marco inclined his head. "You are always welcome, Francesca."

Max leaned over and put his arm around her. "Of course we should go, darling. Make a weekend of it."

Francesca smiled hesitantly at him. She tried to catch his gaze, but he was smiling at the group and not looking at her. Putting a hand down, she squeezed his thigh, trying to get his attention. If they went down to Positano, they would be enveloped by the entire group. It would be very difficult to keep up their pretense. Today had been very trying, and he was pouring it on too thick!

Max put his hand down over hers on his leg. He finally turned his attention to her and leaned over to whisper in her ear two simple words. "Trust me." His breath sent a shiver down her spine that made her eyes widen. She could only nod at his enigmatic gaze. It was a statement, not a question. Did she? All she knew was when he looked at her like that, she wanted to trust him with her whole heart. With a tight smile, she let the conversation swirl around her as her mind and heart continued its duel.

It was only Teresa's comment as their food was being delivered that made her giggle. "Well, I don't care. I'd still wear a tiara."

# fourteen

"What did you do today?"

Sitting on her window seat in her room, she smiled, holding her phone out so she could see Max's smile. She looked forward to their nightly video calls. They had spent one more day in Milan together, poking around the shops and buying a few small things for Max's flat. He had watched as Francesca gathered a throw blanket and a few pillows. A vase then caught her eye. One purchase at a time, Francesca convinced him he needed to warm up the place a little.

Admittedly, it had been hard to leave him. Max had insisted on driving her back to Verona, where they had arrived in time to have a subdued dinner with the family. With Arianna in Milan and Isabella back at university, it was only Luci to entertain them. She had been remarkably quiet.

It was only after they took a walk after dinner that Max told her Luci confided in him she was failing math. He promised to return the following weekend to tutor her for her big upcoming exam. Francesca had been touched by his kindness, and when he was leaving, she had kissed him back enthusiastically, even knowing Luci was probably peeping through a curtain.

"Francesca?" Max asked, staring at her from the phone.

"Oh, sorry," Francesca said, smiling. "I was just thinking about how sweet it was that you offered to help Luci. I looked at her homework today, and Max, I have to say, I didn't understand it at all."

He laughed. "Well, we'll see how much I remember of algebra. It's been a while. So tell me what you did today."

Francesca told him about her day assisting her father in the tasting room. There was a lot to do before harvest began the following weekend. "Are you sure you want to come down? It's chaos at harvest time, and you will probably be put to work," Francesca said. "Plus, everyone will be home, and it will be loud."

Max grinned. "I like loud if you haven't noticed. And by the way, I got my hearing back in my left ear after that soccer match."

Francesca giggled. "I wasn't that loud. You are so dramatic."

"It's nice to hear you laugh," Max said quietly.

"Did you have a tough day?" she asked anxiously. Tired lines surrounded his eyes. "What's happened?"

He sighed. "Nothing important. I'll tell you about it when I come down."

"Tell me now," she said quietly.

"Just a meeting with my grandfather," he said quietly. "I'm just a little worried about him and his stress. And I wish we could talk. Really talk. He's distant with me."

Francesca bit a nail nervously at his expression. "You think it's bad now? Wait until he learns you're engaged to me."

"In the end, he'll be happy once we figure out how to mend this feud," Max said. "But I don't like the way his business is going. I want to help, but it's as if he doesn't fully trust me. Sometimes I think he feels I'm almost too American."

Francesca frowned. "That can't be true. You're blood."

"That may not be enough," he said and shrugged. "Let's

change the subject. What are you going to cook while I'm down there?"

"I'M EXHAUSTED," Max said, slumping into a chair in the tasting room, which was cluttered with numerous boxes of wine, ready to be shipped to clear their inventory. "Your father has the energy of two twenty-year-olds."

Francesca nodded. Slipping off her rubber boots, she sighed. "Aww, that feels better," she said, smiling at Max. "Thank you again for helping with the harvest."

"Of course, I just can't believe what hard labor it is. And your family does this every year?"

Francesca laughed. "Well, as you saw today, we have a lot of help. But yes, that's the hidden secret of owning a vineyard. People think it's so glamourous until they live through a harvest. And Mamma and Luci were busy in here with the annual harvest wine sale." She shrugged. "Of course, they could just hire people, but as you can see, my parents like to be involved. At least with this one, since it was their first. Their baby. Our operation is much more widespread, but my father has allowed those to run at a more corporate level. We have a magnificent manager."

She looked over sympathetically at Max. His faded jeans were stained with mud and grapes, as was his sweatshirt. Seeing him willingly work alongside everyone had filled her with pride. Though he was right about her father's energy, she was secretly happy that he'd been there to jump on to the machinery and take some of the more demanding jobs her father insisted he could still do. Usually, it was a fight between her father and his foreman. This year, her father had easily acquiesced to Max.

"You have a leaf in your hair," Francesca said, admiring his dark unruly curls.

Max grimaced. "I need a shower and a soft bed. You must be tired too. Are you sure you need to cook tonight?"

She nodded. "I told you, it's tradition." Francesca stretched her long legs out before her, trying to get the cramps out. It was difficult to admit she'd rather spend the evening cuddled up with him, watching a movie and eating takeout. "Tomorrow night is the big harvest dinner. We feed the entire crew and even some of the community as a thank you."

"Your family does this frequently?"

She nodded and shrugged. "Actually, my parents frequently organize community dinners. They have always insisted on giving back, and not just with money. Mamma says it's not just about food but about people coming together. Especially the older people in our community who may not have family around. Loneliness is a terrible thing."

"And you cook for these dinners?"

"I'm just one of the cooks," Francesca said. "And I haven't been home for some time. But if I am home, then, of course, I help."

Max smiled at her. "What are you making tonight?"

"Tonight is all the prep work. Getting everything ready to cook tomorrow. I'll be making my Bolognese sauce, but also, I am making stuffed *tortellini*. Other people are bringing dishes. It's only my contribution. It's not that big of a deal."

"I think it is," Max said quietly, staring at her with an unreadable expression. He stood up and stretched, groaning a little. "I think I must be getting old. See you about five?"

Francesca's eyes widened. "But you were here at six this morning. Max, that's only a couple of hours. Why don't you go back to your hotel and just relax tonight?"

"I'm going to help you," he said firmly, walking toward her. He grabbed her hands and pulled her to her feet. "Put on your boots, and we'll walk up to the house."

She smiled up at him. "I have a better idea."

MAX GRINNED as he drove his Alfa Romeo up the hill to Francesca's family's villa. Just two hours prior, he had bounced around on a tractor up the hill with her. The only advantage had been that during every bump, he got physically closer to her. He desperately wanted to kiss her, but her sisters' presence was a natural deterrence. Not that they seemed to care. In fact, they had already become his allies, confiding their thoughts, laughing with him, and providing hints here and there about how to navigate Francesca's moods. Luci had stared at him seriously during their tutoring session the night prior and, without any provocation, stated matter-of-factly, "Francesca is complicated."

Shifting now in the driver's seat, he had to admit his muscles ached. Apparently, his long runs were not using all his muscles to their fullest advantage. With every fiber of his being, he had wanted to stay in the luxurious hotel robe, lounge on his bed, and watch sports on television. Instead, he had forced himself to get dressed, picked up some Chinese food and was heading over for a night of cooking. The only thing he knew how to make was cereal, so he doubted he was going to be much help. However, it was also an opportunity to have Francesca all to himself. Her family had told him they all were conveniently going out.

"You're not going to help her?" Arianna asked in mock horror. He had laughed at the family's expressions but shrugged off their concerns. How bad could it be to cook with her?

Pulling through the open gate, he drove up the hill and admired the view. The villa was certainly a regal and majestic site. Opulent with its turrets and shining windows, and yet it looked like a home. Perhaps it was because he knew all the inhabitants were so happy there. Parking, he grabbed the bag on the seat next to him and quickly ascended the stairs. Raising his hand to use the old-fashioned knocker, he was surprised when Graham answered it swiftly.

"Thank God you're here, sir," the elderly man stated with a serious expression.

"Graham, how are you?" Max asked, laying a hand on his shoulder. He had already adopted an easy relationship with him.

"I'm right as rain," Graham said. "But I can't say the same for the kitchen."

Max laughed. "I think everyone is exaggerating."

Graham shrugged on his coat from a nearby closet. "Miriam and I are going to the movies. I know by now to not be present on this night. As does the entire staff. Good luck to you, mate."

Max watched the older man walk through the door much more swiftly than usual. He made his way toward the kitchen. It couldn't be as bad as everyone was making out. Now, as he entered the kitchen, he realized they were wrong. It was worse.

He guessed every pan and pot in the house was lying on the countertops. Red sauce splatters were all over the marble countertops. Francesca was standing at the island, kneading dough, flour covering her face. Her pink apron was back and now had red splatters all over it. Rock music was bellowing from somewhere, and she punched the dough in rhythm. She stopped kneading for a moment and gave an exasperated sigh as her hair fell below her face. She tried pushing it back with her forearm and spotted him.

"Max, I didn't hear you come in," she yelled.

"Graham, let me in," he shouted back. She pointed at her phone that was lying on the kitchen table, and he went over and paused the music and put down the bag. Lowering his voice, he glanced around. "Uh, looks like a bit of a storm blew through."

She rolled her eyes. "Not you too! That's why I send everyone away. I don't need a commentary on my cooking techniques."

He shrugged off his leather jacket and rolled up the sleeves of his button-down shirt. "What can I help with?"

She grimaced. "I need to get this dough to rise, and I don't want to stop to wash my hands. Can you grab the hair that just fell out of my ponytail? Just help me adjust it so it's not in my face.

Max grinned. Now this was a job he was all in for. Walking behind her, he took the hair tie out of her hair gently. "Sorry, it's a little tangled," he said. Running his hands through her hair was the most intimate gesture they had experienced as a couple. He wanted to make it last, and yet his heart was racing so fast he could barely breathe.

"Just throw it all in a ponytail and make it tight," she instructed.

"Uh, sure," he responded, trying to make his voice sound normal. He gathered her hair slowly and reluctantly put it in the hair tie and tightened it.

"Is that okay?" he asked, clearing his throat.

She nodded and pounded on the dough. He walked around the island. Her movements were sure and smooth. "Remind me not to ever make you angry," he commented.

She looked up at him, puzzled and then laughed. "I love kneading. You just have to show it who's boss."

"I can see who's in charge," he answered solemnly. "So, boss lady, what do you want me to do?"

She rolled the dough into a ball and patted it before placing it in a bowl. She covered it with a towel and looked up at him. "Max, really, I don't mean for you to help."

"I want to," he said huskily. He flexed his hands, remembering the silky strands he just recently touched.

Her beautiful nosed twitched. "What delicious smell is coming from that bag?"

He grinned. "I stopped for some Chinese on the way here. I was thinking you might want something different from Italian. Want to eat, and then I'll do the one thing I know how to do?"

She smiled, "What's that?"

He grinned back. "Wash dishes."

MAX SAT AT THE TABLE, meticulously cutting carrot rounds into tinier pieces. Francesca stopped stirring the meat and onions on the stove for a minute to watch him and smiled gently. "It doesn't have to be precise, just small chunks."

He paused, cutting to narrow his eyes at her. "I feel like there's some smirking going on."

She stared back innocently at him. "Smirking? I'm not sure I know that word," she fibbed.

"Uh, huh. I'm sure. Let's just say I warned you I don't cook."

She smiled a little. "But you did a fantastic job with the washing up," she said, glancing around. All the pans that hung above the island were neatly back in place. "Honestly, you should call it quits."

The kitchen was quiet except for the American pop music she had turned, but this time at a much more respectable level. She had put it on as a joke, but Max whistled away to it. He was sitting back, sipping his glass of soave and smiling at her. "This is fun," he said, his gaze intent.

"You, my friend, have a twisted view of fun," she said, feeling awkward. She turned back to stir her Bolognese sauce, afraid to hold his gaze. Earlier she had cut and stuffed her *tortellini* with a mixture of cheeses, relieved that he was busy washing dishes. Now that they were nearing the end of her cooking, the atmosphere was feeling increasingly intimate, like they were an old married couple.

"Francesca?" his quiet voice came from behind her, his breath on her neck.

"Yes?" she squeaked.

"What should I do with the carrots?"

She winced. "Oh sorry, you can just put them in this pan. I'll sauté them."

She expected him to come alongside her with the cutting

board, but instead, he reached around her from behind and shook the carrots into the pan. She held her breath as his warm body pressed against her.

"I like cooking," he whispered, putting the cutting board down alongside her. He slid his lips along her neck. "This just may convince me to do more of it."

Francesca tried to still her thumping heart by taking a deep breath. "Can you hand me that bowl of tomatoes?" she said, trying to make her voice sound normal. "I squished them earlier."

Max was forced to walk to a different counter, and she moved to pour her mixture into a bigger pot. She avoided his gaze as she reached for the bowl and added the tomatoes to it. For the next few minutes, it was tough to focus as she added wine and herbs to the sauce. Finally, there was nothing left to add, and she turned quickly, only to collide with him. His arms steadied her, and he lowered his head, his lips a breath from hers.

"Do you know what I like more than cooking?" he asked.

She shook her head. "Eating?" she whispered.

"Not quite," he said.

His lips met hers, softly at first and then harder. She wound her arms around him and held on tight. He loosened her hair tie, thrusting his hands through the length of her hair.

Francesca's cheeks burned. Was it because they were standing by the hot stove, or was it his effect on her?

"See I told you," Luci's voice came somewhere behind them. "Everything is going to burn while they do that."

fifteen

Francesca set one last platter down on the long buffet table and smiled. Covered with an Italian linen and with fall décor Arianna had supplied, it was now also filled with plentiful food. As always, neighbors had also arrived with succulent dishes of *polenta e soppressa*, slices of soft polenta served with a locally cured salami, and *radicchio di Verona*, grilled and succulent. There were platters of *risotto all'amarcne*, a specialty in Verona, as well as *luccio in salsa*, fish in a savory sauce. A wide variety of sugar-topped pastries and fritole, small fried dough balls with raisins, were for dessert.

Max stood up to hold her chair out, and her mother gave an approving nod. It had been a little uncomfortable the night before when the family arrived to find them in such a passionate embrace. Later, Francesca was grateful they hadn't gotten more carried away. She had never responded to a man the way she did with Max. It wasn't just the passion. Strangely, he had a knack for just fitting in and making everyone around him comfortable. Francesca was letting her guard down. He didn't seem to care if she was dressed casually or glammed up. She loved when she caught the heat in his eyes. It was as if he wanted to be alone with her as much as she wanted to be with him.

As if he sensed her thoughts, he leaned over and gave her a kiss on the cheek. "Everything tastes amazing. But I think your *tortellini* is the star."

She smiled shyly, and all the Italian mammas were also smiling. They had been grinning all day knowing Max was working in the fields and then still came up to set up the tables and chairs. He had brought a second set of clothes, showered, and changed at the house before dinner. Francesca smiled at his ruffled hair that he hadn't bothered to tame. He hadn't shaved today either, and his beard lightly dotted his jawline. She found she wanted to run her lips along it and run her hands through the curls like he had last night with her own hair. Instead, she grabbed her water glass and took a long drink.

"Frannie, pass the bread," Isabella said, leaning over from the other side of Max. She had been surprised when Isabella claimed the seat and had been talking to Max about a variety of topics. She would have to ask him later what Isabella discussed with him. It was curious that even her sister found him so comfortable to be around. It was also disconcerting. When this ended, her entire family's heart would collectively be broken. Glancing at her ring, she bit her lip, wondering if there was a way to retreat. Perhaps if they had started as just two regular people and slowly dated, they would have a chance. Now they were immersed in this farce that filled her with dread deep down in her soul.

"Is something the matter?" Max had turned back to her and must have seen the tension cross her face.

She opened her mouth, intending to deny that it was anything. Max swooped in, his face inches from hers. "If you say nothing, I'll kiss you till your socks fall off right here," he whispered in her ear.

Francesca felt her heart begin to thud. He was well capable of it. Max leaned back, his gaze searching hers. "How about we go stretch our legs?"

Francesca nodded, and he gently scraped his chair back over the grass and helped her to her feet.

"Are you guys going somewhere to do some smooching?" Luci asked. Suddenly, the table had gone quiet. Francesca frowned at her and was about to admonish her when Max's arm tightly hugged her.

"Bullseye!" he announced, spinning her around. Laughter erupted behind them as they strolled off. Just as they reached the exit, Luci's confused voice carried after them.

"Wait, what did I hit?"

FRANCESCA GRIPPED Max's hand as they walked quickly down the stairs to stand at the stone wall overlooking Verona. Stopping, they both stared silently at the city below them.

"Tell me why you've been so quiet at the dinner," Max said quietly.

"Nothing." Francesca answered automatically, keeping her gaze averted. "I don't know, Max," she finally admitted, clearly frustrated. Turning toward him, she frowned. "Alright, if you want to know the truth, I feel like we've carried this too far. My family is falling in love with you. And so are most of the women at that table tonight!" Francesca added wildly.

"Are you?" he asked.

Francesca gave him a startled glance. "I thought we agreed this engagement was all temporary. I thought these last few days were mostly for show."

"Of course not," he snapped roughly. "Do you think I'm just faking everything? I thought we talked about this, Francesca."

He stood up and walked away from her for a minute, running

a hand through his hair. He turned suddenly, staring at her with narrow eyes. "I thought we were actually getting somewhere. But every time I feel like you're starting to loosen up and let me in a little, you pull back."

"That's not true!"

He nodded. "Yes, it is. You keep questioning my reasons for doing things. We take two steps forward, and then you withdraw. I thought after last night . . ." He turned his gaze away from her and looked out at the view.

"What about last night?" she asked quietly.

"I thought we . . . I don't know. It just felt easy. Like we are able to just enjoy being together and doing simple things. Ordinary things. We weren't looking at cathedrals, ruins, or some other thing that's like a thousand years old while I am pretending I'm interested."

"You have just been pretending this whole time?" she exclaimed.

"No, no. Of course not. I didn't mean that. I'm just frustrated. But, Francesca, I'm not here to be a sightseer or a tourist on holiday. I'm trying to get to know *you*."

She couldn't look at him. For once, she didn't know what to say. He finally continued quietly. "You hold yourself back. You'll tell me the entire history of some ancient building and about a thousand facts to go along with it, but you won't tell me the same about what's going on in that beautiful mind of yours."

She shrugged, feeling tears well up in her eyes. How could she tell him she was so worried about her heart being broken she could never let a man get that close?

"Is it because I'm more American than Italian?"

"No!" she said forcibly. "Max, how can you say that? That's ridiculous."

He walked slowly toward her, looking down at her. "Not so ridiculous. I told you. I'm beginning to sense that my own grandparents feel the same way. I didn't want to get into it on the phone, but my meeting with Nonno was pretty contentious. I tried to make several suggestions about the financial stability of the company, and he shrugged them all off. He'd rather listen to others. He doesn't trust me."

Her heart ached for him. He looked so vulnerable standing there, his curls blowing in the wind, tiredness around his eyes.

She extended a hand and rubbed his arm, almost as if she was soothing a small child. "I'm sure he trusts you. Max, you have one of the kindest hearts of anyone I know."

"Do *you* trust me, Francesca?"

She looked up at him and met his gaze. His expression was uncertain, and she wanted to reassure him. Leaning up, she gave him a small kiss. "I do," she said huskily. "But you know, you haven't exactly been that forthcoming with me. Just now was probably the most you've shared with me about how you feel."

He ran a hand through his hair. "I agree. I need to do better as well." His eyes darkened, and he pulled her into his arms. "What do you say we take this trip to Positano as a chance to really get to know each other?"

She smiled shyly. "I'd like that, Max."

"Now let's do some of that smooching Luci talked about," he said, leaning down to capture her lips again.

Francesca leaned up, and his arms tightened around her. She kissed him back earnestly, wanting him to feel the growing attraction she had for him. A long time later, Francesca finally pulled back. "We should go back to the table," she said guiltily, putting her hands up to smooth her hair.

"They are all still sitting there?" Max asked, shocked, nuzzling her neck.

"Of course. This is Italy, Max. They'll be sitting there for hours! Come on." She grabbed his hand, and they walked up the stairs and headed toward the side yard, where lights had been strung up over the long tables.

Max stopped suddenly and pulled her toward him. "One last

kiss. I promised to help Luci with her homework tonight. Who knows when I'll get another opportunity to be alone with you?"

She gladly lifted her lips up to his and immediately got caught up in the moment. The kiss went on and on. It was only a familiar voice speaking in Italian that snapped her back to reality. "Francesca, we're home!"

Francesca pulled frantically out of Max's arms and instinctively grabbed her hair to pull it to one side. She straightened her sweater and turned to her grandparents standing just a few feet away from them at the edge of the yard, still under the lights. How long had they been standing there?

She rushed toward them, greeting them excitedly in Italian, hugging each of them. But they had confused expressions and hurt in their eyes. "Your papa told us you were with your fiancé," her grandmother stated flatly.

"Nonna, I can explain . . ." she cut in, speaking in English.

"Why are we speaking English? Is he American?" Nonna asked shrewdly.

Francesca took a deep breath. There was time for the truth to come out. First, they needed to grow to like Max before she revealed the truth.

"Come meet him," she said and would have drawn them over to Max, only he had advanced up the hill and was now walking toward them. Francesca's heart was about to beat out of her chest. He emerged under the lights, his expression guarded. He moved closer to her.

"Nonno, Nonna, I'd like to present to you . . ."

Her grandmother had been squinting, and now, as Max got closer, she stepped back and gasped. "Leonardo Valentini," she whispered.

"Nonna, no . . ." Francesca broke in.

"Leonardo Valentini," her grandmother repeated, almost as if she had seen a ghost. Small in stature, her grandfather's round face encircled by a full head of white curls was now also darkening.

"His name is Max," she said wildly.

"Francesca," Max whispered. "I forgot to tell you. I look just like my grandfather."

*sixteen*

"Do you want to talk about it, *Topo*? You've been pretty quiet."

Francesca glanced over at her father, who had been sitting alongside her on an old wooden fence. This was their spot, the place they had come together ever since she could remember to ponder about life's twists and turns. They had been sitting there silently for some time. He still didn't meet her gaze but continued to stare down the hill at the grapevines, which were now mostly bare. They finished with the harvest earlier than usual, thanks to an abundance of helpers.

Francesca had taken off her work gloves. She purposely left her ring in her room rather than risk it being harmed by the hard work. Staring down at her bare hand, she tried to think of how to explain to her father. They had always been so close.

"I don't know what to say, Papa," she finally remarked. "Everyone was so angry at the harvest dinner."

It had been three days. Three long days, and she hadn't talked to Max. She surmised he would want the ring back. He probably realized this ridiculous plan they had conjured up

127

would never come to fruition. She shuddered at how her grand-parents had treated him.

Even after she confessed he was the grandson of Leonardo Valentini, but had been raised in America, they remained hostile. Everyone had begun yelling, Arianna valiantly trying to defend Max. Her parents, Isabella, and Luci were oddly silent with obvious confusion. She had finally whispered to Max that he should leave and give it some time. He nodded and left with a wary glance backward. Francesca had tried to look confident, giving him an encouraging smile as if she could handle her family. She frowned. She had said "give it some time," but had purposely ignored his calls for the last three days, not knowing what to say. Their texts had been short, with her asking him to understand. It was the same with her family, who avoided the conversation. When she tried to bring it up, her father informed her it was more important to get through the harvest before taking on this new drama.

"I just don't understand any of it." Her father's words cut into her thoughts. "I thought you said he was a Rinaldi."

Francesca bit her lip and met her father's confused gaze. "He was. He is. His full name is Massimo Rinaldi Valentini. His mother was a Rinaldi, the daughter of Francesco Rinaldi. He's a distant cousin of Marco. Their grandfathers were brothers. I just knew if I told you right away that he was a Valentini, you might not give him a chance and, well . . . I really like Max."

"I would hope you love him if you are engaged to him," Carlo pointed out.

"Well, yes, but when we first, uh, started dating," Francesca mumbled, trying to cover herself. She felt horrible that she was still covering one lie with another. But she wasn't sure if now was the time to reveal that their engagement was a ruse to end the feud. Besides, she knew deep in her heart she wanted Max to stick around for the time being. "I wanted you and Mamma to give him a chance."

"That feud is between your grandparents and the Valentinis. You know I never cared all that much except that I hated seeing my father so upset over the years." Carlo shrugged. "Personally, I never wanted to be in the fashion business. In a way, it helped me escape that life so I could work with my hands. I always just wanted this feud to end. But you should have told us, *Topo*. You should not have lied," he said, frowning.

At her silence, he turned to her, his gaze growing gentle. "You can tell us anything. We could have helped strategize. Or at least tried to help ease him in with your nonni. I feel guilty enough making you come home to take your place in society. I should have been able to tell my parents no. But they have lost everything and I . . . I just want them to be happy."

Guilt washed over her. "Papa, I…"

"THERE YOU ARE!" Luci shouted, climbing the hill, out of breath. Heaving herself up in between them on the rustic fence, she took great gulps of air before speaking.

"Didn't either of you hear me? I yelled and yelled. I finally had to run up this hill!" she exclaimed, clearly frustrated. "Mamma wants you both home."

Carlo jumped down and looked up at them, his face showing concern. "What is the matter? Is your mamma ill?"

Luci sighed and shook her head. "No, but she probably wishes she was. Nonna and Nonno just arrived." She looked at Francesca and wiggled her eyebrows. "Time for a little chat."

"WHAT ARE YOU DOING HERE?" Francesca whispered anxiously, yanking Max into the dining room and quietly shutting sliding doors. Turning to face him, she frowned. "I told you I would call you!"

"That was three days ago," Max said flatly. He stood there, hands in the pockets of his leather jacket, looking more like a rebellious teenager than a man of his age. He ran his hands through his already tousled hair. "I drove down from Milan this afternoon when you didn't answer my calls...*again,*" he emphasized.

"I was working at the harvest the first time you called," she said quietly. "And now my nonni are here! I've been in negotiations with them for two hours!"

He smiled wryly. "Negotiations? Is that normal?"

"Well, not always," she said and rolled her eyes. "I don't live up to their expectations most of the time. First, I left Verona to work in a shop, like some *commoner,* apparently. I've ignored my place in society, and my social circle is, quote, 'tragic.'"

Max eyed her steadily. "Tragic? What about the Rinaldi family?"

"They are the acceptable part," she said.

"I'm part of the Rinaldi family," Max retorted with a smug grin.

Francesca gave a dismissive wave. "You, my friend, are compromised. That fine Rinaldi blood is diluted by the Valentini line."

He raised his eyebrows. "Compromised. Yikes. That sounds bad. So they are in the living room right now?"

"Yes, they are in there with my parents. We are just waiting for dinner to be served," Francesca said.

"You can't escape to help Prudentia?" he said and laughed.

She rolled her eyes. "Even making sure we have a dinner we can eat won't get me out of this meeting."

He turned toward the door. "Let me go talk to them."

"Are you mad?" Francesca grabbed at his sleeve, her eyes wide. "Let me, um, oil the motor first."

Max blinked at her before grinning. "Grease the wheels?"

"Now is the time to correct my English?"

"Well, you are fluent . . . most of the time," he teased, gently tucking a stray lock of hair behind her ear. "Come on. You've been at this for two hours. Made any progress?"

"Not really," she muttered.

"Well, then, let me try," he said persuasively, drawing her into his arms. "I'm good with nonnas!"

"You haven't met mine," Francesca said emphatically, nestling automatically against his soft leather jacket. She raised her head, and his lips descended slowly toward hers.

"You certainly haven't!" said a cool female voice in the doorway.

They froze. Slowly, they turned to see Nonna standing there, her sharp gaze boring into them.

"Nonna," Francesca began weakly, trying desperately to disentangle herself from Max's arms. He held tight, subduing her attempt.

"Young man," Nonna continued, "if you want to speak with us, then stop romancing our granddaughter and come meet with us." With a pointed look at Francesca, Nonna pivoted and marched back toward the living room.

"God help us," Francesca whispered under her breath.

"What did you say?" Max asked.

"I said good luck!" Francesca lied with a strained smile.

*seventeen*

Francesca sat on a bench in Milan, staring intently at the Duomo. As usual, crowds milled around, taking photos and selfies from all angles. The mass of people didn't bother her, as she was in her own world. Her thoughts were a jumbled mess and staring at the large familiar church somehow brought her comfort. She had arrived in Milan that morning for her last fitting at the designer's salon.

"There you are!" Arianna slid on the bench beside her. She nudged her. "Why didn't you answer my texts?"

Francesca frowned and glanced at her phone. "Sorry, I guess I didn't see them."

"Still thinking about the reaction to your engagement to a Valentini?" Arianna asked, sitting back and gazing at her speculatively. "Mamma said Nonna was pretty harsh. Nonno sounded like he warmed up a tiny bit? At least he spoke to Max."

Francesca rolled her eyes. "Nonno asked him to pass the bread."

Arianna snickered.

"It's not funny!" Francesca said. "They were just awful. They interrogated him like he was caught stealing the silver."

"How did Max handle it all?"

Francesca picked at a thread on her jacket. "You know Max. He was kind, charming, approachable. Completely acting like everything was normal."

Arianna smiled. "That's Max. What did he say afterward?"

Francesca shrugged. "He doesn't seem to be bothered. He says they'll grow to like him. In fact, he doesn't even want to discuss it. Every time I start to, he changes the subject."

"Smart man," Arianna commented with a small smile.

"What do you mean? You know them, Arianna. They'll keep it up. Pretty soon, they'll get Papa riled up to."

Arianna frowned. "Papa already likes Max. He will not go back on that. And Mamma adores him. But you're going to have to speed things along."

Francesca looked startled. "Why would I do that?"

Arianna smirked. "Before everyone else finds out this engagement is fake."

The blood drained from Francesca's face. "Do you think they will?"

Arianna's expression was contemplative. "I mean, I don't think so. But the more you're around family, the more they will ask questions."

"It still may take some time," Francesca said, looking nervous. "We haven't even figured out a way for both sides to meet. And after that, to try to even see if they'll entertain the idea of reuniting."

"When hell freezes over," Arianna said.

Francesca frowned. "It *could* happen, Ari. It might still happen. Don't underestimate Max."

Arianna stared at her. "You really like him, don't you? In fact, I think you're in love with him."

"Absolutely not!" Francesca protested. Suddenly, for some unexplainable reason, the wind was knocked out of her. She tried to take a deep breath.

"What are two of my favorite women so deep in conversation about?" Max asked from somewhere behind them.

Francesca jumped. How much had he heard? "We were just talking . . ." she stammered.

"We were debating your merits and if you are actually going to win our grandparents over," Arianna interrupted smoothly. "Frannie seems to have a lot of confidence in you."

Max smiled gently at Francesca. "Does she, now?" he asked speculatively. "I wasn't sure if you did, Francesca."

Francesca shrugged. "I don't know. At least Nonno spoke to you," she improvised, using Arianna's line.

"He wanted bread," Max reminded her flatly.

"Well, yes, but he said *per favore*," she said with humor in her eyes.

Max laughed. "This weekend, we shall see."

"What's this weekend?" Arianna asked.

"Max is coming to Verona for the weekend, and he thinks if they just get to know him, he might be able to work his magic."

Arianna smiled. "This I have to see. I think I may just take a trip home this weekend. Can I get a lift, Max?"

Max shrugged. "Why not? I need all the support I can get. Now, ladies, how about some lunch before you have to go for your dress fitting?"

Francesca smiled and let him pull her to her feet. "Over lunch, we'll strategize with Arianna about how we're going to pull this whole plan off. She seems doubtful, but perhaps she can give us some ideas."

Arianna linked her arm through Max's. "I'm smarter than I look, Massimo. Feed me lunch, and I'll give you even more wisdom."

"God help us," Max said, raising his gaze to the sky.

"Yes, that's right. You're going to need him, too," Arianna teased.

# eighteen

"What do you suppose they are talking about?" Isabella whispered to Francesca.

Francesca watched her grandfather and Max strolling in the garden. She and Isabella had their noses pressed up against the window. "I'm just glad they are talking."

"Max looks relaxed," Isabella commented.

"Max is always relaxed," Francesca quipped. She studied him as he walked along, hands in the pockets of his black pants. He had arrived wearing a sport coat and a tie, and she had told him to lose them because he looked like he was trying too hard. That had been his only sign of nervousness. He had joined the family for brunch, answering questions, quietly praising the delicious food and generally blending in. Arianna had skillfully drawn her grandmother into the living room on the pretense of wanting to see their vacation photos. Everyone else had followed. It was Isabella, who noticed everything, who had pulled Francesca back to point dramatically at the two men departing out the sunroom door to the garden.

"I really love Max," Isabella said and sighed. "He's the big brother I always wanted."

Francesca glanced at her younger sister with a sense of guilt. "I know, Issy. What are you guys always talking about in the corner?"

Isabella flushed. "He's been giving me tips."

"What kind of tips?"

Isabella suddenly was taking a great deal of interest in her manicure. "He hasn't told you?"

At Francesca's shake of the head, Isabella blurted, "Promise not to say anything? Especially to Luci?"

Francesca put an arm around Isabella's slim shoulders. "Of course."

"Well, it's like this. There's a guy at school, and Max has sort of been helping me with ideas about things to talk about with him."

Francesca smiled a little, pleased Isabella was trying to come out of her shell. "Is he cute?"

"Beyond! He's hot," Isabella said emphatically. "But he's only here for a year. He's a study abroad student from America. So I guess I just thought Max might...you know..."

"Give you some American insight?"

Isabella shrugged, looking out the window. "I guess so. Jacob is probably used to American girls. I don't even know any American girls except the tourists we see here."

"You met my friends Kate and Ellie when you came to visit me in Positano," Francesca remarked.

"Frannie, they're so old," Isabella protested. "I mean like young American girls."

Francesca laughed. "Okay, well, I promise not to tell them they're washed up at their advanced age! And I guess me, too, since I'm near their age! So what has Max told you?"

"He mostly just told me to ask questions. Find out more about his interests and get him talking to relax him. But he told me if Jacob talks about himself and doesn't ask me anything more than to walk away. Max says the last thing I need to do is date some guy who is only into himself. Max is really smart, Frannie!"

Francesca smiled, tightening her arm around her sister. "Yes, he is. I'm glad he's helping you, Issy. So did it work?"

She nodded. "It did. At least he answered my questions, but then he started asking me stuff about me and Verona and what's it like here. And he asked me out for next weekend."

"That's great!" Francesca said, trying to temper her enthusiasm. "Just go out and see if you like him. Play it cool."

"That's what Max says," Isabella said confidently. "He told me from the beginning, guys like it when girls play it cool. He says you played it completely cool, and he liked the chase."

Francesca raised her eyebrows. "Oh, he did, did he?"

"I told you, Frannie. He's super smart."

Before Francesca could answer, she noticed the men coming toward the door. There was no time to move. She stood there with Isabella and waited for her grandfather and Max to come through the glass door.

"Nonno," she began.

"Francesca, where is your sister?"

"Which one?"

Her grandfather furrowed his brow impatiently. "Arianna. Where is she?"

"In the living room. Nonno . . ."

The older man brushed past her and hurried down the hall. Francesca turned to Max, who was leaning up against the door, his hands still in his pockets, his expression unreadable.

"Max, whatever did you say to him?"

Max pushed himself away from the door. Taking a hand out of pocket, he flung his arm around Francesca's shoulders. "Let's go find out."

~

"ARIANNA, THESE ARE FANTASTIC," Nonno said.

Arianna picked up her electronic tablet and looked at her family, her frown darkening. The family was leaning over the older man's shoulder, peering down at Arianna's drawings. She glanced at their faces before holding the pad in front of her protectively.

"*Grazie,* Nonno," she said politely. "But it doesn't matter. I'm not going into the fashion business. And I don't know why Max told you."

"Because you are really, really good, Ari," Max said. "You've taken what you're learned in architecture and applied it to fashion. It's a tremendous combination. You shouldn't keep your talent hidden."

Nonna sat down in the chair next to Arianna. "May I see? I couldn't quite view everything over everyone's heads."

Arianna stared at her for a moment, but respect for her grandparents was instilled since childhood. "*Certo,* Nonna," she said softly, handing her grandmother the pad.

Max pulled Francesca over to a nearby couch and slowly the family sat down in the other chairs. They watched as Nonna slid through Arianna's designs on the electronic tablet. Some she stopped at for quite a while, and then others she smiled.

"How did you know?" Francesca whispered to Max.

He shrugged. "She told me. I convinced her one day to show me, and I was blown away."

"But I don't understand. Why did you tell Nonno?"

He smiled at her and pulled her close. "Just watch," he said.

Nonna was finished looking at the designs now, and she sat with the tablet in her lap. "God has given you a gift, Arianna. You must use it."

"Nonna, I don't . . . that is, I'll use it in architecture."

"No, fashion," Nonna said, her expression becoming determined. "We built a fashion empire. It's time we returned to it."

"You mean you'll make peace with the Valentinis?" Luci

asked incredulously. Francesca gave her a speaking look. It was too soon to ask that question.

"No! Never!" exclaimed Nonno. "We will not speak to them. But it is time we return to Milan with our heads held high."

Antonia was the first to speak. "Giancarlo, do you think we can start a business at our age?"

"We could," Nonno said thoughtfully. "We are still relatively young. We are capable." He looked at his wife and spoke rapidly in Italian to her.

"What did she say?" Max whispered. "I heard the part about returning to Milan and that they should try to make a go of it again. That's good, right?"

Francesca sighed. "Yes, except the end part. That's when he said if they return to Milan, it will give them the opportunity to burn your grandparents' business to the ground."

*nineteen*

"So, how long has your grandfather been an arsonist?" Max asked, glancing at her briefly before returning his gaze to the road. His eyes were hidden by sunglasses, and it was unclear if he was joking or not. They were driving down to the Amalfi Coast for a few days to celebrate Margherita's birthday party.

She played dumb. "I'm not sure I know that word. 'Arsonist?'"

"You know, someone who plays with fire?" Max asked with a wry smile. "Likes to burn things down."

"Well, yes, that part of the motivation to return to Milan is unfortunate," Francesca remarked dryly. "But you should have talked to me about this idea of yours ahead of time."

"I tried!" Max said. "Remember the night you came to Milan? After your dress fitting, I told you I wanted to talk, and you told me to wait until after dinner."

Francesca bit back a retort, and color heated her face. They had gone to the corner *trattoria* and talked for hours over a decadent meal. She never met a man who loved to sit back and have her order for him. In fact, she learned he'd try anything. It was a challenge, and sometimes she ordered something a little out of the ordinary to see what he would do. He just smiled and ate it for the most part. Secretly, she hadn't wanted to ruin their dinner by even bringing the subject up.

Whether it was their conversation that just flowed, the wine that had flowed even greater or just a feeling of closeness, but when they got home, they kissed for hours. She finally nestled her head on his cashmere-sweater-covered chest and promptly went to sleep. In her defense, she had gotten up early in order to drive to Milan. Still, when she woke up early the next morning as the sun peeped into the massive windows, she was startled to find herself exactly in the same position. Glancing up, Max was staring at her with a hard-to-read expression. Apologizing, she had sat up awkwardly, pushing her tangled hair back. She hadn't snored, had she?

"What are you thinking about?" Max's voice cut into her thoughts. He glanced over at her and smiled a little. "Thinking about sleeping with me last night?" he asked, perceptive as always.

She rolled her eyes. "I didn't sleep with you," she retorted. Fidgeting in her seat, she finally continued. "Well, fine, I guess I did. But not the way you're making it sound. We just slept. And I still don't know why you didn't wake me up!"

"I was comfortable," Max said quietly. "I told you to stop apologizing. Other than being stiff when I woke up, it was a lovely night."

Francesca gave an unladylike snort. "Next, you'll be telling me that my snoring was musical."

"You don't snore," Max stated. "At least you didn't with me."

"That rat!"

"Excuse me? Max asked, glancing at her quickly.

"Arianna has told me for years I snore!"

Max grinned. "Well, I guess you can tell her I can verify you don't."

"I can't tell her that!" Francesca protested.

"Tell Nonna then?"

She shoved his shoulder. "Great idea! Let's just announce it to the world."

He laughed but kept his eyes on the road. The twists and turns of the infamous road from Naples to Sorento were increasing. He handled them carefully, but also confidently. "Speaking of announcements, I was thinking we shouldn't let down our guard with the Rinaldi Family."

She looked at him quizzically. "What does that mean?"

"It means we should just continue acting like a normal engaged couple in love."

"You said Marco might sense the truth," Francesca commented. "He knows you just met me. Which means Katie will also know. He would never keep anything from her."

Max nodded. "Yes, they do know. I should have told you before now. Marco asked a lot of questions, and I had to tell him. But Marco reassured me it was our business. I just think at this point we ought to keep the circle small. You haven't even met my grandparents yet. You know how Italians are. Everyone likes to talk. I'm not saying any of the Rinaldis would speak out of turn, but an odd word here or there and the next thing you know, both our grandparents know this is a farce."

Francesca turned to look out the window, fearful she couldn't hide her surprise. Their relationship had become deeper. Sure, the engagement was still fake, but why did he always have to remind her of that? At least he had promised her this trip would be a time to get to know each other. She certainly hoped so.

"Francesca?"

She hesitated before speaking. "If you think that's for the best, I guess so," she answered. "It's just difficult. They are all my friends, and I don't want to lie to them."

"I understand," he said soothingly. "Let's just take it day by day and see how it goes. I want you to be comfortable. If you really want to tell them the truth, then I'll support you."

Francesca agreed quietly and went back to gazing out the window. The problem was she didn't know what the truth was anymore.

~

"I REMEMBER when I first met Francesca," Katie said, leaning earnestly across the table toward Max. "She was so statuesque and beautiful. I was instantly envious of her."

Marco slung a casual arm around Katie and hugged her to him. "She was envious of Francesca's height the most," he teased, smiling down at his five-foot-five wife.

Katie pushed at his chest but immediately raised her head for his kiss. Francesca sighed softly, and Max looked at her sharply.

The family was sitting outside relaxing after a delicious dinner cooked by Stefano. Though it was brisk out, the tall gas heaters kept them warm. Stefano and Teresa were there along with Nico, who had explained that his wife Georgina would arrive the next day. She was a pilot and had a last-minute flight to help transport a medical team to a hospital in Spain. Margherita had added that Katie's sister Meara and her husband Alec and their cousin Lucca and his wife Ellie would be there the next night for Margherita's party. It was to be held on the family's lemon grove estate at the stunning venue on the top of the hill.

Katie leaned forward on her elbows. "I was just thinking about it the other day and how funny it all was. That Marco told me to just go find a dress in Positano for the shareholder's gala, as if I was just going to pluck something off a tourist's rack." She stopped to roll her eyes. "Thank goodness Rita told me to go to Capri. The next thing I knew, Francesca and her friend Allegra whisked me away to buy me the most gorgeous dress ever. It was this amazing blue with no back to speak of. Francesca gave me the courage to wear it, though."

Marco sighed dramatically. "I loved that dress."

The family laughed, and Teresa leaned forward now. "Francesca chose all of our wedding dresses. Honestly, she knows fashion so well. She should work for one of those big fashion houses in Milan!"

Francesca was staring at her plate uncomfortably. Putting a comforting arm around her shoulders, he squeezed a little. "You are right, Teresa. Maybe we should look into that, my love."

He almost started laughing at her expression. While he knew she didn't want to mislead her friends, he was thoroughly enjoying playing up the proud fiancé. He saw Kate's startled look as she glanced at Marco. Marco gave a small shrug. They were even confused.

Wouldn't they laugh if they knew how confused he felt? This had all started as a lark and had grown and twisted into the most convoluted muddle. He now had genuine feelings for Francesca, but also her parents and sisters. They had practically adopted him as if he was already a member of the family. He had never felt that acceptance before. And now that he was getting to know the Rinaldi side of the family, he was feeling it with them as well. Yet he was lying to them.

Or was he? True, their engagement wasn't real. There was little chance of him marrying Francesca. She was completely out of his league. While she and her family were authentic and down-to-earth, she was meant for great things. And while he also came from a prominent family, he was not royalty. Most of the time, he felt like a visiting American tourist. He had purposely tried to remind her the engagement was only a farce for that reason. At some point, he would need to walk away and let her marry someone in society that her grandparents would approve of.

"Max, do you have a minute to come into my study and look at some figures that were just sent from the Rome office?" Marco asked.

"You're not going to make him work at this hour, are you?" Kate asked, frowning up at her husband.

"Relax, *cara*, I promise it will just be for a few minutes," Marco said, rubbing his wife's shoulder as he stood.

Max dropped a kiss on Francesca's head and stood as well. What was Marco talking about? The Rome office didn't generate any numbers.

"I'm going to clear the table, and Nico is going to wash the dishes," Stefano announced. Nico got up dutifully, rolling his eyes. "The youngest always has to wash," he grumbled, picking up dishes, giving Stefano a dark look.

Margherita laughed and stood as well, gesturing toward the doorway. "I think I will go ensure those two don't kill each other or break my dishes."

Once everyone had exited through the French doors leading to the house, Teresa and Kate eyed Francesca speculatively. Leaning forward across the table from her, they identically rested their chins on their hands.

Teresa smiled a little. "And now you can tell me the real story." Glancing at Kate with a frown, she continued. "My best friend won't crack, but I know something is up. You are engaged, and yet you almost act like you are just getting to know one another."

Francesca swallowed hard. "It's complicated."

Teresa laughed. "We all do complicated in this family. I'll make it easy. Start with when you fell in love with Max."

# twenty

Francesca sat at the window seat in her expansive bedroom as the sun rose. The pink and orange lit the sky, casting a glow over the rows of lemon trees below her. She frowned. It should have been the most comfortable and relaxing night of sleep in the quiet bedroom with its neutral colors. It seemed so serene compared to her frenetic home, where someone was always barging into her bedroom and voices could be heard drifting upward throughout the house. Instead, she had laid awake most of the night, her mind a tumbling mass of emotions.

When Kate and Teresa had said the words "fall in love," her heart had skidded and bounced erratically. It first happened when Arianna asked her in Milan, but she was too afraid to visit those emotions and stuffed them way down. Why hadn't she realized it? She was hopelessly in love with Max. In fact, she loved everything about him. The way his hair always looked just a little unruly. How he teased her yet made her feel special all at the same time. The hot look he would give her when he would pull back from kissing her. It was as if he wanted to grab her and...oh she didn't know. He never did, though. Perhaps he wasn't as into her as she thought. Often, she went over their time together in her head. It was ridiculous how happy he always was and so very confident in any circumstance. And she loved the gentle way he treated her sisters, already like a big brother. Her parents adored him as well.

Sighing, she hugged her knees tighter. She was cold in her short jammies and grabbed a nearby throw to put over her. Shivering a little, she wondered if it was the temperature in the house or her shattered nerves.

Kate and Teresa were kind the night before. Kate explained that Teresa had figured out something was up after the soccer match. Kate had been steadfast in her refusal to talk about it, but Teresa had formed her own opinions.

Francesca ended up telling them the entire story from beginning to end. It felt great to tell her friends everything, including her feelings. She hadn't done that with anyone, even Arianna.

"What are you going to do?" Teresa had whispered. "How far are you going to take this whole charade? It could end happily. I mean, he seems like he really . . . er . . . likes you," Teresa remarked, looking unsure. Kate had shot her a dark look before agreeing. "He seems fond of you," Kate remarked thoughtfully.

More than anything, that had made Francesca wince. Fond of her. Though she knew her friends were trying to help, no one wanted to hear the man they were in love with was *fond* of them. Suddenly, the next few days seemed like they were going to stretch on endlessly. Today, more family would be arriving, which meant more pretense. This had been a terrible idea. The likelihood she and Max would have time to learn more about each other in this crowd seemed slim.

A sudden whistle shattered the still morning. It stopped, started, then merrily shrilled again. Francesca glanced down, her confusion melting into a grin. Below her stood Max, his curly hair blowing in the wind. He wore a plaid shirt and jeans, looking rugged and annoyingly handsome, and at his side stood a golden retriever, sitting perfectly, as if it was smiling up at her.

The whistle sounded again—this time in jaunty little bursts like a secret code.

Francesca twisted the knob on the window and pushed it open. "Shhh, you're going to wake everyone up!" she hissed down at him.

Max grinned up at her, boyish and utterly unrepentant. "Get dressed and come down, and I won't have to."

She raised an eyebrow. "Where are we going?"

"Get dressed and find out."

Rolling her eyes, she started to close the window. "Who's your friend?"

"Get dressed . . ." he repeated, and the whistling began again. This time, a little softer.

She grinned. "Okay, I'll be down in a few. But I'm warning you, this better involve coffee."

Francesca ran into the massive closet and grabbed a pair of jeans and a blue-and-white-striped sweater. Putting her hair in a French braid took just a few extra minutes. It would be worth it, though. It looked pretty windy out there, and her hair would be a fright.

Grabbing a jacket, she ran down the massive staircase, her nose twitched at pastries in the oven. Darn, someone was baking. She hoped this little adventure of Max's would get them home in time to indulge in a *cornetto* or whatever deliciousness was in the oven.

When she opened the massive mahogany front door, Max and the dog were almost right where they had been standing. Max gave a small whistle, and the dog jumped into an extra-long golf cart that was parked in front of the house.

Max grinned. "*Buongiorno,*" he said. "Care to take a spin?"

"*Buongiorno,*" she answered automatically, sliding into the front seat of the golf cart. "Where are we going on this little journey? Christmas tree hunting?"

He laughed and kicked the golf cart into gear. "Why do you say that?"

"I've seen movies where men wear plaid shirts to chop down Christmas trees."

Max chuckled. "We would be a little early for that. But yes, I wear one then, too." His grin grew, as he glanced at her again. "I wore this for you. Knowing how you like a man in a plaid shirt!"

Not knowing how to respond, Francesca only smiled and hung on to the seat as they bounced up the hill and then headed toward the right. Soon they came upon a newly built house.

"Oh, my! It's gorgeous. Is this Katie and Marco's?" Francesca asked.

Max set the brake and climbed out. "Yes, it is. I guess Rita gave each son a plot. They took their time designing it, but at least the outside is finished. We are just going to borrow their back deck." Grabbing a picnic basket out of the back, he whistled again. The dog jumped out and joined them. Francesca bent over and petted her. "Wait, is this Sophia? Lucca and Ellie's dog?"

Max nodded and indicated they were going to walk around the house. "She is. They arrived late last night. We're borrowing her as well. Ellie was muttering something about decorating a cake, and Lucca said he'd help her. I said we could dog sit."

Francesca laughed. "Ellie has decorated all the cakes for special occasions. It's a tradition now. I can tell you the story later." She followed him around the house, which was finished on the outside, but after a quick peek inside, told her there was still a lot of work to be done. They climbed the steps to a massive empty deck. Sitting down on the top step, Max snapped his fingers, and Sophia lay down below them.

"She's so well-trained," Francesca remarked, settling down next to Max. "I remember hearing stories about when Lucca first got her. But then he really got into training her."

"I love dogs. We had one while I was growing up, but now

my life isn't very conducive to having animals. Not being committed to either country doesn't help."

Francesca kept her expression neutral. Was he thinking about going back to the States? There was so much to ask and yet, she felt like she shouldn't. Instead, she changed the subject as they gazed out at the vista before them. "This view is amazing. Especially at this time of the morning."

"I thought you'd like it," Max said confidently. He shook out a cloth and placed it on the deck within their reach. Next came *cornettos* that he carefully put on the plate. He brought out cheese and prosciutto. Finally, he carefully retrieved a basket of raspberries. He poured coffee into a mug and handed it to her. "It's a cappuccino, but I made it a while ago, so it's probably a little settled," he said. "Sorry about that."

"Did you pack this all yourself?"

He laughed. "No, Rita helped me. I told her I was going to try to put together a breakfast picnic, and she happily offered her assistance."

Francesca took a big sip of her cappuccino and smiled. "Rita is the best."

Max nodded. "I agree. She just makes everyone feel special."

"Oh my gosh, it's her birthday today," Francesca said. "What was she doing up so early?"

Max shrugged and handed her a plate with a *cornetto*. "She was sitting at the kitchen table talking to Lucca's security manager, Mike Donnelly. If I didn't know better, I'd say there was some chemistry there."

Francesca shook her head. "I don't think so. She's been dating Sergio for a couple of years."

"Hmmm, I'm probably wrong," Max said, taking a sip of his coffee. "She had these pastries warming in the oven. Take a bite."

Francesca took another sip of her cappuccino and then bit into a cornetto. "Oh, these are good. I bet Rita got them at my favorite *pasticceria* in Positano. No one makes better Italian pastries than them. Not even Nonna."

She glanced over. Max was staring at her with an odd expression. She reached up to her hair. "What, do I have something in my hair? Why are you looking at me like that?"

"I just don't know many women who would answer a morning whistle, get dressed in five minutes and then chomp on a pastry with no questions asked."

Francesca delicately put the *cornetto* back on a plate and wiped her hands with a napkin. Frowning at him, she said, "I'm not chomping. That is decidedly an unladylike way of putting it."

He laughed. "Sorry. It was all meant to be a compliment."

She seized the opportunity. "Okay, I'll bite then. Max, why did you plan this little morning getaway?"

He clasped his cup and stared at the view. "Honestly?"

She rolled her eyes. "No, I want you to lie to me! Of course, I want to know the truth."

He stared at her, his brown eyes intent. "Truthfully, I just wanted to be alone with you."

Francesca looked down at her pastry, running her finger over the dough. "Really?" she whispered.

"Really," he said, smiling at her. "I'm not sure what was up with Marco and his mysterious nonexistent numbers last night. He seemed determined to get me away from you, though."

Francesca gave a small wince. "It was premeditated. It was so Katie and Teresa could grill me. They both know we aren't really engaged."

Max laughed. "They should work for the FBI or the CIA or something. Those two are good. What did they ask?"

Francesca waved a hand. "Oh, you know. What you would expect. Katie didn't tell Teresa, though. Teresa figured it out," she rushed to tell him.

"Are we somehow bad at this?" he asked huskily, leaning

over and grabbing her braid, tugging on it gently. "Don't we act like a newly engaged couple?"

"I . . . I don't know," Francesca stammered, averting her gaze as she thought about the questions they asked. "I think they were more interested in what our plan was. I just told them we weren't sure," she muttered. "That we're just taking this day by day."

"I'm sorry if I put you in an awkward situation," Max said, putting her braid down. He stared into his coffee cup. "I didn't know it was going to become this complicated."

"I didn't either," she whispered. "It will be alright in the end."

"Hey," he said, and she looked up at him. He nudged her with his elbow. "Can I have a bite?"

"There's more pastries on the plate!" she protested.

"I know, but that's the only chocolate one."

She grinned up at him and dutifully held it out for him to take a bite.

He chewed and swallowed, his gaze never leaving hers. "You have a little piece of chocolate near your mouth," he said softly.

She reached up to wipe it, and he stilled her hands. "Let me," he said huskily. His lips descended, and she leaned into his kiss, putting an arm around his neck to pull him closer.

After a few minutes, he pulled away slowly.

"Did you get it?" she whispered.

He shook his head. "Let me try again," he said and slowly lowered his mouth.

# twenty-one

The picnic was a success. After a few fervent kisses with Max, he had gotten a blanket out that was strapped to the picnic basket and thrown it around them. They cuddled together, her head on his shoulder, and just talked. She never wanted it to end. They shared memories about growing up that were poignant and funny. She told him a little more about her family members and what it was like to live in their controlled chaos. He shared his university days and a little about his New York life. At first he had loved it, but after a few years he found himself wanting more. It had sounded like he had an active social life there, though, and she wanted to ask more. She held her questions since neither had brought up much about any past romances.

Finally, they had reluctantly stood, gathered their picnic stuff and headed up the hill to the venue. The family had gathered to oversee the last-minute setup for Margherita's birthday party.

"We just want everything to be perfect," Katie explained when they arrived. "The staff knows what they are doing, but we wanted to be a part of it. We left Rita watching Frankie so she wouldn't be tempted to come up here and check it out."

Francesca smiled. "It's truly perfect, Katie." The rooms were filled with flowers and greenery, and lights were intricately woven throughout.

"It will look better in the evening when the lights and candles glow," Katie said, moving a planter and standing back to admire it. "This is where we'll have cocktails. Come see where we'll dine."

The women walked into the next large room that had been transformed, with three long tables intricately set with crisp white linens, glistening plates and silver. Candles and greenery wound down the tables. A trellis of flowers was suspended above them with greenery, flowers and lemons.

"Are those real?" Francesca asked, her eyes wide.

Kate laughed. "Yes, as well as all the other flowers. Who knows where Marco got them from? He had everything flown in. Rita is going to love it. And we hired her favorite band to play. The dance floor is in the next room, and that's where the dessert trolly and her birthday cake will be."

"I can't wait to see her face!" Francesca exclaimed.

Kate laughed. "She'll be appalled. She definitely doesn't want all this attention, but we just had to. Plus, she has so many family and friends. Why not?"

"Is there anything I can do to help?" Francesca asked. Staff members were bustling everywhere, and there probably weren't any tasks left undone. Max was outside with his cousins who were stringing lights in the trees, looking like they were laughing more than working. Sophia was bouncing between them, barking, and running joyfully.

Kate shook her head. "Not unless you want to go out there and tell them they have a lot more trees to do," she said, rolling her eyes. "This will take all afternoon at this rate. But I guess, if nothing else, they are having a great time."

Francesca nodded and stifled a giggle. Nico had a stick, and

Max was helping thread lights on it as they tried hoisting them up into the tree. The men were laughing at their attempts.

"Max looks happy," Kate remarked softly.

Francesca agreed. "He loves being with family."

"He loves being with you."

Francesca felt her heart thud. She glanced at Kate nervously. "I hope so. It's better than him being *fond of me.*"

Kate grimaced. "I probably should have phrased that differently. I didn't want you to get your hopes up, but after watching you two together, I feel like you both have deep feelings for one another. Remember when you told me I should give Marco a chance? That men like him rarely come around?"

Francesca could only nod, finding it difficult to talk.

"And then you told Teresa the same thing. And I believe you also said roughly the same thing to Georgie before she married Nico."

Francesca tried to look cool. She turned her back and went to straighten a tablecloth on the dessert table. "What's your point, Katie?"

Kate grinned at her. "Take your own advice. Lean into this. I know this started as fake, but it doesn't mean it can't turn into something very real. He's a Rinaldi, too. And men like him are few and far between. So no matter what, give me the chance he deserves."

Francesca stared at her, trying not to show her uncertainty. Her throat felt dry. "I will try," she finally squeaked out.

"Try what?" Max said from the open French doors.

Francesca gave Kate a stricken look but quickly adopted a neutral expression when she turned. Outside, the men were still arguing about the best way to hang the lights. She laughed. "Try to help you guys figure out this light situation," she said, walking toward him.

He raised his eyebrows. "And how are you going to do that?"

"Well, climb a tree, of course," she said, strolling confidently past him.

"YOU LOOK STUNNING," Ellie said as she sat on the bed with Teresa, admiring Francesca's gown.

Francesca turned slowly around so Ellie could see the back. It wasn't a new dress. In fact, she had burrowed to the back of her closet to find it, but it was a special one by a local designer that she had only worn once but loved it.

"This old thing?" Francesca said and laughed. "Are you sure it's okay? I don't usually wear pink."

Ellie whistled. "Why not? It looks so good on you."

Francesca glanced back in the mirror. The pink dress had a fitted bodice of Italian lace and then flared at her hips whimsically in a silken material that fanned out when she walked.

"Man, you make this look so easy, Francesca," Ellie said and sighed. "I needed you when I ordered my dress last month. I should have sent you some photos from the designer's gallery."

Francesca smiled at her friends. "I'm here. Any time."

Ellie stretched. "I guess I should go get changed myself. It took me longer to decorate that four-tiered cake. Lucca was getting impatient with me. I re-did three parts over. I wanted it to be perfect for Rita."

Teresa stood. "I'm sure it's amazing, Ellie. I'll go with you. I only have my dress to put on. Meara insisted on having a glam squad for all of us. They arrived early and helped me, as you can see," she said, dramatically patting her hair.

Ellie laughed. "I better go get some glam. I wish I had time for a nap. Francesca, did they do you first? You look beautiful."

Francesca shook her head. "I didn't know until Katie told me, and I had already finished my hair and makeup. It's fine. I'm just a guest here."

Teresa rolled her eyes. "You're more than that. You're family. But it's not like you need it. You'll steal the show or a special someone's heart as soon as you walk in! We'll see you up the hill."

Francesa waved, and they departed before she went to perch on the window seat so she wouldn't crush her dress. Why had she had gotten ready so early? Probably because there wasn't much else to do when they returned. They had all descended the hill together, laughing as they went. Max had stopped the golf cart and grinned at her, picking a twig from her hair. "You climb trees better than anyone I've ever seen," he said.

She beamed at him. "Practice!"

They had joined everyone in the kitchen briefly for a hasty lunch before retreating to their rooms to get ready. Max gave her a quick kiss on the cheek, telling her he and Lucca were going to go for a walk to catch up.

Francesca couldn't help feeling disappointed, as she was looking forward to spending more alone time with Max. Obviously, he was soaking up his family time. She understood that was important as well. Resting for a while in her room, she had dozed a little before waking up startled and then jumped into the shower. Secretly, she was glad she hadn't known about Meara's glam squad. She preferred doing her own hair and makeup. Strangers always wanted to put too much makeup on her and do her hair in ways she wasn't comfortable with.

A soft knock on the door interrupted her thoughts.

*"Puoi entrare."*

The door opened slightly, and a paper airplane sailed through, gently landing on the plush carpet near her. The door quickly closed.

Francesca giggled. "What in the world is he up to now?"

Picking up the plane, she admired its crisp folds and intricate details. She was about to regrettably unfold it when she saw the words on the side. *Meet me on the back veranda when you are ready. I'll be the dashing one in the black suit with the pink tie.*

Francesca bit her lip. She didn't remember telling him her dress was pink. She rolled her eyes. It must have been her friends. Her bet was Teresa.

Walking slowly back into the bathroom, she took another appraisal of herself. She applied another layer of lipstick and patted her hair, which she had decided ultimately to leave down, but had used her curling iron extensively to give it soft waves.

Not wanting to appear too eager, she descended the stairs carefully in her high heels. The glam squad chattered in one of the bedrooms. Sophia barked in the distance. Francesca walked through the house and toward the French doors and opened them slowly. She took a few steps outside, and Max was standing off to the side, his back to her, his hands clasped. Solar torches cast a warm glow on the veranda, while fairy lights twinkled in the nearby bushes, creating a magical atmosphere.

"*Buonasera*," she said softly.

He turned, and his expression changed from serious to a slow, warm smile. He stared across the veranda at her, and her heart jumped. Nervously, she twisted her hands in front of her. "What time does the next flight take off?"

Max chuckled and approached her, still staring intently. He grabbed her hands, and his gaze swept over her. "You look breathtaking," he said and swallowed hard. "Sorry, I'm a little nervous."

She smiled a little. It was hard to picture the always confident Max nervous. "Who told you my dress color? It's like we're going to the prom."

"Teresa, of course. She even went and found one from Stefano's closet for me." His eyes glittered in the amber lighting. "Did you go to your prom?"

She shook her head. "We don't really have those here. We have school dances but not like an American prom. I've watched a lot of movies, though," she remarked confidently. "I bet you took the most popular girl in school."

"Nope. Not me. I took Mary Alice Wojesky. She had an unfortunate overbite that meant she had braces for all four years of high school. And I dare say she was *not* popular, but I thought she was the nicest girl in school."

Francesca stared up at him, feeling the warmth of his gaze. "Why are you nervous now?"

"Because tonight I am taking the prettiest girl to the party, and I have no idea what to say to her."

She rolled her eyes. "Max, you always know what to say."

He gave a subtle shake of his head, and she made a sudden decision. Snaking a hand up around his neck, she brought his lips down close to hers. "Then there's no reason to talk, is there?"

She felt his sudden breath hot against hers, and then his cool lips met hers and quickly changed to a searing intensity. His arms closed around her like a vise. She could barely breathe. His mouth moved over hers sensually, and she threw herself into the kiss. She was surprised when Max pulled back, his breathing labored. She followed his startled gaze over her shoulder. Turning, she saw Kate's sister Meara and her husband, Alec, standing in the doorway. Meara's eyebrows were raised, and Alec was smirking.

"Katie told us you two should ride up the hill with us," Meara drawled. "But perhaps we should leave you to your . . . private party?"

## *twenty-two*

Max's arms went around her, holding her close. "Finally! I haven't hardly been able to hardly dance with you," he whispered in her ear.

Francesca smiled and laid her head close to his chest, listening to the band play a slow ballad. "Sorry about that. I didn't realize how many people I would know at this party."

He squeezed her a little tighter, his embrace warm and comforting. "That's alright. It was Marco and my other cousins that were the problem. They all kept rotating, each one dancing with you. Even Alfonso was in the mix. I never thought I'd get a chance. They were just messing with me."

Francesca giggled. "They are all sweet."

"Sweet doesn't even come close to describing it," grumbled Max. "I told Alfonso he better find some other fans if he keeps this up."

Off to the side, Alfonso was flirting with some of the local women. "I think he already has," Francesca pointed out and laughed.

"Rita is sure having fun, isn't she?" Max observed, glancing over at the older woman. She had been surrounded by guests all evening, laughing and mingling.

"Yes, I'm so happy for her. I know she didn't want all this, but it's been a spectacular party," Francesca said. "Ellie's cake was gorgeous with all those colors, and the sparklers shooting out of it were incredible."

"It all reminds me of another night," Max said softly. At Francesca's curious expression, he hugged her tighter. "Marco and Kate's wedding. The night I first saw you. But you didn't notice me."

"I noticed you," Francesca responded. "I even thought you might approach me, but you didn't come close."

"I told you. I was too nervous."

She smiled up at him. "There's that word again. Max, I've seen you hold your own with my grandmother. How can I make you nervous, but she can't?"

"Oh, so many reasons," he murmured, smoothing her hair back to the side. "Have I told you how gorgeous you look tonight?"

"Yes, but you can say it again. You look pretty dashing yourself."

He grinned at her. She leaned up for a kiss. His lips met hers briefly, and he smiled. "Anyone looking at us would completely think we're in love and have a normal engagement."

Francesca disengaged herself slowly and blinked at him. The music had stopped, and couples around them were exiting the dance floor. Max gazed at her questioningly and tried to pull her back into his arms.

"Oh my God, get a room," Meara said as she strolled by. Turning to Meara, Francesca gave her a cool look. The stunning redhead was known for her dry sense of humor.

"Meara, your timing is perfect. Keep my *fiancé* company, will you?" she asked, emphasizing the words. "I need to go find Katie."

"Oh good. Max, we need to get to know one another since you're part of this family," Meara said. "Come sit down, and let's chat."

Francesca walked away, her back straight, her shoulders held high. She purposely did not look back.

# twenty-three

Francesca and Max were sitting at a local pizzeria overlooking Positano with a view of the Tyrrhenian Sea. They had dined on an exquisite lunch of salad and pizza. Francesco explained it was where Marco and Kate had first dined together and started Kate's obsession with pizza.

"It's a beautiful view, isn't it?" she asked, keeping her gaze averted.

Max stared at Francesca's lovely profile. "Beautiful," he agreed, as he rubbed a frustrated hand over his eyes. He had been trying for the last twenty-four hours to get to the bottom of whatever was wrong between them. Mentally, he had tried to recall what he said to bring about the strange coolness that had set in. He was so caught up in the moment of dancing with her that he couldn't even remember what he said. It couldn't have been that awful to bring about this change in her. Perhaps someone else had said something to upset her. All he knew was that every time he attempted to get near her, the walls went up.

The evening had ended soon after she had foisted him on to Meara. He was relieved as he tried to answer Meara's probing questions, yet remained preoccupied with what had just happened. Meara had probably thought he was a simple moron, listening with half an ear as he scanned the crowd for Francesca.

Eventually, they had all piled in various vehicles to go down the hill, and the family gathered for a nightcap to reminisce about the party. Francesca had drifted away, busy talking with Ellie. He had barely received a backward wave. Had there been regret in her expression? He wasn't sure.

They had already planned to spend their last day on the Amalfi Coast in Positano before hitting the road to Milan, where he was finally going to introduce Francesca to his grandparents. Was that the cause of her shutdown? Perhaps she was nervous about the meeting.

Whatever it was, had sent Francesca back into tour guide mode. They had wandered the small shops and local venues with her running dialogue about what they were seeing. She had shown him the shop she worked in with Allegra, who had looked him over with interest. He frowned, remembering how Francesca had only introduced him as a "friend." Allegra had been obviously confused, glancing at the ring on Francesca's finger, but it was obvious she knew better than to ask questions. Francesca had become lively during her time with Allegra, laughing and joking with her. The women had hugged several times, and he saw how much Francesca cared for her friend. But when they left, Francesca transformed back to being distant.

They had then gone to her small flat where she had grabbed a few clothes, stuffing them into a shoulder bag nonchalantly. She had been non-committal as to her future when it came to the Amalfi Coast.

Gazing at her set profile now, he felt the urge to nudge her. Even if she yelled at him, it would be better than this politeness that had swept over them.

"Francesca," he began hesitantly. "Why are you keeping your flat here?"

His question seemed to startle her. She glanced quickly at

him and then looked away. She answered coolly. "Why wouldn't I? I still have a good job here. You saw for yourself how nice it is."

He would not back down this time. "So, you aren't thinking of making Verona home again?"

Her expression was shuttered. "Verona will always be my home. But after this gala and things calm down a bit, I'll break it to Nonna and Nonno that I will return to Positano. I've been happy here," she said, her voice wistful.

"What if we're successful?" he asked, trying to keep his tone even.

"What do you mean?" she asked guardedly.

"If by some miracle we are able to bring our families together and the fashion house can resume. You saw the look in your grandparents' eyes when they looked at Ariarna's sketches. Even if they have a twisted motivation, it's obvious how much they love the business of fashion. Wouldn't you want to be a part of it?"

"I'm not a designer like Adrianna. I can't even draw a straight line," Francesca informed him quietly.

"There's more to fashion houses than just designers," Max pointed out. "Your friends went on and on the other night how you were responsible for choosing their gowns for their biggest day of their lives."

Francesca shrugged, finally turning to meet his gaze. "I've always known what looks good on a person. I can look at someone and see them in colors and shapes . . ." she trailed off and looked uncomfortable. "It's hard to explain," she muttered.

He covered her hand with his, and when she went to withdraw it, he gripped it tighter. "I believe that," he said quietly. "And I think you can take that talent and use it. That's what it is, by the way, a talent. A special skill. You obviously made each of your friends feel special by finding them the perfect dress. Think of how you could leverage that in our fashion house."

She looked away, and it was difficult for him to read her expression. "Francesca?"

She glanced at him warily and he continued. "Is there something else bothering you? I feel like something came between us. And I'm not sure what I did or said."

She was staring down at their hands that were still joined. "No, not at all," she said slowly. "I think this has all just been a lot, you know? Playing like we're engaged in front of everyone, and the lines got blurred."

"What are you talking about?" he asked roughly. "What lines? What did I say last night? What caused this rift?"

She removed her hand gently from his, and he let it go. Eyeing him steadily, she finally spoke. "Watch the game tape."

"Watch the replay?" he asked incredulously. "How do you even know what that is?"

"I know a lot of things," she said defensively. "I've seen American sports. It means rewatch the tape and see what happened."

"I know what it means," he said, shaking his head and trying not to laugh. "But there is no film of last night's conversation, or I wouldn't be asking you."

She sighed deeply and averted her gaze again before standing abruptly. "I think it's time we got back. Rita was counting on one last family dinner."

He stood quickly. Having already paid the check, they were free to leave. Putting his hand gently on her back, he led her out to his car that was parked in the small area near the pizzeria. They drove silently back to the lemon grove. Max glanced a time or two in her direction, but she calmly looked out the window.

Punching the code into the gate, it swung open. He waved to a couple of Lucca's security team, who were stationed nearby. Last night, he had casually mentioned to Lucca that his security director Mike Donnelly should have come to the party. Lucca had looked puzzled. "But why?" When Max had gone on to explain the chemistry he witnessed between him and Margherita, Lucca's jaw had dropped. "Well, I'll be damned," was all he said. "Now I'm going to have to watch for that."

"Where are we going?" Francesca asked, as he ignored the turn toward the family's estate.

Max smiled. "Back to the field," he said. And continued to drive up the hill toward the reception venue.

FRANCESCA BIT HER LIP. Max wasn't playing fair. The last thing she wanted to do was talk about last night. She had been a dreamy-eyed fool who had gotten lulled into the idea that they were truly an engaged couple in love. All Max's hot looks, his even hotter kisses, had made her insides melt. Worse, she had let her guard down for the first time in her life. Her cheeks burned with shame now, just thinking about how she had been putty in his hands.

His sudden stop sent the gravel spraying, and she glanced at him. His mouth was in a firm line, and he looked determined. He got out of the car without speaking and went around to open her door. He held his hand out, and she automatically let him help her out of the car.

"Where are we going?" she asked, trying to keep her tone casual.

"We're going to go back inside, we're going to dance, and then we're going to recreate the conversation that we had last night in lieu of the game tape," he said calmly.

"But we can't! The staff is in there cleaning up. They'll think we've gone mad!"

He shrugged. "I don't care. Just as long as we get to the bottom of it."

He tugged her hand, but she held firm, rooted next to the car. "Max, please. We don't need to go in. We can talk through it."

He turned and searched her face. Brushing a piece of hair out of her eyes with gentle fingers, his mood seemed to alter. Finally, he spoke. "Tell me what I said," he pleaded huskily.

She sighed. Now she felt foolish for making such a big deal of it. She might as well go for broke. "Let's just say you reminded me yet again that we aren't really engaged."

Now he was confused. "Well, we aren't."

"Yes, thank goodness, right? Don't you think I know that?" Francesca exploded. "You take every opportunity to remind me. And yet, you keep asking me to pretend it's real. And then sometimes I feel like it's real. Like we *are* a couple. I feel like some ping-pong ball bouncing all over. I don't know what is reality and what isn't any more. Worse, I've misled my family and now my friends."

He edged even closer, and she had to strain to look up at his intent face. "What if you haven't?"

She was confused. "What do you mean?" she whispered, her heart pounding. He was gazing at her so intently she almost couldn't breathe.

"What if this all hasn't been a lie? What if we *are* a couple falling in love. Perhaps not to the engagement stage yet, but nevertheless with serious feelings."

Francesca's knees were going to give away. "Last night you laughed about people thinking we are in love. Are you saying it's not a joke? You are falling in love?" she whispered.

"I am."

Two words that made her want to crumble. "With me?" she asked ridiculously.

Max smiled gently. "Well, of course with you." His lips traced her jawline. "I can feel your heart racing, Francesca," he said. "Do you feel the same?"

She gave him a tremulous smile. "I think I do."

He pulled back and gave her a tender smile. "Only think?"

"I do," she said sheepishly.

"Then let's try this again," he said. "We are a couple falling in love. And by the way, I'm perfectly serious. I'm sorry if I was flippant last night. I didn't mean to be."

She nodded, her cheeks growing pink. She wanted him to kiss her desperately. His lips were now nearing her mouth, and his hot breath touched her.

He pulled back a little and stared at her. "What?" she asked anxiously.

"You better start the game tape," he said quietly. "Because this is going to be a kiss to remember."

And when his lips met hers, she knew he was right.

*twenty-four*

Francesca stared intently out the window on the way to Max's grandparents' villa. It was tough not to mull over what Margherita had discussed with her following dinner last night. Last night, when Margherita asked her to come help her with dessert, she knew something was up.

Asking her to sit down, the older woman looked concerned. "I'm going to speak out of turn," she confided.

"Rita, you can say anything to me," Francesca reassured her.

"I am worried about you," Margherita said softly. "I've watched you and Max, and you are perfect together. But I know all about the feud between your families. It was widely discussed, not only in the papers but amongst all us old Italians," she said with a laugh. "I know Max's mother, not as well as I should, since she spent so much time in America. But we grew up around one another, and we have written over the years. I know she has had a difficult time and is finally happy. But she has worried about Max spending time with her in-laws."

"Why is she worried?"

"They are very stubborn people. Like most Italians, but even more so. I don't know them well, but I know his grandfather has become bitter over the years," Margherita said. "I'm sure some of it had to do with losing their only son and not seeing their grandson as much as they wanted. I'm afraid some of that bitterness can't easily go away. If they can't accept you, what do you think Max will do?"

"I'm not sure," Francesca answered honestly. "Neither of us wants our grandparents upset. We want them to reunite."

"I know your grandparents, too," Margherita remarked. "I am not sure they will budge either when it comes to ending this feud."

"You are probably right," Francesca agreed softly.

"Do you have plans to marry?" Margherita asked.

"Well, not yet," Francesca said awkwardly. "But that's because . . . look, Margherita, I'm not going to lie to you. Max and I started this as a lark. Our first idea was just to end the feud, but well, we now have genuine feelings for each other."

"I know, dear," Margherita said, patting her hand.

"Marco or Katie told you?"

Margherita laughed. "No. By now, you should know I figure most things out. I'm glad we had this talk. I just wanted you to go in with your eyes open, knowing it may not be that easy. These old feuds have strong tentacles. But you hang in there. Remember, Max is worth it."

"That he is," Francesca said and stood up to hug Margherita tightly.

Shaking off the conversation, Francesca now turned to Max. "How much farther?"

His lips twitched. "About five kilometers less than the last time you asked."

Francesca twisted in her seat nervously. "And what is the plan?"

Max took a deep breath. She knew he was trying to be patient. "I've told them I met someone very special. We're going to go in, and I'll introduce you by your first name. After a little social chit chat, I'll tell them we are engaged and want to be honest about who you are. They'll bluster a little, but honestly, I don't think they will be as violently opposed as your grandparents have been."

"Why not?" Francesca asked, remembering Margherita's claims about their temperament.

His expression was serious. "Because I'm an outsider, remember? They aren't as invested."

Francesca reached out and put a hand on his shoulder. "Max, you can't mean that. You're their grandson."

"I am," he said quietly. "But they have others who stayed in Italy. I know they love me, but they still see me as American."

"I thought your grandfather allowed you to look at his books?" Francesca asked.

"He did and then proceeded to not take much of my advice," Max said dryly. "Only bits and pieces of it."

"You should try to talk to him about it," Francesca suggested. "At least tell him how you feel."

Max's profile grew stern. "Possibly. I had a long talk with Lucca about it the other day. He was raised mostly in America, too. If nothing else it was nice to know he felt some of the same outsider feelings I do."

"But you're not an outsider!" Francesca protested.

Max stayed silent. Turning into massive wrought-iron gates, he guided the car up the drive lined with cypress trees. At the top, Francesca caught her breath at the massive Renaissance-inspired villa. Its stone walls were surrounded by lush gardens with neatly trimmed hedges. While it resembled her grandparents' villa to a certain extent, this villa was much larger and opulent.

Max parked the car and turned toward her.

Francesca glanced up at the massive stone building. "It looks . . ."

"Cold?" Max supplied. "Wait until you see the inside."

Snapping off his seatbelt, he came over and opened the door for her. She got out and nervously wiped her hands down her simple navy blue dress. She had dressed conservatively for the meeting, wearing a simple high-necked dress with a matching cardigan. She wore her hair in a chignon.

Max smiled before leaning over to nuzzle her neck. "I love when you wear your hair up so I can do this," he whispered.

She pulled back. "You told me you love my hair down."

He grinned. "I love it both ways." He leaned in to kiss her.

She shoved at him. "Max, not now!"

"*Signore* Max," a quiet voice said.

Max grinned at her before turning. "Preston, how good to see you." He went forward, clapping the older man on the back. The man's expression didn't alter. "Your grandparents are waiting for you in the drawing room."

"Preston, this is my fiancée, Francesca," Max said, not missing a beat.

Preston gave a stiff bow. "It is very nice to meet you, *signorina*. I will pull your car around to the garage, *Signore* Max. There is a weather front coming in. Please do not keep your grandparents waiting."

They entered the massive entrance, and Francesca turned to him. "That's a real butler. Not one like ours who just likes to act like one," she whispered. She glanced around, taking in the massive, expensive oil paintings, heavy antique furniture, and gold fixtures. "It's like a museum."

"You haven't seen anything yet," he whispered back. Their footsteps clicked on the marble floor as he led her toward a set of mahogany doors. Opening one, he indicated for her to pass through, and then he followed her.

Max's grandparents were sitting on formal chairs near a fireplace. It was as if they were sitting on thrones. Max's grandfather was on the taller side, wearing a well-tailored suit, his gray hair perfectly styled. Despite his formal dress, she saw instantly why her grandmother had seen the startling resemblance between him and Max. So this would be what Max would look like when he got older.

Turning, she took in his grandmother, who wore a tweed skirt, silk blouse, and matching jacket. Her hair was a mixture of brown and gray, and she wore it pulled back and carefully styled. Francesca thought back to her own grandparents, who dressed formally when the occasion called for it, but were more casual when at home. They also seemed approachable. It was almost as if these two should be royalty and not her grandparents. How in the world did these couples ever come together? She was startled out of her musings by the couple standing up to face them.

Max shook hands with his grandfather, and gave his grandmother a small peck on each cheek. "Nonno, Nonna, I would like you to meet Francesca," he said. "Francesca, these are my grandparents, Leonardo and Elisabetta Valentini."

Francesca had been standing a little behind Max's shoulder, and he gripped her hand in solidarity and pulled her next to him. She smiled nervously.

"*Signore* Valentini, *Signora* Valentini, it is very nice to meet you," she said in Italian, getting ready to approach them.

They stared at her for a moment, their expressions stunned. It was Max's grandmother who finally seemed to snap out of it. She gave a small curtsy. "Princess Francesca," she acknowledged.

Leonardo watched her and then turning, he also gave her a small formal bow. "Princess Francesca, we welcome you to our home."

Francesca's stomach turned over.. Max had an uneasiness in his expression.

"*Grazie.* But how did you know who I am?" she asked in Italian, a little more sharply than she intended. She took a breath. "Most people don't."

They looked uncomfortable at the directness of her question. "We have certainly followed your family in the society papers,"

Max's grandfather said smoothly. "Though we have only seen an occasional photo of you in the Verona community, we have paid attention. Please, sit down."

He glanced at Max. "We will speak English now, as Max is still *uncomfortable* with our language."

Francesca glanced warily at Max's features, which tightened. Was that the first dig? She perched delicately on the uncomfortable small sofa next to him. This was the first time she had seen a less-than-confident Max. He cleared his throat. "Nonno, Nonna, I think you should know Francesca and I are engaged," he said, grabbing her hand again and giving her a small smile.

"But, Massimo, you never said," Elisabetta protested. "And to the princess, no less!"

Francesca squirmed uncomfortably. "*Per favore*, I do not use the title. No member of my family does."

"Your grandfather used to. In fact, he liked to throw that in my face," Leonardo remarked dryly.

Francesca opened her mouth to defend her grandfather and then closed it, glancing anxiously at Max. He was grasping her hand, but he was sitting forward, his expression serious.

"I had intended on us talking about this later, but yes, Francesca and I are very aware of the disagreement between the families. It doesn't matter in the least to us," he said, his tone even.

"Disagreement," snorted Leonardo. "This is an all-out war, son."

Max's mouth formed a thin line. "We will marry regardless."

Francesca glanced at him, surprised. They had never used the M word.

"Have you set a date?" Elisabetta asked shrewdly, almost as if she was calling his bluff.

Max glanced at Francesca, and his gaze was steady, as if telling her to allow him to guide the conversation. "We have not. As you can imagine, we have a lot to work out. We have met with Francesca's parents and grandparents, and they are aware of my intentions."

Leonardo stood abruptly and prowled around the room. He finally turned. "You do understand the implications of marrying a Ricci?" he roared. "First, they steal the crest, and now they are stealing my grandson! What did they offer you?"

Max looked confused. "Offer me? What are you talking about, Nonno?"

He rolled his eyes. "I know Giancarlo. I can sense he is up to something. Did he offer you money? Part of the wine business?"

Max stood abruptly, dropping her hand. "Nonno, that is out of line. Why in the world would Francesca's family have to offer me anything? I have fallen in love with an intelligent, funny, witty, and talented woman. She has transfixed me from the start. That should be everything you need to know!"

Francesca felt her heart thudding. Was he being honest? Did he really feel that way?

Leonardo shook his head. But the bluster had gone out of him. He suddenly looked at Francesca, his expression skeptical. "Wait, you were betrothed to Mario Bianchini, Elisabetta's nephew. Not that she talks to her sister, but we heard that years ago. Was that dissolved?"

Francesca felt her face flush. "It wasn't a real betrothal," she said quietly. "It was a wish between our grandparents, but it wasn't a formal arranged marriage. I would never agree to that!"

"And Mario has run off to America with his latest love," Max told him. "He is completely out of the picture, and so therefore, I made my move," he said smugly. "Swept her right off her feet," he said, coming back to lay a hand on Francesca's shoulder, smiling down at her. This time, she read his expression, and her heart swelled.

She met his penetrating gaze and smiled slowly.

Leonardo ran his hand through his hair, a gesture similar to what Max usually did when he was frustrated. The genetics were stronger than they realized, Francesca mused.

Leonardo finally spoke, his voice raspy. "Massimo, it is difficult to understand you. First you go to work for your mother's family, those Rinaldis. Everything they seemingly touch turns to gold. Now you've brought home the granddaughter of our enemies."

Max looked astonished. "Nonno, I went to work for the Rinaldis because they offered me a fantastic position. I wasn't aware there was anything available at your company. And as for your enemies, I found them to be kind and decent people."

"Kind and decent!" bellowed Leonardo. "What do you know about it? You aren't from Italy! Your father left for America! You do not understand the past, our family's heritage!"

Max sat down and rubbed his face with his hands. When he raised his head, his eyes held sadness. "And now we have finally succeeded in airing the actual issue here."

Elisabetta stood now, her eyes spitting fire at Leonardo. "Leo, stop! It is true, our son left. But only because he saw the opportunity. He did not forsake us or our country. You are being dramatic. We lost him through death, not by choice! And Massimo has tried to connect with us! You are the one holding him back! And I won't allow it anymore, do you understand? You are to fix this and fix it now!"

Elisabetta turned to Francesca, who was sitting like a statue, trying very hard to keep her expression neutral. She gave Francesca a small smile. "Prin . . . Francesca, why don't we go stroll in the garden? Leo and Massimo have some talking to do."

Francesca scrambled to her feet. "Certainly," she said, glancing at Max. His head was bowed, but he raised it, and for the first time, he held uncertainty in his eyes. Without stopping to think, she bent her head and gave him a soft kiss before whispering in his ear, "Talk to him! This is your opportunity! You've got this. Keep your eye on the prize!" She drew back and saw she at least put a small smile on his face. She frowned a little and leaned in again. "Go big or go home! And remember, when the going gets tough . . . " she stopped, flustered. "I can't remember how that one goes."

This time he did laugh and gave her a wide grin, his body relaxing. "I'll tell you later," he whispered.

As she followed Elisabetta out the door, Max spoke, more confident now. "Nonno, why don't I pour you some wine? Nonna is right. We need to talk."

"MASSIMO WAS SUCH A SWEET LITTLE BOY," Elisabetta said as they walked on the stone-paved path. "Though he was constantly into mischief, if you can believe that," she said and chuckled.

"Oh, I can definitely see that," Francesca replied, glancing nervously back at the villa.

"Don't worry, dear. They will be fine. It's been a long time coming. In fact, thank you for bringing it to a head. My stubborn husband. He is his own downfall," she said, shaking her head.

Francesca remained silent. "*Signora* Valentini..."

"*Per favore*, Elisabetta."

Francesca smiled. "Elisabetta, if you don't mind me asking, your husband made it very clear how he feels about my grandparents and the feud. Do you feel the same way? What I mean to ask . . ." She broke off uncomfortably.

Elisabetta had stopped walking. "Your nonna, Antonia, and I were the best of friends. I miss her," she said wistfully. "First my sister and I became estranged, then the feud started with your family. I began to question if it was me. Do I drive people away?"

Francesca saw the anxious look on the older woman's face. "I think the feud was bigger than you," she said reassuringly. "It sounded like it was something that grew and grew and then exploded between your husbands."

Elisabetta nodded. "To be honest, I only found out when it was too late. I should have known. I blame Leo a lot for it. I believe he felt inferior to your grandfather being a duke and, therefore, tried to control things too much."

Francesca shrugged. "I think it was complicated for my grandfather. When Italy became a republic, the royal lines were abolished. Yet, he had grown up with the old ways. While I find it a bit of nonsense, it was difficult for him to let go," she said. "Despite the fact that they don't really embrace it that much, they still insist that I take my place in society. I don't even know what that means."

"There is still the old guard, dear. You would be very sought after if you wanted to be as the eldest daughter of a prince. There are parties, charities, foundations, even private companies that would love to have you be a part of their circle."

Francesca's eyes widened in horror. "I would hate that!"

Elisabetta stopped walking to stare at Francesca. "I do believe you mean that," she said. "I apologize, my dear, but when I first met you, I wondered how in the world you and Massimo would work. He is so . . ."

"Casual?" Francesca asked. "Yes, I know. Flannel shirts and all," she said, her smile growing.

"Flannel shirts?"

Francesca grinned. "Sorry, just a joke between us."

Elisabetta nodded. "I can imagine life with my grandson would be full of joy. I just hope those two hard-heads in there can build something together. But I am pleased Massimo found a place with the Rinaldi family. Though my husband is envious of them as well. They are a wonderful family."

"They are," Francesca agreed. "But they have had their hardships as well." She closed her mouth abruptly. It wasn't up to her to remind Elisabetta that Margherita's husband had walked out on her and their three small boys.

"I understand hardship. Rising in society used to be important to me," Elisabetta said wistfully. "But after all the sadness in our lives, I have had to realize what is important. I can only hope my husband can at some point." Turning to her, she raised an eyebrow. "And what about you, dear? What do you do with your time?"

Francesca startled a little. Max's grandmother certainly got to the point. "I'm making some changes," she said. "I'm not certain yet, to be honest." At his grandmother's sharp look, she continued. "I can't believe I'm telling you this, but I think Max may be right. I may look at something in fashion. I'm not a designer or anything. My sister could be. But I understand fashion, if you see what I mean. I like to dress women."

"It certainly is in your blood," Elisabetta commented. "Thank you for confiding in me. I think Massimo has chosen wisely. Your marriage will be successful."

Francesca felt her face flushing. Once again, she felt like a fraud. Even if they were falling in love, an engagement was way in the future, and now it was once again rearing its ugly head. She opened her mouth and closed it again.

"It's alright, dear. You don't have to say anything. It's obvious how much Massimo means to you," she said. "In fact, let's go back in and see what progress has been made. He may need you at his side. I've enjoyed our little talk."

"I have, too," Francesca said. And she meant it.

# twenty-five

Francesca lay in bed, staring at the ceiling. Once again, she adjusted the fluffy pillows and sank down, trying to get more comfortable. Nope, it was impossible. She heaved backward with a frustrated sigh.

The drive back to Milan from Max's grandparents had been performed in silence. When the women had returned, they found Max and his grandfather talking quietly. There didn't seem to be any animosity toward each other. Francesca and Max had stayed and dined with them and made casual conversation. Francesca felt that both Elisabetta and Leonardo tried very hard to keep things light. Max took part in the conversation, but he was more subdued than usual.

When they left, the driving rain all the way back to Milan forced Max to keep his eyes on the road and conversation to a minimum. She saw Max's hands tighten on the wheel several times, and she inadvertently bit back a shudder once or twice. She felt very confident in Max's driving skills, but the weather conditions were challenging for even the most experienced driver.

By the time they entered Max's flat, he looked exhausted and told her so. His lips had brushed hers and he thanked her for coming with him but sent her to the bedroom she had used in prior visits without another word. His quiet footsteps a few minutes later passed her door, stopped briefly, and then continued to his own bedroom, where the door quietly clicked shut.

Why had he shut her out? She urged herself not to ask questions but to let him reach out to her. Perhaps he would share more the next day on their drive back to Verona.

A crack of lightning lit up the sky, and its answering thunder rocked her room. The storm seemed to be right on top of them now. Francesca snuggled in. She loved a good storm when she was safe and warm. Another boom thundered, and then her room lit up temporarily.

After a few minutes of nature's give and take, a frantic knock pounded on her door. She smiled and sat up. Max was sweet. He must think she might be nervous. Before she could call for him to come in, he poked his head in the door.

"Are you awake?" he whispered.

She laughed. "Who could sleep through this? Besides, I love a magnificent storm!"

He walked in, slowly closing the door. The sky lit up and illuminated him in pajama bottoms and no shirt. She swallowed hard. His bronze chest was strong and perfect, even in the darkened room. His hair was all ruffled, but what stood out the most was the incredibly tense look on his face. She had never seen that before, even earlier, with his grandfather.

"Max, are you okay?"

He shook his head. "Will you think I'm a terrible wuss if I told you that I'm afraid of storms?"

She raised her eyebrows and motioned for him to come sit down on the bed. "What's a wuss?"

"You know, like a scaredy cat. A weakling."

"Of course not! A lot of people hate storms."

A crack of thunder bellowed over them. "That sounds like a close one," she remarked. "We could sing 'My Favorite Things' like in *The Sound of Music*," she teased.

"You're not helping!"

She stifled a giggle. "Sorry. Papa likes storms, too. We always get up and say things like that." She eyed him cautiously, longing to comfort him. "Do you want to lie down next to me?"

He seemed to think about it for a minute and then nodded. She was surprised when he stayed on top of the covers, but she instantly put her arms around him. She couldn't resist touching his skin. It was as soft as she imagined, but also clammy, as if he had been sweating. At first he held himself stiff, but then seemed to relax a little. Another bang of lightning shot through the sky, and he tensed.

She smoothed his hair back and encountered the same clamminess on his forehead. This wasn't just a dislike of storms. This was outright fear. Now guilt hit her about teasing him.

Francesca pulled back, wanting to see his face. "Max, tell me about it," she whispered. "It's more than the storm, isn't it?"

He pulled her back and snuggled into her neck. She took a deep breath of his spicy cologne, and she stroked his curls. He was silent for a long time, almost as if he was weighing telling her the truth. When he spoke, his voice was husky. "My father died in a storm."

"I didn't know that. I'm sorry," she said. "Do you . . . do you want to talk about it?"

He remained silent, and the storm continued to rage outside. He finally spoke. "He was driving home from the hospital, and he was in a car crash."

"You told me that before. But what happened?" Francesca murmured.

"He lost control of the car. The rain was pounding down, just like it does a lot in Seattle. He was an experienced driver. It's hard to say what made him crash."

"I'm so sorry, Max."

"I just remember the police officers coming to the door. The storm was raging. I got out of bed to see if my mother was okay. I wasn't scared of the storm. But when I saw them in our front room and my mother sobbing, I just knew."

"How horrible."

He sighed. "It was tough. I wanted to blame someone. I wished I had someone to be angry at. I wanted to rage at a drunk driver or the hospital for keeping him so late. I even wanted to be angry at him. But there was no one to be angry at. Except the storm and Mother Nature."

"How did you overcome it?"

He shrugged, drawing closer to her. "It's hard to say. I guess it was tiring being so angry all the time. And eventually I realized I was now the man of the house, and I needed to take care of my mom and sisters. We had enough money, but I had to be the rock. So, I just moved on."

"You were still so young," she whispered.

"Papa would have wanted that," Max said simply. "But I've hated storms ever since. All I see are those police officers and my mother every single time. And tonight, when I was driving, all I could think of was if I made one wrong move, something could happen to you. And I could never live with that."

"Oh, Max," she said and sighed. "You drove fine. I was perfectly safe with you."

He let out a long breath. "You were scared. I heard you bite back a shriek."

"It wasn't your driving! It was just how horrible it was. It was raining so hard I knew you could barely see. You looked so tense."

She rubbed his neck a little, and he sighed again. "That feels good."

A crack of lightning lit up her room, and he instantly stiffened. "It's okay," she said. "You got this."

She heard his soft laughter. "Yes, about that, by the way. What are you, a motivational speaker now? How did you know all those sayings?"

She giggled. "I told you! I watch a lot of American shows. I tried to think of everything I could. I hated leaving you with your grandfather. You don't have to talk about it, but did you at least clear the air?"

He sighed. "We did more than that. I'm sorry, I just needed some time to process it. It was like the floodgates had opened. We talked about my father and Nonno's abandonment feelings. And how I felt about never belonging, either here or at home."

"Oh, Max, that can't be true."

He shrugged and snuggled closer. "It's the way I feel. But we were both bluntly honest with each other, and we have a lot of thinking to do. By the way, how did you fare with Nonna? You two looked almost conspiratorial when you came back from your walk."

"We understood each other very well. But she sure cuts to the run!" Francesca observed.

He pulled back like he was trying to see her face. "Cuts to the run? Oh, cuts to the chase." He laughed despite the loud thunder outside.

"Go ahead, make fun of me. Here I am trying to protect you, and you're laughing at me."

She could feel him smile. "You're doing a great job distracting me. Tell me something else."

"Like what?"

He turned on his back, and she instantly swung an arm around him, her hand stroking his chest. He intently played with her hair. "Try another saying. I like it when you mess them up."

She sighed. "What if I use the one you used earlier today?"

He kissed the top of her head. "What was that?"

"I think you swept me off my feet," she whispered.

"Really?" he whispered back.

She didn't raise her head but nodded. His arms tightened around her.

There was a long silence. Finally, he heaved a great sigh. "I should leave you, Francesca. I think the storm is almost over. It sounds like it's further away."

She used an elbow to prop herself up to look at his face. She could see his serious expression from the small light coming through the curtain.

"What if I asked you to stay?"

He studied her face for a moment before a small smile tugged at his lips.

"Really?" he asked again.

She nodded, her expression tender. "Really."

"Then I'd say," he murmured, brushing a strand of hair from her cheek, "I'm hooked, line, and sinker."

# *twenty-six*

"Whatcha thinking about?" Max asked, glancing at Francesca as they drove up the hill close to her home.

"Last night," she murmured with a smile.

"Me, too," he said and grinned back. "I may just change my mind about storms."

She giggled, and he reached over and grabbed her hand. "I just want to touch you one last time. Your family will be on us in about two seconds. This is our last chance to be alone before the gala," he remarked.

She sighed. "I really can't believe it's almost here," she said and swatted his hand away. "And I'm still mad at you for not telling me you were going to be gone this whole week!"

"I know, I'm sorry. It's just that we were having such a good time, and I didn't want to think about it. But Marco needs me to travel to London with him. We'll be back on Friday, but I know you have a lot to do to get ready. I'll see you on Saturday. We'll talk as much as possible. I'm sure I'll have a lot of time on my hands while Marco calls Katie all the time," he teased.

"I know, and I'm usually not this needy. But this gala is just overwhelming. All those eyes on me," she said with a shudder. "And then, on top of it, our grandparents will be in one room."

"Do you think they'll be a duel? Fistfight? Wrestling match?" He joked.

She groaned. "Max, this isn't funny! I feel like I'll be on edge all night."

He grabbed her hand again and held it firmly. "Don't be. We can't control them. Remember baby steps? They'll see each other and get that first awkward meeting over with. Then perhaps there will be a second and a third."

"But that could take forever," she said, turning to him.

He parked the car at the front entrance and turned to her. Taking his sunglasses off, he had a wariness in his eyes. "Are you so eager to get rid of me?"

She looked down, picking at a thread on her jeans. "Well, of course not! Especially after last night. I...I mean..."

He interrupted, "Francesca, there's something I need to tell you..."

"YOU'RE FINALLY HERE!" Luci shouted, running toward the car. They looked at each other helplessly. Finally, he gave her a small smile. "I was right. Two seconds."

Getting out, he threw a casual arm around Luci's shoulders. "Hey Luce, how's it shaking?"

Luci's laughter rang out before she started chattering away, as Max went to help Francesca out of the car.

"Hey, remember me?" Francesca asked.

"I see you all the time," Luci said dismissively. "But I wanted to tell Max how well I'm doing in math. The last tutoring session really helped!"

Francesca was confused. "But that was weeks ago!" She looked from one to the other. A quick look passed between them, and guilt flashed across Max's expression.

She smiled. "What did I miss?"

He shrugged. "I might have video chatted with her a couple of times from the Amalfi Coast."

"Max! Why didn't you tell me?"

Luci grabbed her hand. "Because you would have told him that I should do it myself," she said. "But Max is so good at explaining it all. Even if he does make really bad jokes."

"Hey, my jokes aren't that bad!" Max protested. "Way to turn on me!"

Luci laughed. "I'm on your side. Just remember that before you go in there."

Francesca frowned. "Nonna and Nonno are here?"

"You guessed it," Luci said. "But they are in a good mood. The gala is less than a week away."

Francesca sighed. "I know."

"Aren't you excited? You get to wear that amazing dress, and everyone will notice you! And you can dance with Max," she gushed. Turning to him, she gave him a skeptical look. "You *can* dance, can't you?"

He laughed. "Of course I can! I am the best line dancer at our local pub at home."

Luci looked at him, her eyes wide. "I don't know what that is, but something tells me we have work to do."

Max's intent gaze met Francesca's over Luci's head. Slowly, he grinned. "Don't worry. We've got this," he said.

MAX SIPPED his beer and gazed out at the Thames and the Tower Bridge from his hotel penthouse. As predicted, Marco had gone to his room to call Katie and Max had worked for another hour until he got restless. Francesca had texted him earlier that she would be unavailable for his call that night. An old friend from university was in town, and they were going out together.

She claimed she needed some downtime after her grandparents' constant drilling on protocol.

Now he wished he would have asked her where they were going. What if she went back to that restaurant where that guy from school was? He still wanted to go punch him for hurting Francesca, even if it was a long time ago. He could tell that it still affected her, though it wasn't obvious. Anyone looking at her would think she was the most confident person in the world. He was happy she shared with him her true feelings. Now he saw the guarded expression on her face when she was feeling old uncertainties. They were a lot alike that way.

He thought back to the night of the storm. She had been so caring and loving listening to him. Some of the stuff he had eventually told her he had never even said out loud. It was like having a huge boulder lifted off his back. He had felt lighter ever since, and he wanted to be with her.

Guilt also washed over him. Terror had indeed brought him to her room, but he never wanted her to think that he had other motivations. In fact, he purposely had not advanced anything physical until they determined what was real and what was a charade between them. In his heart, he knew they both cared for each other, but things were more complicated than just their feelings. That's where his own uncertainties came in. She was so poised and regal, and nothing could change the fact he was the guy who often forgot to brush his hair and was happiest in jeans and a flannel shirt. Even without the princess title, she would always stand out above most women. Could she be happy with someone who was still learning her culture even though it was his birthright? At the lemon grove, he couldn't help confessing he was falling for her, because he had to know her feelings. It was eating him up inside not knowing if she felt the same.

And then there were their grandparents. True, her grandparents had been a touch warmer when he had entered the house earlier that week. They both actually spoke to him without

Francesca nudging them to. He still had work to do, though. And his own grandparents already thought highly of Francesca, even despite the feud. Nonna had called to tell him that earlier that day. She credited Francesca for bringing about his talk with his grandfather. He had agreed with his grandmother, telling her how Francesca had given him a lot to think about.

There was one thing he had wanted to tell her before Luci came to the car, though. He should have told her on the phone, only he wanted it to be in person. He just hoped it wasn't going to make a huge difference in their relationship.

"We'll see," he said to the empty room. "We've got this," he repeated.

# twenty-seven

Francesca stood before the full-length mirror. Nonna had reviewed the program with her several times to prevent any surprises. Francesca pasted on a smile. Her gown had ultimately turned out to be exquisite. Nonna had insisted it be debutante white, and Francesca had opted for a higher neck in the front and a low dip in the back. There were no ruffles or pleats, nothing fussy. It fit her like a glove and was obviously cut by a master. When she tried it on for her grandparents and parents, she had worried they would find it too plain, but they had cheered and clapped. Luci had proclaimed her fabulous. Arianna had traveled down to do her hair, since she had a special skill at it. Twisting Francesca's hair into a complicated updo, she had pinned and curled and woven it intricately into a chic style. When she was finished, they both looked into the mirror and burst into uproarious laughter.

"You don't look like you at all," Arianna said between giggles.

"Maybe that's a good thing," Francesca said dryly.

Arianna shook her head. "You should wear your hair down."

Francesca frowned. "Not for tonight. I need it to be up. That's what Nonna wanted. For once, I want to be the perfect grand-daughter. Someone they are proud of."

Arianna stared at her in the mirror. "Oh, Frannie, you don't feel that way, do you? They love you, and they *are* proud of you!"

Francesca shrugged. "I left home. I became a shopgirl, and now I'm engaged to a Valentini. I think three strikes and I'm out, as Max would say."

"Well, for once, I disagree with Max. And remember, you are with him for a good reason. You're actually trying to help our stubborn grandparents get their business back."

An image of her with Max the last night they'd been together made her flush. "Yes, being with Max is completely selfless."

Arianna stuck one more pin in Francesca's hair and stood back. "Are you in love with him, Frannie? You didn't answer me the last time I asked."

"I've grown fond of him," Francesca said, thinking back to Katie's term. If she told Arianna the truth, she worried it would spread throughout the family.

"Fond? Who are you? Some Victorian maiden? What does that even mean?"

Francesca stood up before Arianna could fuss any more. "It means things are complicated, Ari," she said more sharply than intended. At her sister's expression, she hugged her. "Max and I are still figuring things out," she said. "But yes, we are happy. Thank you for doing my hair."

Arianna grinned. "Next time, we'll do it down. But you look amazing, Frannie. Max is going to fall even more in love with you."

Francesca blinked and nodded. The lump in her throat was too big to answer.

FRANCESCA TOOK the chauffeur's hand and gently stepped out of the vintage Rolls-Royce her grandfather specifically used for special occasions. It was disappointing she couldn't have Max with her, but etiquette required her father to formally present her.

"*Grazie,*" she murmured and tried not to notice the chauffeur's stare.

"*Bellissima, Topo,*" her father told her, as he joined her, giving her a reassuring smile. He knew her nerves were on edge. "We'll just go in and get this done."

She nodded, her expression grim.

Her father nudged her. "You are going to have to smile, though."

She grimaced, and he laughed. "You'll get there. Especially when you see your young man."

The idea that Max was inside waiting for her did make Francesca smile. She missed him, although they had talked most every night. Though it would have been nice to confide in him how nervous she was becoming, she had kept their conversations light. Max had probed once or twice, but she had stayed firm in her resolution to not whine about something so silly. It was only one night, after all. She could do this.

Lifting her gown, she walked toward the entrance. Her new designer shoes pinched a little, but she adored them. They were even higher than she usually wore, but Francesca secretly delighted in towering over people. Some people might find it awkward, but she felt powerful when they had to look up.

They entered the gala, which was being held at the Palazzo Reale in Milan. Its grandeur wasn't lost on Francesca, who loved its old-world opulence and historical significance. Arianna had once told her Napolean used it for his palace during his reign. It was regal and elegant and just right for this occasion.

Francesca took a deep breath. Slipping her hand through her father's arm, she nodded that she was ready. Her name was announced, but it was as if the voice was muffled. She knew it was her own hearing. Everything was closing in on her. They approached her grandfather, and her father bowed formally as he presented her to him. Her grandfather's comforting hand guided her to the dance floor.

She glided effortlessly across the dance floor in an elegant waltz that her grandmother had insisted she learn years ago. While doing so, she discreetly turned her head. The faces were a blur as they rotated by, but surely, she could see Max? Thundering applause rose, and more people joined them on the polished dance floor that sparkled under the colorful frescos on the exquisite gold-rimmed ceiling. The gold chandeliers cast a warm glow, and if she hadn't been so tense, Francesca would have admired the exquisite ambiance. She finally let out a breath when her father came to claim the second dance.

"You're doing splendidly," he murmured. "I know this is your night, but thank you for making my parents so happy."

"It's not really my night," Francesca said, staring into her father's kind face. "It is really for them. You know I couldn't care less about all of this."

Her father's arm tightened around her. "You take after me. I've never sought the limelight either, and I was more than happy to leave all of this in Milan behind."

Glancing over his shoulder, she bit her lip. "Papa, I haven't seen Max."

"He's right there, *Topo*."

She glanced around, bewildered. "Where?"

Her father danced her over to the side and spun her around. The final note faded. The orchestra began another dance, but the music was a distant hum as she spotted him. There he was, standing in his formal white tie attire, his hair carefully styled. His brown eyes intently gazed at her, his expression unreadable. Her father gently pushed her toward him a little. Max walked slowly forward, staring at her. It unnerved her.

"Say something," she whispered tremulously.

Slowly, he smiled, a tender, loving smile she had never seen before. It was for her only, and she beamed back at him.

"Now this is really like a prom," he said. "I should have brought you a corsage."

She giggled, and he touched her shoulder lightly. "I'm almost scared to touch you," he said quietly. "You look every inch the princess tonight."

Francesca frowned a little at him, which made his grin wider. "Are you allowed to dance with me now?" he asked, already gathering her in his arms.

"Of course I am," she responded.

"Was I supposed to bow or something?"

She tapped his shoulder hard. "If you do, I'll slug you."

"That just might make the headlines," he said, gathering her close for a minute. He pulled back and stared at her. "Nice necklace, by the way," he murmured. She put a hand up to the extravagant diamond and amethyst necklace her grandmother had retrieved from the safe earlier that night. Diamonds and amethyst flowers were intricately woven together in a stunning jewelry piece. It had been passed on for many generations.

"It's vintage," Francesca said, her eyes dancing.

"It's like the crown jewels or something," Max remarked.

"Max, stop it," she whispered.

His arms tightened. "I'm sorry. I make bad jokes when I'm nervous."

She pulled back to stare into his eyes. "Why are you nervous? It's just me."

"You and the three hundred pairs of eyes staring at us."

She gave a dismissive wave with the hand on his shoulder. "It's just because people are curious about me. They'll get over it very soon. It's a passing fancy."

"They're wondering what you're doing dancing with the

American. And by now they've seen the ring on your finger, and our engagement will soon be public."

"I didn't think of that," said Francesca. "But Max, you're Italian, too."

"And a Valentini," he pointed out.

"Yes, that, too," she said. Glancing around, she kept a smile pasted on her face. "I don't see your grandparents, but there's just so many people."

"Oh, they're here," Max muttered. "I can feel their beady eyes boring into my back right now. Nonna is telling me to stand straight and not step on your toes. At least I combed my hair!"

Francesca laughed and whirled around, holding her gown out. For once, she did feel like a princess. It felt heavenly to be in Max's arms, and she relaxed. She pulled back to smile at him, still completely in rhythm with him. It was as if they had danced together their entire lives. He was staring intently again, searching her face. His hand came up and traced her jaw with a finger. He looked like he wanted to kiss her.

"Francesca, there's something I need to tell you," Max began.

Her heart began to thud. Max's expression was serious. This couldn't be good news. But why would he tell her now? Couldn't she sidetrack him? Her nerves were already on edge. Marco and Kate danced near them. She gave them a wave that her grandmother would probably tell her later was not very regal. They grinned at her. Beaming at Max, she said, "Finally, some more friendly faces."

"I'm glad to hear you say that, *cara*," came a familiar voice behind them.

Max's expression had grown more serious. The music had ended, and Francesca broke away from him and turned to the attractive man staring at her with his trademark smile.

"Mario," she whispered.

She turned to glance at Max and wondered why he didn't

look surprised. "It was what I wanted to tell you," Max explained flatly. "Mario has returned, and he's single."

Francesca looked confused and glanced back at Mario.

"You don't think I would miss your big debut," Mario said with practiced charm. He glanced at Max. "*Mi Dispiace*, Massimo, but as her betrothed, I should have this dance."

Francesca's eyes widened. "But, Mario," she protested. She was whirled away suddenly, her gaze snapping back. Max was standing where she had left him, his expression unreadable.

"Aren't you glad to see me, *cara*? It's been so long," Mario asked.

Her startled gaze went to his. "Of course," she said absent-mindedly. She glanced back to see Max walking over toward his grandparents, who were anxiously staring at her.

"I thought you got married in America," Francesca said. "That's what Max told me."

"What has *mio cugino* been filling your head with?" Mario murmured in her ear. "Of course not. How could I marry when I am betrothed to you?"

Francesca looked helplessly at him. "Mario, *per favore*. You know that's not real. It was a wish from our nonni. We used to laugh about it."

"It was more than a wish. It was a promise," he insisted, his arms tightening.

"But I'm engaged to Max now," she said quietly, impatiently glancing around, intently keeping her voice low.

"You're what? Engaged to another man? To a Valentini?" he asked in what seemed to be a purposely loud tone.

"Shhh, will you please keep your voice down," she hissed. "I'm not your betrothed. I was perfectly free to do what I wished. And I chose Max."

"How could you? How could you disrespect your family? The feud between your families is longstanding. Are you sure he's not using you?"

"The feud is ridiculous, and it's time everyone got over themselves," Francesca said, breaking away. They were standing in a corner, and she didn't care anymore who heard. "He is not using me! Max would never do that! Mario, just because you have returned . . ."

"*Mi dispiace*," he said suavely. "But clearly, Francesca, you must understand my feelings for you. I've been in love with you since we were children."

Her mouth fell open. "That is not true! I was a faithful friend. The one girl who would sit and listen to your love adventures. You had no interest in me."

His expression darkened. "I can't believe you question me! I have always cared for you. And while my back is turned, my cousin sweeps in and covets the woman I love."

Francesca peeked around Mario, trying to see where Max was. He had disappeared in the crowd. "Mario, this is a pointless argument. We both know there was nothing between us. Please, this is a big night for my family. Can we continue this tomorrow?" she asked anxiously.

"Certainly," he said with a sulk that she suddenly questioned was genuine. "We can have lunch and discuss this further."

She frowned at him and opened her mouth to tell him she was in love with Max when she felt a light hand on her back.

"Francesca, I've been looking all over for you. Surely the belle of the ball can dance with her old friend?"

Francesca smiled into Marco's kind smile. His gaze gave her a speaking look, and she almost slumped in relief.

"Marco, of course," she said and gave a small laugh. "If your lovely wife will let me, I would love to dance with you."

Marco gripped her hand tightly, and they began to walk away.

"I'll see you tomorrow, *cara*," Mario said loudly from behind them.

Francesca didn't turn around but pasted the smile on her face and began to waltz with Marco. "You look very dashing in your white tie," Francesca said, smiling weakly at him.

"*Grazie*. Katie thinks so, too," he said, his eyes dancing. "But I told her I must leave her to save a damsel in distress. And you did look in distress, Francesca. You must know that Mario Bianchini is an opportunist and nothing more."

"Well, of course I do," she grumbled. "I'm not stupid, Marco. But he just grabbed me and took me away, insisting we are betrothed. It's all silly. An ancient promise between our grandparents. We were never really engaged," she said, glancing up at his set expression. "Marco, what's wrong? Are you upset with me?"

He shook his head. "Of course not, Francesca. But *mio cugino*, doesn't understand these old customs. Max may be confused."

"I'll explain," Francesca told him confidently. "I'll make him understand."

"You'll have to do it tomorrow," Marco said, as he swung her around, smiling politely at interested stares around them.

"Why?" she asked, glancing around and then at Marco's firm expression.

"Because he just left."

# twenty-eight

"Are you awake, Frannie?" Caterina poked her head in the door of her adjacent hotel suite in Milan. "I brought you a cappuccino."

Francesca was sitting on a nearby sofa, her legs stretched out over the cushions. She wore her violet-colored bathrobe, her hair pulled back in a simple ponytail cascading down her back. The family had stayed in the luxurious set of suites, knowing they would have a late night. Unfortunately, Francesca had little sleep. Following Max's departure, she had no choice but to stay and smile, looking confident and composed. She had danced with a number of people, made all the right conversation and nibbled on her the late-night dinner. The highlight had been when Marco received the award on behalf of the Angelo Foundation for its role in improving women's healthcare. She had almost put two fingers in her mouth to whistle but was stalled by a frown from her grandmother. While no one was rude enough to acknowledge what had transpired, she felt the question in gazes her way. Relief washed over her when the night ended.

"Mamma, you didn't have to bring me *caffe*," Francesca said, but reached for the cup gratefully.

"I wanted to, dear," Caterina said, sitting in a nearby chair. "When you didn't come down for the hotel's breakfast, I was worried."

Francesca shrugged and glanced out the penthouse window at the city of Milan, still waking up. Usually the streets were bustling, but since it was Sunday, there were few people out yet. In the distance, church bells rang. "It looks so peaceful down there," she remarked.

"But it's not peaceful up here," Caterina stated.

Francesca turned and grimaced. "You've seen the headlines?"

Caterina nodded slowly.

Francesca hung her head. "And nonna and nonno?"

"Oh, they've seen them," Caterina remarked dryly.

Francesca leaned her head against the wall. "Mamma, that reporter must have been standing near us in the corner. It's like she printed exactly what Mario said."

This morning, without even thinking, she had looked at her phone and almost immediately had come across the photo of her dancing with Mario. A stranger would assume her expression was almost dreamy. But those who knew better would understand it was Francesca's polite smile. The headline still rung in her head. "Two Suitors, One Princess: A Royal Love Triangle Turns Explosive!" She had thrown her phone across the room, where it still lay. It was impossible not to feel completely humiliated.

"Francesca, why did you have this conversation in public?" her mother implored. She took a deep breath. "I'm sorry. I shouldn't have snapped at you. Nonna and Nonno are beside themselves. Obviously, they were . . ."

"Embarrassed?" Francesca asked, her eyebrows going up. "Once again, I disgraced them."

"Absolutely not!" Caterina said, sitting up straight. "Francesca, you can't believe that. If you want to know, they were angry at Mario for showing up like that unannounced and pretending somehow he was a victim!"

"Oh, Mamma," Francesca said and covered her face with her hands for a minute. "I'll never forget the look on Max's face. He looked so...I don't know. Disappointed, I guess. He's probably furious with me."

"I doubt that, dear. Max is a level-headed man, though he *is* Italian," she pointed out, raising an eyebrow. "He probably needs time to blow off steam. He'll be fine."

"Perhaps," Francesca acknowledged, folding her bathrobe into pleats absent-mindedly. "I just want to talk to him."

"FRANNIE!" Luci burst into the room.

"Luciana, you know better! Please knock before entering someone's room," Caterina admonished.

"I am sorry, Mamma, but Papa sent me up to tell Frannie to get dressed and come downstairs right now."

Francesca sat up eagerly. "Is Max here?"

Luci rolled her eyes. "I wish. No, Mario Go Kart is here."

Caterina stood. "Luciana, don't call him that."

"He's an even worse bore than he used to be," she replied promptly.

Francesca giggled despite her dark mood. "Tell him I've left already."

"Not going to work. Papa already told him you would be right down to the lobby."

Francesca stood and took one last sip of her cappuccino. "I might as well get it over with," she remarked.

"Are you going to break his heart?" asked Luci.

"I doubt his heart can be damaged," Francesca said, walking to her closet. "I'll just be kind and tell him no, thank you."

"No, thank you?" Caterina said. "That's how you're going to end the engagement?"

"Mamma, you know it's not a proper engagement!"

Francesca protested. "I will tell him that and send him on his way."

As Francesca began rifling through her closet, Luci smirked and leaned casually against the doorframe.

"Well, if you're going to break his heart, at least do it in something fabulous," she quipped. "Nothing says 'I'm not into you' like looking too good for him in the first place."

FRANCESCA SAT in the window of a nearby *trattoria*, sipping a glass of lemonade. Her head was aching. Bored, she popped a piece of cheese in her mouth and chewed. For the past hour, Mario had droned on about all his adventures in America. Why did she never notice that he was so self-absorbed? Luci was spot on when it came to that.

She had taken her sister's advice and put on a killer dress. Why not make Mario drool just a little? The old Francesca, with the braces and glasses, wanted to own the moment. Let him see what he lost! Now, as she tugged the royal blue dress down a little over her thigh, she was regretting it. For one, Mario's eyes had been focused on her chest half the time. This dress showed a little more cleavage than she was used to. In fact, that's why she had packed it purposely to wear for Max.

She snapped her fingers. "Mario, my eyes are up here."

He smiled charmingly. "*Mi dispiace, cara.* It's just that you are so gorgeous. I had no idea." He broke off, like he was realizing his mistake.

"Why didn't you have any idea?" she asked sweetly, but there was an edge to her voice.

He looked uncomfortable. "Let's just say you have matured into a beautiful woman," he answered smoothly.

His hand covered hers, which had been lying on the table. He frowned. "Must you insist on wearing Massimo's ring? I thought you would leave it off, given our discussion last night."

"He is my fiancé, not you," Francesca replied sharply, withdrawing her hand.

She looked at him shrewdly. "Why are you here Mario? What's in it for you?"

"Francesca, you didn't use to be so crass. Why, of course I'm here because of you," he explained suavely.

Francesca frowned at him and popped some salami in her mouth. Finally, swallowing, she stared at him.

He finally squirmed a little. "Why are you looking at me that way?"

She smiled. "I know every expression on your face, Mario. I studied you since I was a small child. So out with it. You're up to something. I just know it."

He leaned back and chuckled a little. He sipped his wine. "You're right. I feel badly teasing you. I just couldn't resist, especially with you now being such a breathtaking woman and engaged to my cousin, the American," he said, his tone a little bitter. "Forgive me? I would hope that we are friends, at the very least. Can you keep a secret?"

At her nod, he continued. "There is a woman. A very lovely woman that I would like to marry. She's an American heiress."

"The one you went to America to marry?" Francesca asked.

"No, no, that didn't work out," he said, with a wave of his hand. "But Daniella is exquisite. However, her father is a little skeptical of me."

"Where do I come in?" Francesca asked, raising an eyebrow.

"Well, if you must know, I played it cool. I told her I was already engaged. To a princess, no less. Of course, she's American, and thinks all royals are like the ones in England. She knows nothing of Italy."

"And the fact that my title is meaningless," Francesca filled in dryly.

"Not meaningless. It's still important to society," he informed her. "But, yes, she's thinking you're a famous princess walking around in your tiara. She begged me not to go, but I told her I would return to Italy and do the honorable thing. You know, let you down easily and all that."

She rolled her eyes. "Mario, you never change, do you? So you just wanted to get in on the photographs. That's why you showed last night?"

"Well, of course, Frannie. By the way, you could have pulled out an old tiara or something. And how was I to know Massimo and you . . . well who would have guessed?" His face grew dark. "Now my plan is ruined. She's going to see those headlines and know I have competition."

"So that's why you wanted to go out today? You're hoping some paparazzi might snap a photo."

He averted his gaze, and her eyes widened. "Really, Mario? You called them, didn't you?"

"Just one photo, *cara*, and you'll be done. Can you see to do it for an old friend? Daniella will see that I am with a princess, and she is competitive. She'll want me back in a heartbeat," he said smugly. "And I'll cement my future with her papa. He'll believe I've chosen his daughter over a princess."

Francesca rubbed her neck, feeling her headache worsen. "If I let you have your one photo, will you leave me alone? Stop all this betrothal nonsense?"

"Of course," he said smoothly. "I will get out of you and Massimo's way. Though frankly, you could do better than him."

"Mario, don't say that! He's your cousin! Max is a smart, sweet, and funny human being. And I love . . ." she broke off.

"It's worse than I thought," Mario said, grabbing the bill. "You've fallen for him. Well, I know when I'm not wanted. Just be sure he's not using you for his grandfather's business," he said darkly.

"Max would never do that!"

He stood and looked down at her. "We'll see. Let's go and get that photo taken, and I'll be off. I do want you to be happy, Frannie."

She smiled, thinking of Max. "I am." Standing, he helped her into her matching jacket.

They strolled out to the piazza in front of the Duomo. Mario tightly gripped her hand. "We can pretend we're going to look at the Duomo for our wedding," he murmured.

She rolled her eyes. "As if! I would never get married here in this giant cathedral. One photo, Mario, and then I have to go. Where is this photographer?"

Mario stopped dead center in front of the Duomo and put his arms around her. He smiled. "One photo. Let's get this right." Francesca gasped as he bent her over his arm with a flourish and his mouth descended. Bent like this, she couldn't very well struggle or he might drop her. Fortunately, the kiss was brief, and as she straightened, a man scurried away with his camera. "I ought to slug you, Mario. I thought we were just going to take a photo. I never agreed to kiss you."

He smiled. "A kiss among friends," he said. "And now, princess, I'll be off." Giving her a brief hug, he turned and began to walk away. "By the way, your Nonna called mine this morning and broke our engagement. So, you are truly free," he said with a grin.

"Are you kidding me? Why didn't you start with that?" Francesca hissed. "I wouldn't have done any of this."

"Exactly! *Ciao,* Frannie," he said. Giving her one last grin, he walked away.

Francesca's temper bubbled up over the top. She fought the urge to kick something. Returning to her hotel, she would meet up with her family and then call Max. Her heart raced. Now he would see that photo! She had to get to him before he saw it! Running as fast as she dared in her high heels and short dress, she sped back to the hotel. She would fix this. She had to!

# twenty-nine

"He just left," Luci said dully. "He drove away just a few minutes ago."

"What? Why didn't you stop him?" Francesca asked, clearly frustrated. Tears welled up in her eyes.

"I'm not sure what happened. Max seemed in kind of a weird mood, but he agreed to stay for dinner. Mamma told him you were driving home with Nonna and Nonno. She was pouring him a drink when he suddenly said he had to go and roared away."

"Perhaps he got called into work," Carlo said, anxiously trying to appear positive.

"I doubt there was some financial crisis, Papa," Francesca said, dejected. Now she really felt like kicking something. It had taken her grandparents longer to collect their bags, and Nonno's chauffeur had driven slowly with Nonno instructing him from the passenger seat. Francesca had sat in the back with Nonna and had wanted to scream to let her take the wheel. It had only been out of kindness that she had agreed to drive with them when she returned to the hotel after her lunch with Mario. It would be a good opportunity for them to talk. And talk they did.

Fortunately, it had been much nicer than she thought. They both had rushed to reassure Francesca that they did not blame her for the headlines or Mario's appalling behavior.

"I called his Nonna this morning. I said, 'Marisella, the deal is off. Our Francesca deserves better than that,'" Nonna snapped indignantly.

"What did she say?" Francesca couldn't help but ask.

"She asked if a Valentini was better."

"And how did you respond?" Francesca prodded, anxious to hear her grandmother's answer.

There was silence. Finally, Nonna spoke. "I told her far better."

"Francesca, you're not listening," Luci's shrill voice broke into her whirling mind.

"Sorry, what did you say, Luci?"

"I told you to call him! Tell him you're here and to turn around."

Francesca nodded. "Good idea," she replied, and walked away for privacy. Biting her lip, she wondered if he would pick up. Max hadn't answered any of her phone calls or texts, except one cryptic one that afternoon that said he would meet her in Verona so they could talk. Not very encouraging, but she felt sure once she explained Mario's warped and twisted motives, Max and she could laugh it off. Then they could focus on their relationship and decide if they wanted to continue their initial plan to bring their grandparents together. Now, as she looked off into the distance at the vineyard, she wondered if that was even a motive anymore.

Last night Max had simply strolled off, leaving Francesca to hurry over to his grandparents. His nonna had been kind but, his nonno was gruffer. Clearly, they were confused as to what was occurring.

Picking up the phone, she quickly called Max. Luci was right that he could easily return. The call went immediately to voicemail. She frowned. Either he was on the phone, or he declined the call. She tried again. Voicemail. At the tone, she began to ramble, "Um, hi, Max. I'm home, and Luci said you left suddenly. I hope you're okay. I thought . . . well, I thought we could talk. I'm not sure why you left. Call me back. I'm worried about you. Okay. Well, call me back."

She hung up and sat down on a nearby stone bench.

Luci came skipping up. "Is he coming back?"

Francesca shook her head, a lump in her throat growing.

"Oh, Frannie, you didn't blow this, did you?"

Francesca frowned at her sister. "You're not helping, Luci."

Luci sat down next to her, staring down the hill as well. "Sorry. I just love Max," she said quietly.

"So do I," Francesca responded.

"THERE'S a big black car coming up the hill!" Luci yelled up to Francesca's room.

Francesca hurried downstairs, despite knowing it wasn't Max's car. Two nights had gone by and she was getting increasingly stressed about what Max was thinking. One cryptic text from him told her nothing. Checking her phone hundreds of times, she had yet to see the photo of Mario kissing her. Confused why it hadn't been published, she almost wanted to text Mario to find out. At least it was buying her some time.

Dressed in jeans and a pink cashmere sweater, she rushed down the stairs two at a time and came to a screeching halt, watching Graham admit Kate Rinaldi into the home. "Katie!" Francesca shouted from the top of the stairs and descended the last several at a quick pace. She hugged her friend.

"What are you doing here?" Francesca asked, getting directly to the point.

"Well, you always spoke so highly of Verona, I thought you

could be my tour guide," Kate said. While her words were casual, she gave Francesca a speaking look. Francesca glanced over her shoulder to see her parents coming into the entry hall. They had all been introduced to Kate the night of the gala and rushed to greet her.

Francesca made a quick decision. Grabbing a light coat from a nearby closet, she said, "Katie is visiting Verona, and I'm going to show her around." She quickly disengaged her friend from her parents, hustled her out the door and into the black SUV, where a driver was waiting.

Luci stood with her parents at the front door and watched them go. "They're going to plot about what to do with Max," she proclaimed. "My money is on Katie. Maybe she'll have a good idea to clean up this mess. After all, she caught Marco!"

FRANCESCA STROLLED across the *Ponte di Castelvecchio* with Kate. They stopped to admire the view of the water. "You were right. It's lovely here, Francesca," Kate said with a small smile.

"It is beautiful, but something tells me you didn't come all the way to Verona to tell me you like the scenery," Francesca said, turning to eye Kate speculatively.

Kate looked uncomfortable. "Have you heard from Max?"

Francesca bit her lip. "I finally got a text. He just said we need to talk, but he didn't set a time."

"That won't be an easy meeting," Kate murmured. She turned to Francesca, her expression serious. "Why did you throw Max over so . . . publicly? Couldn't you have just broken it off quietly? The whole thing was just a farce to begin with," Katie finished. Her cheeks were flushed, but then just as suddenly, the color drained from them.

"Katie, are you okay?" She saw her friend sway a little and

grabbed her arm. Francesca guided her to sit down on a nearby stone bench. "Your face went from red to white to green! Tell me you're alright! Should I call Marco?"

Kate shook her head and rubbed her temples. "I'll be okay. Just give me a minute. Marco doesn't know I'm here," she said quietly. "But I had to. I just wanted to know why."

"First tell me! Are you sick?"

Kate glanced up and gave a small smile.

"You're pregnant?" Francesca breathed.

Kate nodded. "This one was a little more planned than the last one. We wanted Frankie to have a little brother or sister closer in age to him. He'll already be three on his next birthday."

"Aw, Katie, I'm so happy for you guys," Francesca said. She sat down and put her arm around her.

"That's what I don't understand, Francesca," Kate said, turning to her. The color had come back to her cheeks. "You're a good friend. I thought I knew you. And I was sure you had fallen in love with Max. I saw how upset you were after he left the gala so abruptly."

"I did . . . I do!" Francesca insisted.

"Marco thought the same thing. He still does, despite seeing the photo. It's me who is confused."

"I know the photo was bad and I'm staring at Mario like I care for him, but I was just so startled. I was trying to not draw even more attention to the situation."

"What are you talking about?" Katie exclaimed. "You were kissing him!"

Francesca felt the color drain from her face. "I . . . uh . . . he kissed me in front of the Duomo."

"I know," Katie said flatly.

"How do you know?"

Kate took her phone out of her pocket and flipped through it. "Because Max sent us this," she said. Francesca glanced down and saw her worst fears were true. There she was in her short blue dress, cleavage, and all, being dipped down and thoroughly kissed by Mario. "I don't want to think Max was giving away any secrets. Marco was on the phone with him, trying to sort it out. He was defending you, but then Max sent this as I guess proof that you and Mario were back together."

Francesca mumbled in Italian.

Kate smiled a little. "I know that word. Marco uses it when he's angry."

"I'd like to say a lot more words," Francesca said, slowly handing back Kate's phone.

"Then start talking," Kate said, sitting back.

# *thirty*

"This is the craziest thing I've ever done," Francesca said, glancing nervously up at Max's building. She had let Kate convince her to just get in the car and head for Milan to explain to Max what happened. Francesca had quickly texted her parents but didn't even return to the house to change. Glancing down, she wondered if she should have taken the time to put on something different. She shrugged. Max was used to her dressing casually. Glancing at Kate, she asked anxiously, "Do I look okay?"

"You look beautiful as always," Kate said, "But maybe take your braid out and fluff up your hair."

Francesca nodded and smiled. "Max likes my hair," she told her confidently, feeling that familiar race of her heart at the thought of his expression when he touched it.

Francesca stared at the building uncertainly. Kate nudged her with her elbow. "My father always says to take the bull by the horns." Francesca glanced at her, giving her a worried look. "And what do you do if the bull charges you?"

Kate laughed. "I think you're taking that saying a little too literally. Listen, Francesca, you told me you and Mario aren't together, and in fact, he just used you for his own gains. All you have to do is explain it all to Max and he will understand."

"You're right," Francesca said. "None of this was my fault." She paused and bit her lip. "Well, maybe the kissing part. I let him talk me into the paparazzi photo. But at that point, I just wanted to make a deal for him to leave us alone. I had no idea my nonna had already handled it."

"Sounds like she handled it quite well," Kate remarked. "Now go up and get your guy."

Francesca grinned and got out of the car. She glanced back at Kate, smiling at her from the back seat. "I can never thank you enough, Katie. Tell Marco thank you, too."

Kate grimaced. "I will, once I admit I did this! He was adamant about not interfering."

Francesca laughed and allowed the driver to shut the door. She turned to go into the building and suddenly remembered the security. They would have to announce her. What if Max said no?

Fluffing her hair again, she pasted a sweet smile on her face. Convincing the young security officer who had seen her coming and going with Max to let her upstairs without announcing her took no effort. He blushed as he ran his key card for the elevator, holding the doors and tipping his hat.

It was only when she was in the elevator alone that her heart started beating fast. She wiped her sweaty hands down on her jeans. Perhaps she should put on some lipstick. It was then, with a sinking heart, she realized she didn't have her purse with her. Oh well, it didn't really matter. Max would take care of anything she needed.

Getting off the elevator, she walked down the hall and took a deep breath before knocking on Max's door. After a few seconds, he opened it, and she wanted to throw her arms around him. He looked so attractive standing there with his hair ruffled as always, the slight growth on his jaw that looked like he hadn't shaved for days. He was dressed in jeans and a long-sleeved plaid shirt, with socks on his feet.

Staring at her, he crossed his arms, his expression serious. "Francesca, I wasn't expecting you. How did you get up here?"

Heat crept into her cheeks. Better not to give Kate away. "I got a ride."

"I meant the building. Guests are supposed to be announced," Max said succinctly.

"Please don't be upset with the security officer," Francesca rushed to explain. "He's young, and he recognized me. I told him you would want to see me . . . " She broke off. "It's not his fault," she rushed to explain.

"Well, I guess as long as you're here, you better come in," Max said quietly.

She walked in and he quickly shut the door. His gaze was averted. "I was going to text you tomorrow and ask you to meet. I was just trying to finish up some work for Marco," he said as they walked into the living room. His laptop was open on the sofa and takeout containers littered the coffee table. He picked them up quickly. "Sorry, I wasn't expecting company."

She bit her lip. This was going to be more difficult than she thought. "It's fine, Max. I'm sorry to barge in like this. We...I thought it would be easier just to take the bull by the horns," she finished lamely.

He stood holding the containers and eyed her. "Another saying, Francesca? But you used it correctly, and it's spot on, I guess. I'll be back in a second."

She stood frozen and waited for him to return. "Please sit down," he said, indicating a plush chair opposite from the sofa. He was being so odd and polite. She felt her heart plummet to her feet. Balancing on the edge of the chair, she stared at him. They both spoke at the same time

"You first," he said. "I imagine you're here to give me your ring back."

She felt the color drain from her face, and she fingered the ring on her hand protectively. "No, I wasn't...Max, I really have to explain everything to you."

"I saw the photo," he said. "I get it. Mario and you have a history and he doesn't come with any baggage like I do."

"Max, that's not true!" Francesca protested. "And where did you see that photo?"

"It was online in an American tabloid," he said. "My mother sent it to me."

"Your mother?"

He gave a twisted smile. "Yes, my mother. I have one like everyone else. I had told her about us. I was excited . . ." he broke off and looked away from her before continuing. "I needed to tell her after I introduced you to my grandparents. I wanted her to hear about everything from me. Anyway, she saw it first. She texted me the photo while I was waiting for you at your home the day after the gala."

"Oh," Francesca said inanely, trying to swallow. "Listen, Max, it wasn't anything."

"It sure looked like something," he commented dryly.

"Will you just listen to me!" she burst out. "Mario was just using me! He staged the whole thing to make a woman in America jealous."

"Did you know that when you kissed him?"

She nodded and stared at her feet.

"And you went along with it?" Max asked roughly. "And you wore that dress to meet him? Were you trying to see if there was an attraction?"

Putting a hand to her hot cheek, she rubbed her temple. "Yes . . . I mean, no. Call it vanity, I don't know. And then I went along with the photo but only to get him to go away. I wanted him to drop this whole betrothal stuff. He told me he'd release me and then you and I could resume . . ."

"Our farce?" Max asked, his eyebrow going up. "So you faked a kiss so you could go back to a fake engagement?"

"It wasn't like that! You're twisting my words. Will you just listen for a second?"

He ran a hand through his tousled curls, upsetting it further. "Francesca, I'm sorry. I . . . that's why I didn't want to have this talk until I was prepared. I needed time to process everything."

"You and your processing," she said, feeling the anger bubble up.

"What are you saying?"

"You needed time to process your talk with your grandfather. Now you need time to process your relationship with me. Max, has it ever occurred to you that you should just stop *processing*?" She enunciated the last word. "Really, what you do is shut down. You just don't want to deal with things."

"Okay, amateur psychologist, why do I do that?" he asked roughly.

"It probably stems from your horrific loss of your father," she said and shrugged. "You shut down when it happened, and then you couldn't think about it. You needed to just carry on and step in for him. That's really admirable, Max. But sometimes you have to just forge ahead and communicate about things. Not everyone has the luxury of processing first."

Standing, she prowled around the condo, walking over to the window with the view of Milan. Taking a deep breath, she felt guilty for her outburst. "I'm sorry. But it's the truth." She turned to him on the couch, looking defeated. She had never seen that look on his face.

"Max," she said urgently, starting to walk toward him.

He shook his head and stood, his expression clearing. "I don't know if you are right or not, but if you want, we can deal with everything now," he said. "Let's start at the beginning. I heard from a mutual source that Mario was back in Italy and that he never got married. I texted him, but he didn't answer. I wanted to tell you a few times if you remember. I hoped it wouldn't make a difference to you."

She smiled a little. "It doesn't. Do you understand about Mario then? It wasn't any of my doing, and he's gone now."

He nodded slowly.

She smiled. "Oh, good. Because I . . ."

"Francesca, it doesn't really matter in the end," he interrupted. "While I believe you, the situation ended up making something very clear."

She eyed him warily. "What is clear?"

"That we are wrong together. I'll never be in your class, Francesca," he said softly. "That whole gala was far more intense than I imagined. I'm not from this world. I can barely be a part of my own family's world. In fact, I've decided to go back home for a little while."

"Home?"

He nodded. "To the States. I'm going to return and decide where my life should be. Figure out where I belong."

"I thought you said it was here!" she exclaimed.

He shrugged. "I enjoy working for Marco. But we'll see. I have things to figure out. I think deep down, we both knew you and I would never work. It's not just the ridiculous feud, it's everything. I looked at you dancing in that ballroom, and I felt it even before Mario appeared."

Francesca sighed and tears welled up in her eyes. "That's not true, Max. None of it is. Do you think I'm some kind of snob? That my family is?"

He shook his head. "No, not at all. You . . . everyone has treated me with kindness. But I feel like an imposter. I'm just a kid from Seattle. Yet there's a part of me that belongs here as well. I need to figure out what is best for me."

"And what about me?" she asked softly.

He walked toward her, gently smoothing her hair from her face. "You're going to do big things, Francesca. You're the smartest, kindest, and most authentic person I've ever met. The moment you walked in the other night, you had control of that ballroom. You always will, no matter what room it is."

"But . . ."

His lips brushed her cheek, and with his finger, he gently rubbed a tear away. "It's so much better this way."

She nodded, the lump in her throat making it difficult to talk. "I should go," she finally uttered.

"I'll see you out," he said.

Pride now had swelled within her. She wasn't about to tell him she had on a light jacket, and it was freezing outside. Then she remembered she had no purse and no money. It didn't matter. She was too miserable to care.

They walked to the door together, and he opened it. She hastily took off the ring and handed it to him.

"Please keep it," he said roughly. "Donate it, melt it down. I don't care. It doesn't matter."

She felt a searing pain at his words. Slipping it into her pocket, she eyed him coolly. "You're right, Max. It doesn't matter." And then she hurried away, down the hall and out of his life.

*thirty-one*

F rancesca exited Max's building. Blindly, she took a right and started walking. The fresh air felt great at first. She had no idea how long or far she walked, her mind mentally retracing everything he just said. It hadn't mattered about Mario. Max had made up his mind even before that by the sound of it.

It was only when she ended up on a darkened street, teenagers laughing in a deserted park, that she got a little nervous. Walking quickly toward a well-lit street, she picked up her phone. Arianna was gone for the week at a conference in Switzerland.

She longed to call Kate, but what if she hadn't told Marco about her involvement yet? Biting her lip, she hit the only number of someone she knew who might be in Milan.

Ten minutes later, Alfonso roared up in a bright red Ferrari. He quickly got out and ran to her, embracing her tightly. "Francesca, *Dio*, you're freezing." Ushering her in the car, he immediately turned up the heat. "I'll drive you home," he told her, his tone comforting.

She appreciated her old friend didn't ask her any questions.

Instead, he chattered nervously about his last few soccer matches, how much he was enjoying the team and still worried about fitting in.

"You're going to do great," Francesca said with false brightness. She was truly happy for Alfonso, but it was difficult to sound excited when her heart was shattered. "This is a really nice car," she remarked absentmindedly.

He nodded and grinned. "All the players get them," he said smugly. "I hope you will come to another match soon."

"I'd love to," Francesca answered truthfully.

"I'm sorry I wasn't able to come to the royal gala and see your debut," he commented. "We were on the road."

She gave a bitter laugh. "Oh, it doesn't matter. I didn't invite any of my friends. I was trying to keep it low-key."

He glanced at her but turned his eyes back to the dark road. "That photo I saw didn't seem too low-key."

"Which one?" she asked dully.

"There's more than one?" he asked. "The photo with you dancing, and it said you had two fiancés."

"Oh, that one. Well, yes, but it wasn't really true."

He nodded. "We don't have to talk about it if you don't want to," he told her quietly.

"Thank you, Alfonso. You're a good friend."

FRANCESCA CAREFULLY DROVE her father's luxury sedan toward Verona. It had been a month since she walked out of Max's condo and his life. A lot had occurred in that month. Admittedly, she had stewed and mulled things over for some time at home. Initially, her family had tip-toed around her. Even Luci hadn't said a word, probably under severe duress from her parents. Francesca's grandparents visited many times and had been oddly silent about anything to do with her.

One day over breakfast, Francesca calmly announced she was returning to Positano to pack up her things. She saw her mother glance quickly at her father.

"What are your plans?" Carlo asked gently.

She shrugged. "While I love the Amalfi Coast, I feel like it would be moving backward to go there. I think I want more. I'm just not sure what that is."

She had given Allegra most of her furniture and donated the rest. The only thing she took were her clothes and personal items. Calling Marco to officially resign had been the most difficult of her tasks, and she had agreed to meet him to discuss it.

It was over lunch that she learned he had flown down specially to see her. It warmed her heart to see how much he cared.

"Is this about Max?" he asked roughly. "What did my cousin say when you went to his flat that night?"

"Katie?" she asked, her eyebrows raised.

"Broke down and told me everything that night."

Francesca gave him a small smile. "She was right. I needed to take the bull by the horns. Only the bull didn't want me."

He covered her hand with his. "Tell me what happened."

An hour later, she had spilled the entire story to Marco from the time Max walked in her front door to their agreement, to Mario's re-entry into her life.

"*Mio cugino* is an idiot," he commented, sipping his wine. "It's amazing we're related."

She giggled and dabbed at her eyes with her napkin. "I'm sorry I've taken up so much of your time."

"Don't be sorry, Francesca. Katie and I are your friends. I am pleased Alfonso was there for you."

She looked at him with surprise because she'd purposely had left that part out. Skimming over how she had gotten back to Verona had been intentional. She didn't want Marco asking why she didn't call him first. Biting her lip, she stared at him. "Alfonso ratted me out?"

He laughed. "No, never that. He was concerned and he . . . well, he knew I would be as well."

She shook her head and hung her head. "It was ridiculous of me to think Max would just welcome me with open arms."

"He should have! What in the world is he thinking? All this talk about not being good enough. He's a Rinaldi, for goodness' sake!"

She raised her head and laughed. "That's true. But I think in the end, Max has a lot to process," she said, trying to keep the bitterness out of her tone.

"He'll never do better than you!" Marco proclaimed.

At her silence, he continued to sit back and observe her. "And you're sure moving back home is the right thing to do?"

She shrugged. "It's only temporary until I can figure things out. But I want to move forward. I'm grateful for everything you've done for me, Marco. You were always there for me. You're a good friend."

He smiled. "Always."

She straightened in her chair and leaned forward earnestly. "I'd like to return the favor, Marco. If I can lend my name to the Angelo Foundation, I will. That is, if you think it will help in any way."

"I would be proud to have your endorsement," he said solemnly.

She shrugged and gave a wry smile. "This royalty thing *does* come with a few perks."

MAX SAT OUTSIDE on the ferry's deck, gazing at Seattle's skyline. It was freezing outside, and everyone else with half a brain was sitting inside the heated area. He felt the mist hit his face and roughly wiped it off.

He hadn't been long in the Seattle area. First, he traveled to New York and checked in with some business contacts, half wondering if he should return to his life there. It had only taken three days for him to realize that moving back to New York was not in the cards for him. While he had enjoyed his time there, everything seemed different. The city didn't look the same to him, and the magic had worn off. His friends were welcoming and kind, but even they asked why he would even think to choose New York over Italy. He struggled to explain and just murmured he was exploring his options. Exploring his options. That phrase came up a lot in recent conversations with his mother, his sisters. Francesca's name had been uttered, but the look he gave when it did had quelled any further questions.

When he left for the States, he had emailed Marco and asked him if it was a good time to take a few weeks off. He had finished his reports and could still work remotely if needed. His phone had immediately rung even though it was late in Italy. "What the hell do you need time off for?" Marco bellowed. "And what the hell are you doing in America? Max, we need to discuss this. I want my CFO here in Italy. If you're moving back to the States, then we'll have to talk about the best way to make a transition."

"I don't know yet," Max told him honestly.

"You don't know a lot of things," Marco grumbled.

Max sighed. "Is there something on your mind? I know you're probably upset about Francesca and me splitting up, but it was the right thing to do."

"Really?"

"Yes, really. We come from two different worlds."

"Please. I know an excuse when I hear one," Marco sneered.

"Oh, really?" Max said roughly. "What excuse?"

"You have stuff in your life you need to deal with, *mio cugino*. Katie taught me that the hard way as well."

"What do you mean?" Max asked.

"We both lost our fathers, and that's a lot to deal with. Your father died. My father chose to leave," Marco said. "That kind of grief stays with you."

"Have you been talking to Francesca? That's the kind of psychology stuff she was throwing around."

He heard Marco's snort. "Well, of course I talked with her. Someone had to. You thrust her aside with some ridiculous excuse about not being good enough. I don't know what the hell is wrong with you. You portray this confident man, like a Rinaldi should act. Then you throw over the most amazing woman and run away to the States when she gets too close. And she did, didn't she?"

Max frowned. "Sounds like you already have your opinion," he said coolly. "But the reality is you're not involved in this, Marco."

"You involved me when you treated my friend so poorly," Marco said angrily. "Thrusting her out your door with no coat, no money. What the hell were you thinking?"

The air whooshed out of his body. "What are you talking about?"

"Katie convinced her to hop in the car and take the bull by the horns. My lovely wife didn't notice that Francesca brought nothing with her. And she should have told Francesca if things didn't work out to call us immediately."

"Is she okay? What did she do?" Max asked, running his hand through his hair, frustrated.

"She called Alfonso, and he took her home."

"Why didn't she call you?" Max asked.

"She wasn't sure . . . uh, that Katie had confessed that she went down to see her. I told Katie it was none of our business."

"And it isn't," Max insisted.

"My wife is very emotional right now. When she's pregnant, she's like a human waterfall."

"Marco! That's wonderful news."

"*Grazie*. And now, you have some decisions to make. You have two weeks."

A click confirmed that Marco had hung up. Max stared at his phone for a minute. It would take time to process what Marco had told him.

# thirty-two

"You were the last people we expected to see here," Leonardo Valentini said roughly, after sitting down in the back room of a Milan *ristorante* with his wife. They stared across the table at Giancarlo and Antonia Ricci.

The Riccis glanced at each other uncertainly. "We didn't know you would be here either," Giancarlo answered sharply.

They hear high heels clicking on the marble. A figure emerged from the *ristorante's* double doors.

"Thank you all for coming," Margherita said from the doorway, smiling at them. "I appreciate you accepting my invitation." Sitting down, she made a slight gesture to the server, who came over and poured glasses of wine. He gave a small bow before departing, as if he also was in awe of her presence.

Margherita sat back, her expression serious. "I apologize for bringing you here under false pretenses, but I believe we all have the same desire. And that is always to see our children and grandchildren happy."

"Our grandson isn't even here," Leonardo interrupted briskly. "He's taken off for the States."

"And abandoned our granddaughter," Antonia retorted.

"After we graciously accepted him into the family, no less. Although he is a Valentini."

All four of them started talking at once, accusations flying across the table quicker than anyone could respond. Margherita sat back for a moment and watched before standing. "*Basta!*" she said, her voice rising above them. "You are acting like children. It is time for this ridiculous feud to end! I am here, way overstepping my boundaries as my oldest son would gladly tell you. But I am also here because I love both Francesca and Massimo, and I want to see them together."

Sitting again, she addressed the women. "Elisabetta and Antonia, you were once best friends," she observed.

"It's been many years," Elisabetta remarked.

"Too many," Antonia said softly. The two women stared at each other, each with tears in their eyes.

Margherita smiled a little. "That's a start." Now turning to the men, she said, "My assumption is that you are both too stubborn to end this feud on your own."

Giancarlo's dark frown was aimed at Leonardo. "We appreciate what you are trying to do, Margherita, but it's even worse now. Unless they can explain why their idiot grandson hurt our precious Francesca. She wouldn't hurt a fly."

"Gian!" hissed Antonia. "Be quiet! That's not going to help the situation."

He grimaced. "I know. But you also want to know why he left! Let's first get that answered!"

Elisabetta put a hand on her husband's arm to steady him. "The truth is, we do not know," she said quietly. "We saw that smug Mario Bianchini make a show at the gala. We were in disbelief when we saw the headlines."

"That has been taken care of," Antonia said firmly. "Francesca will no longer be bothered by him, and there certainly is no betrothal."

"Good!" Elisabetta said. "Massimo called before he left and

explained that Francesca had nothing to do with it. He also warned there would be another photo that would probably make its way into the Italian tabloids. But Massimo told us not to be angry and that she was doing her best to get him to leave her alone."

Antonia nodded. "She did not know that I had taken care of it. But if Massimo understood, why did he leave?"

Leonardo snorted. "That young man doesn't know which way is up sometimes. I tried talking to him! And what does he do? Take off for America the first time things get rocky here."

Elisabetta now glared at her husband before turning to them. "I think Massimo has always struggled with his own identity. It is difficult to grow up, a part of two countries," she said gently. "And though I . . . we, Francesca and I, that is, were happy that Leo and Massimo finally talked about things. I know my grandson. He takes a while to come around. It's also taking someone else time to come around." She glared at her husband. "Massimo is too much like his grandfather."

Antonia frowned. "Our son asked us not to bring up the subject with her. But I do know that Francesca told her mother some nonsense Massimo had in his head about not being good enough for her."

Leonardo leaned across the table, his eyes blazing. "That's not true! I can believe it! All this royalty nonsense. She probably made him feel inferior! Remember when you told me I should address you by your title?" he roared at Giancarlo.

Giancarlo looked embarrassed and glanced quickly at his wife. "A simple joke," he said weakly. "Alright, not a very funny one," he added. "I will admit that I was once caught up in that way of life. It was how I was raised," he said simply, laying his hands on the table. "And we only wanted Francesca to have a small taste of it in case it opened doors for her."

"It cost us our business," Leonardo pointed out.

"No, it wasn't that, and you know it, Leo!" Gian sat forward.

"It was your controlling nature. You wanted to do everything yourself. You would tell me about decisions *after* you made them. Important decisions!"

"That's a lie," Leonardo hissed.

The men stared at each other angrily for a moment. Margherita watched silently. Finally, she leaned forward, staring at them seriously. "Are you all aware that my husband left us when my sons were just small children?"

The men looked down at the table, and the women glanced nervously at each other. Antonia spoke first. "Yes, we have heard about it, Margherita. I've very sorry that happened to you. But what does that have to do with us?"

Margherita twisted her wine glass. "It's a long story. But let's say there was a disagreement of sorts in our own families. So much could have been solved with communication. I made peace with Giacomo before his death. It breaks my heart to think if only . . . if only we had talked more. If only I had taken seriously some of his feelings."

"How did you ever forgive him after that?" Antonia asked softly.

Margherita shrugged. "It takes so much energy to hate. I didn't want to live like that anymore. And he said he was sorry."

The room was silent.

Elisabetta suggested, "Perhaps we could all apologize."

"It's not that simple," Leonardo replied.

"Why can't it be?" his wife challenged him. She turned toward Antonia. "To be honest, I have wanted this feud to end for years. I miss you, Antonia." She held out her hand and after a moment's hesitation, Antonia grabbed it. "*Ti amo,*" Elisabetta whispered, tears welling in her eyes.

Margherita smiled at them. She turned to the men. "What can we do to make you move forward?" she asked abruptly.

Giancarlo raised his eyebrows. "I can forgive. It was a long time ago, if that's what you all want," he grumbled.

"If he forgives, I'll forgive too!" Leonardo said competitively. "But you're not talking about reconciling the business, are you? You left us with the headaches and the bills."

"You took our crest!" shouted Giancarlo.

Margherita rolled her eyes. "You once co-owned one of the best fashion houses in Milan. Don't you think there was some kind of magic there? Some reason that brought you together? Some kind of fate? And now fate struck again with Francesca and Massimo falling in love."

Antonia glanced quickly at her husband. "Gian and I were just talking about returning to Milan to start something new. Something that would involve our granddaughter."

Elisabetta startled. "Francesca? She told me she wasn't a designer."

Antonia shook her head slowly. "Well, no. We recently learned that Arianna is quite the designer. We had no idea. We'd like to give her a start. But now that you mention it, Francesca would excel at being part of a sales team. She understands how to dress women."

She sat back and looked at her husband. "Giancarlo," she said softly. "Think of it. Our granddaughters involved in fashion."

"Antonia, we have only begun to discuss it. There would have to be many steps before we could think about it. We'd need a solid business plan."

Leo stared at them before clearing his throat. "We had a successful business plan."

"That was a long time ago," Giancarlo commented.

Leonardo stared at him thoughtfully. "Think about it. We could start again. This time, I promise we would be equal partners."

Elisabetta grinned. "And think about it. We could also involve our grandson. He would have to return, and he would have a role, a place with his family."

The four of them stared at each other for a moment.

Margherita smiled at them all. "Now we are getting somewhere! And I want to remind you all that business should be the least of your priorities."

Giancarlo glanced at her, confused. "What could be bigger than the business?"

"Our future great-grandchildren," Antonia said, smiling at Elisabetta.

# thirty-three

"What do Nonna and Nonno want to speak to us about?" Francesca asked, forming dough into tortellini. "And why do I have to make a special dinner? It's Sunday. They know it is everyone's day off."

"They didn't tell me anything," Caterina replied. "Just what I've already told you. They asked Ari to come down, which thankfully she agreed to. I don't know what they have on their minds."

Francesca sighed and finished with the *tortellini*. She went to the sink to wash her hands. "Everything is finished until it's time to cook it. I guess I'll just change, and we can have a drink before dinner. Something tells me we're going to need it."

An hour later, Francesca's mouth dropped open when her grandparents entered the living room. Right behind them stood Elisabetta and Leonardo Valentini. She rose automatically to kiss her grandparents. "This better be good," she whispered in Nonna's ear.

Her grandmother's eyes twinkled, and she beamed at Francesca. "Francesca, greet the Valentinis. They have driven down from Milan just for this meeting."

Francesca frowned quickly at Nonna but quickly smiled a little, greeting them formally with a kiss on each cheek.

"*Buonasera*," she said quietly.

"You're probably wondering why we are here," Elisabetta said. "But I'm going to let your grandparents start the conversation."

Francesca turned to Caterina, shooting a confused look at her husband. Francesca sighed. At least her parents weren't in on whatever her grandparents' plot was. And it was a big one, based on the smugness of their expressions.

Everyone sat, and drinks were served. Giancarlo said, "We want you all to be the first to know that the Riccenti Fashion House is once more!" he said. "It is going to be re-worked by both of us," he said, tipping his glass toward Leonardo. "The Ricci crest will be released and once more be a part of the branding."

"But how . . .?" stuttered Francesca.

Elisabetta smiled gently at her. "That doesn't matter now, dear. We are happy to be reunited."

Antonia nodded. "And we want Arianna to come on board as a designer, and you to head up sales, Francesca."

Francesca shook her head. "I know nothing about running a sales department," she said slowly.

"I do," Antonia promptly replied and smiled. "And so does Betta. We were both excellent, weren't we?" Her smile grew wider. "And you have had plenty of experience in sales."

"But I . . ." Francesca started to say. She turned to her sister. Arianna's smile couldn't be any bigger. Her parents clasped hands in astonishment.

"What do you say, *Topo*?" her father asked gently. "Do you need time to think about it? Don't feel pressured," he whispered. "It may not be for you."

She shook her head, taking in the celebratory atmosphere.

Swallowing hard, she finally answered. "I think it's a wonderful idea."

MEETINGS STARTED in a flurry at the revamped company. Francesca moved in with Arianna temporarily until she had time to look for a new place. Tentatively, she had approached her grandparents about asking Marco for business advice. She assumed they would rebuff her, but her grandfather readily agreed. "A sound idea, Francesca. We will set something up."

Over the next few weeks, she watched her grandparents in meetings, laughing and excited. They looked years younger as they enthusiastically bent over charts and graphs on a computer. Meanwhile, Francesca delved into the current company's operation and finances as well. Max had been right. Things were chaotic at best, and it was obvious sales weren't just in a slump. They had stalled out. It was a surprise then to see that the offices and the salons were freshly painted and sported new furniture and functional office space.

"That was Massimo's doing," Elisabetta had informed her when Francesca inquired. "He saw immediately that we needed to invest in our surroundings to attract new personnel. We put some of our personal savings into it," she explained. "The company has had little profit, but Massimo convinced us that we needed to modernize the computer systems and he helped Leo hire a few people to begin the process."

Francesca bent over her laptop and tried to focus. She didn't hear her grandmother approaching until she spoke. "Francesca, there you are, dear. We're having our first directors' meeting today. We have hired an excellent Chief Executive Officer. I know we already told you our plans, but it's final. We all agreed someone other than Leonardo or Giancarlo should run this company. We intend to just be advisers," she said with a smug smile. "You'll see him at a meeting this afternoon."

Francesca glanced down. "Nonna, there is nothing on my calendar," she said, looking confused. "Are you sure it's today?"

Her grandmother waved a dismissive hand. "An oversight, my dear. Things are happening quickly around here. We'll see you soon!" Francesca watched her grandmother happily depart, almost skipping down the hallway.

Shaking her head, she sat back in her comfortable leather chair, overwhelmed. It would be some time before she would understand and feel confident in her new role. Turning to her laptop, she began the tedious task of evaluating the timetables for launching new lines. It was going to take a lot of effort. In fact, she had visited her sister already bent over an electronic drafting table in a room filled with fabric swatches and mannequins. Sewing machines sat empty near a wall.

"Isn't this wonderful, Frannie?" Arianna said, grinning. "I haven't slept for two weeks. I just keep drawing and drawing."

Francesca was thrilled for Arianna and her grandparents. There was just a piece missing. This had been Max's idea and now things were finally coming together, and he wasn't there to see it. Her heart still ached at the mere thought of him and daily she wondered if working so closely with his grandparents was good for her. Still, she felt compelled to help re-launch the business. Perhaps once it got successful again, she could move on and accept a life without Max.

Her watch revealed it was time for the afternoon meeting. Hopefully, they had made a wise decision with this hire. The Chief Executive Officer was vitally important to the success of the business. Gathering her laptop, she straightened her slim skirt and put her matching brown jacket on over her cream silk blouse. Might as well look her best when she met this new employee. Technically, he would be her boss. Smoothing her hair, she walked down the hall toward the large conference room. Opening the door, she entered and saw the pleased expressions of her grandparents and the Valentinis. Smiling a little in greeting, she glanced to her right.

"*Ciao,* Francesca," Max said softly. He was standing at the head of the table in a gray suit, wearing a violet tie. His hair had been tamed in a style. He smiled slowly at her, but his gaze was unreadable.

She stood frozen in the doorway.

"Come in, Frannie," her grandfather urged. "We spoke to Marco as you suggested, and he had an idea. We have a lot to talk about."

Francesca's heart raced and her knees wobbled. "I . . . I can't," she stammered. Her eyes widened at Max. "I need time," she muttered, turning away.

"Time for what?" Antonia asked loudly, watching Francesca's fleeing back.

"To process it," Max told her quietly.

thirty-four

Francesca walked slowly across the *Ponte di Castelvecchio*, following her long run. She zipped up her sweatshirt a little and shivered. It had been two days since she had bolted from the conference room. She had borrowed Arianna's car and driven home as fast as she could. She needed to be in Verona to think, back to her majestic bridges and calm water. Taking a deep breath, she felt calmer. Even the air smelled better in Verona.

She knew her parents had learned about Max's arrival from her grandparents. They sensed her desire not to talk and instead gave her the space she needed. Still, she felt their troubled eyes on her and Luci was oddly quiet. It was disconcerting. She found the most peace, going on long runs or walking through the city, letting her mind unravel what had just occurred. Of course, there was no way she and Max could work at the House of Riccenti together. That was unthinkable. But seeing him again almost physically hurt her heart. She would have to find something else to do. While it was a dream come true to see her grandparents revive their fashion house as well as work beside her sister, it would be too much to work alongside Max. What were they thinking? What was he thinking?

Swinging her leg back, she kicked one of the stone railings of the bridge in frustration. Her foot, clad in a running shoe, instantly felt sore.

"That's a good way to break your foot."

Max.

She turned to see him standing a few feet away. He was wearing a sheepskin jacket, his curls blowing in the wind, tousled as usual. He stared at her, his expression unreadable. "Were you imagining that to be my head?"

She turned back to look at the river, choosing not to answer him. "I told you I didn't like surprises," she said flatly. She remained silent for a minute. "How did you know where I was?" she finally asked in a wooden voice.

"Um, binoculars?"

She frowned at him darkly. "Is Luci spying on me again? I told her to stop!"

He walked toward her and leaned down on the bridge's balustrade. "I asked her to," he said softly.

"Why?"

"Why did I ask her?" he asked, glancing warily at her. "Or why did I leave you? Or why have I come back?" His eyes searched her face.

"All of the above," she whispered.

He stood and stared at her. Her ponytail had come loose, and strands of hair blew around her face. He tenderly touched it, sliding it behind her ears. She stepped back, as if his touch burned.

"I asked her to find you because I wanted to talk to you," he said quietly. "I left because I'm an idiot. That's been the most agreed upon term between Marco, my mother, my sisters, as well as my grandparents. And I came back because I want to build a life. A life in Italy and a life with you."

He was staring at her so tenderly, she felt a lump grow in her throat. "You want a life with me?" she asked roughly. Suddenly, she was angry. Angrier than she had been in her whole life.

"I realize that I am asking a great deal," he said slowly, his expression guarded. "I left a very confused man. But I have much more clarity now."

"You do?" she asked skeptically.

"Oh, yes," he said, smiling a little. "A very smart psychologist summed it up for me. It still took me a while, Francesca, but I realized you were right. I had a lot of unfinished business. I did a lot of soul searching, and then it just came to me."

At her raised eyebrows, he continued. "I never felt more at home than when I was with you. You're my home. So it doesn't matter if we are in Italy or America or you decide to pack our bags for somewhere else. I'll go because you're home for me."

"What about all that 'you're not in my class' business?" she asked, trying to keep the bitterness out of her voice.

"I was wrong about that, too. While my bloodline is not royal like yours, it's pretty darn good," he said with a slight grin. "I'll always feel half Italian and half American, but it's time I got over myself and realized I have a lot to offer you if you'll let me."

She couldn't help a tear from sliding down her cheek. He gently stroked it away. This time she stood frozen at his touch.

"Make no mistake, I will be in awe of you every day as you will always bewitch me, fascinate me, and make my heart race. But I'll be proud of you and grateful that I found you. If I promise to continue to love you to the end of our days, do you think you would be interested in building that home with me? I am desperately in love with you."

The tears were falling more rapidly, and she wiped them away impatiently. Stepping away from him, she took a deep breath.

He looked at her, concern in his eyes. "Francesca?"

She stared at him through her tears. "I've waited for you to say that."

"And now? Did my stupidity kill my chances with you?"

"Of course not, Max!" she said sharply. "But for once in my life I'm going to have a spine. You can't just come back and make everything better with a kiss on a bridge. You were the one who told me my old insecurities would come out at the strangest times. And guess what? They did and they have. And it's taken me weeks now to put myself back together. Then our grandparents sweep me into this business, and it's been overwhelming and exciting. But mostly bittersweet."

"Bittersweet?"

She nodded. "Because you weren't here!" She swore softly in Italian. "And I love you, too!"

When he reached for her, she backed up even more.

"But now it's my turn. I'm finished with everyone telling me what to do. We play by my rules or forget it!"

"What are your rules?"

"You gain my trust back. We'll work together at the business and start to build something. And then personally, we'll date again. Slowly," she said firmly. "And only after I am sure . . . we both are sure . . . that we should move forward."

He cautiously advanced, his hands sliding up and down her arms. She was trembling now. "Forward to what?" he questioned softly.

She gazed up at him. "Forever."

epilogue

"Nonna said you need to wear it," Arianna insisted, her mouth firm. "I styled your hair specially to hold it in place." In her hand, Arianna held the family's tiara. With its pink tourmalines and diamonds, it dated back to the eighteenth century.

Francesca smiled at her sister's reflection in the mirror behind her. "I appreciate you doing my hair for our wedding, Ari, but that thing is not going on my head."

"I'm going to wear it when I get married," Luci said confidently as she twirled in her violet-colored bridesmaid dress. Isabella snorted. "Of course you will. But first we just have to get Francesca married.

Arianna shrugged and gently set the tiara on the vanity. Caterina, who had been sitting on the bed, wiping tears from her eyes, spoke up. "I have a compromise. Every Ricci bride has worn it," she pointed out. "What if you put it on for a few photos? The ones you wanted to take down at the *Ponte di Castelvecchio*."

"Those are for Max and me," Francesca protested. "It's where he proposed again." At her mother's frown, she gave in. "Alright, Mamma, just a few photos."

Max only requested photos taken at the bridge because it was special to them. The first time they'd visited the bridge, he'd realized his life was changed forever. They had reunited there, and, months later, Max had proposed again.

After Francesca had declared they needed to date each other slowly, Max had willingly complied. She had dug the ring out of her jewelry box where she had stuffed it in sadness and gave it to Max solemnly. He had silently pocketed it.

They spent their days creating a business plan and revitalizing the company. Max had hired a well-known publicist who had helped them announce the merger of the two families and the re-introduction of the House of Riccenti. The energy behind the company was growing and their days were hectic. They often didn't even see one another, except for meetings.

At night, they went on dates, some casual and some more formal. It was different this time. Francesca found Max opening up much more and because of that, she felt confident to share her innermost thoughts with him. There was nothing they couldn't talk about, and they spent hours absorbed in each other. Christmas came and went, a bustle of activity, and they spent it together with Francesca's family. His grandparents were guests for Christmas dinner.

A visit home for Sunday dinner on a February night turned into a walk on the *Ponte di Castelvecchio*. The sun was setting in the cold sky, and Francesca was completely content, facing the pink and gold sky with Max's arm around her. She was startled when he withdrew his arm, and a rustle revealed him down on one knee.

She said yes before he could even speak.

"You're supposed to let me propose," Max teased.

Francesca apologized and listened while Max spoke. It was adorable that he was nervous. "Francesca, it seems like a long time ago that I bought this ring for what was intended to be an engagement that wasn't real. Somehow, I knew even then that I wanted it to become real. But we had a lot to learn, you and me. About each other and ourselves. I said I would play by your rules, and I hope I have earned your trust again. Your love again. But I am getting eager for you to be my wife. Will you marry me? Accept this ring for real this time?"

She hauled him to his feet and kissed him, admiring the ring again on her finger. "Better tardy than ever," she said, beaming up at him.

He looked confused. "Better late than never," he said with a laugh.

She gave a little wave. "Whatever. It's back where it belongs."

Glancing up, she gave him a questioning look. "Why now? Why today?"

He smiled. "It's February fourteenth. La Festa di San Valentino. Or Valentine's Day, as we call it in the U.S. I know it's a cliché, but after all, it is part of my last name. And so on this day, it seemed fitting to ask you to become a Valentini."

She smiled, pulling his head down for a kiss. "It's perfect. *Buon San Valentino,* Max."

"YOU SHOULD HAVE KEPT your crown on," Max said, twirling her on the dance floor at their wedding reception, bringing her closer to him. "I found it strangely very sexy," he breathed in her ear.

"It's a tiara," she told him with a teasing frown. "And that's the last time you will see it on this head."

"I'll have photos," he whispered. "Have I told you how beautiful you look today? And happy," he added.

"You have mentioned it," she said, smiling up at him. He

bent and gave her a brief kiss. "I'll tell you more later," he said huskily.

The couple had opted to marry in the Basilica di San Zeno Maggiore in Verona with a reception at the vineyard. Their grandparents had been less than thrilled, since their sights had been on a magnificent wedding in Milan.

Max and Francesca had held firm, and the grandparents had grumbled but relinquished. They were more intent on the wedding occurring. Max's mother, stepfather and sisters flew in, and Francesca had spent a wonderful week getting to know them.

"I like your Mamma," she told him. "And your sisters and my sisters are having a wonderful time together."

"Everyone is having fun," Max said. "Though it was so nice of Margherita to offer the lemon grove, I'm glad we decided to stay in Verona."

Francesca smiled. "I had the most amazing talk with her. Did you know she played a hand in all this? Ending the feud, I mean."

Max grinned back. "I heard. For once, Marco told her to meddle and thank God she did. She ended the feud. Something you and I hadn't done."

"We could have eventually done it," Francesca said smugly. "We hadn't even gotten to that point yet."

"If you think so," Max teased and whirled her around.

Francesca glanced over to where Kate was sitting, laughing with Teresa. "I'm so happy to see all my friends. I'm glad Marco and Katie made it. Katie's almost due, and she said she was afraid Meara would lock her in a hospital room since she had complications last time."

"Katie looks uncomfortable, but she wouldn't have missed this for the world," Max remarked, glancing over. "We have wonderful friends and family. Stefano was in overseeing the catering staff, and Teresa planned the spa day for you and the girls."

"I appreciated Ellie decorating the cake, and it's so beautiful," Francesca added. "And Meara was the one who actually helped me choose my dress. She has an eye. Maybe we should hire her!"

Max laughed. "I don't think Alec wants to leave Rome, and besides, she would want my job!"

"Not a chance," Francesca reassured him. "You're too great at it. Did you see your Nonno cry during my dance with him?" Francesca said. "I never thought I'd see it. Everyone is so happy."

Max grinned. "Everyone but Alfonso," he said, nodding his head toward where Alfonso was standing with Marco in the corner.

"It looks like they are arguing," Francesca said, watching closely. Marco put an arm on Alfonso's shoulder and was intently discussing something with him. "Should I go see if I can help?"

"Leave Marco to handle it," Max said. "After all, he helped get me on track eventually. And here we are . . . finally."

Francesca grinned up at him. "Verona wasn't built in a day," she said.

"Rome," he corrected.

She looked smug. "I like my version better."

# *upcoming books*

Looking for your next sweet romance from Italy?

Check out the next in the series—
Alfonso and Lena's Story:
My Lake Como Love

E-Book Available Now!
Paperbacks available at Amazon or your favorite bookstore

## MY LAKE COMO LOVE: CHAPTER ONE

Alfonso Bellini stood at the curved gray-stone railing of his sweeping balcony, the deep blue expanse of Lake Como shimmering below. Despite it being a spring day, the sky was darkening and the threat of rain was ominous. The mountains rimmed the lake in the distance, dark shadows with snow still capping their peaks.

It was unusual for Alfonso to have idle time on his hands, and he rubbed his face in frustration. Perhaps he had made the wrong choice. He longed to be at home, or what he used to call home: his beloved Positano. Born and raised in the seaside town on the Amalfi Coast, he had experienced an idyllic childhood with his parents Enzo and Gina. Their love had seemed so effortless, so completely ordinary. They were a happy threesome, tending to their small ceramics shop that sold planters, dishware, ceramics, and linens that were locally crafted. Alfonso went to a nearby school, and encouraged by his father, he played *calcio*—what he later learned was called football in much of the world, and in America, soccer. As he grew, so did his *calcio* skills. His heart swelled with joy and pride seeing his parents in the stands cheering him on as he played a sport he adored. Despite their simple lifestyle, the family was content and grateful for their little piece of serenity. Their bond was unbreakable. Until it wasn't.

Alfonso rubbed his eyes again. Even now as a grown man, he couldn't forget the day his father's best friend, Angelo Rinaldi, came with the local *poliziotto* to tell him that his parents had been killed in a car crash. They had left early that morning, driving to Naples to meet a renowned ceramics dealer. It was to be a big sale they had boasted that would greatly benefit the family.

The days following had been surreal for him. At seventeen years old, Alfonso's whole world was ripped apart in an instant.

Angelo, who had been like an uncle to him, immediately sprang into action. A wealthy entrepreneur who founded and operated a company called Oro Industries, Angelo was used to taking charge. While Alfonso sat in a chair staring off into space, Angelo made the dreaded phone calls to friends. There was no family. His parents, raised in the Lombardy region near Lake Como, had long lost their parents and though there was said to be cousins around, they had moved away and were sprinkled around Italy. After marrying, Gino and Enzo moved to Positano to begin their life together and then later welcomed their only child.

Angelo's first call had been to his nephew, Marco. A short time later, Marco burst through the door of the small shop and swept Alfonso into his arms. It was only then that Alfonso gave himself permission to cry. Marco was like an older brother to him, and his presence enveloped him and provided comfort in a way no one else could. When Alfonso was a young teenager, Marco came to live in the family's small two-bedroom home carved into one of Positano's hills. Angelo was determined to tame his nephew's wild ways and believed that living simply would do just that. At first, Alfonso had been awkward and shy, sharing his bedroom with the charismatic and handsome man in his early twenties. While Alfonso had known Marco his entire life, since their mothers were close, Marco was older and had paid little attention to him. But now sharing the same roof, Alfonso eagerly observed him, quietly yearning to be like him. Marco softened under the kind guidance of Enzo and Gina, who worked hard and expected Marco and Alfonso to do the same. It wasn't all about work, though. Marco seemed to soak in the family time, sitting around the table, following a delicious fresh meal prepared by Gina. That was their time to laugh and tell stories.

Alfonso questioned Marco about his own childhood one evening as they lay awake in the darkened bedroom. Marco had shifted on the opposite twin bed, finally sitting up to face him. Despite the shadows obscuring his face, Alfonso could see the grim set of his jaw and his sad expression. Marco confided in him about his father, who had left his mother when he and his two younger brothers, Stefano and Niccolo, were young. While he adored his mother and was close to his brothers, he never felt the unbreakable closeness of doting parents. Even with Angelo's unwavering love, he always felt different from other families. That, plus a learning disability, had hampered him as he grew up. Later, as Marco helped Alfonso navigate life without his parents, Marco confided how much their unconditional love impacted him.

Despite Marco's assistance, the first couple of years following the loss of Alfonso's parents were difficult. Alfonso soon learned his parents had faced unknown challenges. He was shocked to learn it was Angelo who owned his parents' small ceramic shop, investing in it during a time when the town was still sleepy, before tourism surged. Angelo immediately told Alfonso the shop was now his if that was his desire. He accepted, thinking he would naturally follow in his parents' footsteps. Marco's frequent visits bolstered him and helped him manage the business.

Fate intervened with the arrival of an acceptance letter to an elite soccer academy in Milan. In the turmoil following his parents' death, Alfonso forgot he had even applied. Encouraged by Angelo and Marco, he departed the only home he knew to attend the academy, reasoning to himself that his father would have wanted him to. His first few weeks were grueling, as professional coaches put him through the paces. He pushed himself to work hard, but in his mind, he knew his focus kept slipping.

When Alfonso's first match began with the initial whistle blow, a crushing wave of anxiety struck him, culminating in his first-ever panic attack. The familiarity of being on the pitch and the shouts of the spectators did nothing to ease his racing heart. Glancing into the stands, he knew rationally his parents would not be sitting there, but the raw reality hit him like a gut punch that they *never* would be sitting there. Crumbling to his knees, he could not stand. His teammates and coaches thought he had injured his leg, but he shook his head to dismiss them. Standing slowly, he walked determinedly off the pitch. Soon after, he packed and returned to Positano, declaring he would never look back.

That decision had been made with no thought of the blows still to come. Yet the hardship continued. Angelo fell ill, and after only a brief stay in hospital, passed away. The weight of the expansive corporation—the nation's largest exporter of olive oil and lemon products—fell on Marco's shoulders. Though he tried to be there for Alfonso, his visits grew hurried, his calls less frequent. Everything shifted, however, when Marco stepped back from the boardroom and returned to Positano, seeking distance from the anxious shareholders who doubted his leadership. It was during this turbulent period that he met Kate, the woman who would one day become his wife.

Alfonso smiled just thinking about that day. He had been there when Marco walked through the door of the ceramic shop carrying the pretty brunette in his arms. Kate had fallen and hurt her ankle upon arriving in Positano. Marco was immediately enthralled, and for some inexplicable reason, he cautioned Alfonso not to say anything about his billionaire status or that he ran a prominent company. Kate assumed Marco simply managed a ceramic shop. Things quickly unraveled as they fell in love, and Marco was forced to explain he had not been honest with her. Alfonso wished he had been there to see the look on Kate's face when she discovered she was dating the most eligible bachelor in Italy.

He still felt fortunate to have shared so many moments with the couple. After his parents' death, the entire Rinaldi family had enfolded him as one of their own. Angelo and Marco had been constants, but it was Marco's mother, Margherita, who became the most unexpected anchor. She had been so close to Gina that she seemed to understand his grief more deeply than anyone. Out of respect, he had always called her *Zia Rita*, but over time the title came to feel less formal—she truly was an aunt to him. Gradually, he also grew closer to Marco's brothers, finding his place among them.

Alfonso was no longer just a guest at family gatherings—he was one of them. He stood proudly at Marco and Kate's wedding, celebrated the cascade of family unions that followed, and rejoiced at the birth of their first child, Frankie. He had been in the front row at Frankie's baptism. Now Marco and Kate were celebrating the birth of their daughter, adorable Arabella.

During these last few years, Marco cajoled, encouraged, and finally threatened Alfonso to take to the pitch again. It felt different the second time. He began slowly, playing in local amateur leagues. When he looked in the stands, he always knew a member of the Rinaldi family or extended family would be there, even for the smallest of matches.

It soon became apparent that Alfonso's skills were way beyond those of his teammates or opponents. A scout helped place him in a *Serie D* league. That time was a blur as Alfonso honed his skills with almost a feverish intensity. *Calcio* became everything to him, and he rose through the leagues, eventually reaching Serie A. It was a surprise to him—but to no one else— when he was called up to the national team. He remembered the pride he felt, pointing at Marco and Kate who cheered him on during his first match. Stefano and his wife Teresa were there as well. But the voice that rang through the crowd the loudest had belonged to his good friend, Francesca. Alfonso had been friends with the statuesque blonde for years when she managed a shop in Positano. Once, she had confided in him that she was of royal lineage in Verona. Attending the match with her boyfriend Max, she yelled louder than anyone, pumping her fist in the air. Anyone looking less like a princess at that moment was

Francesca. Alfonso had been so proud he thought his heart was going to burst.

His first two years had been heady. Given a Ferrari on signing, Alfonso's jubilation turned to disbelief when he seemed to become famous overnight. Photographers loved to capture his expressive face during matches. Women flocked to him. He grimaced at the memories. So many women. Most of them were models, draped in designer clothes, their makeup flawless. He brought them to every extravagant event in Milan. Now, he realized he had let it all go to his head, living dangerously on the edge in the limelight of what he knew now to be mostly a fake and empty world.

It was at Francesca and Max's wedding when Marco gave him a stern lecture about it all. Marco believed Alfonso was falling into the same trap he had when he first embraced his billionaire fame. Alfonso reacted angrily, pointing out rudely that he was an adult and he no longer required a lecture from anyone. He regretted the words flung at Marco that evening. Now he wished he had. Marco had been right, and now his world was in chaos. He was facing earth-shattering accusations that threatened his entire career, and the world believed him to be guilty.

Taking a deep breath, Alfonso squinted to watch the boats in the distance, bobbing happily on the lake or whisking travelers to their destinations. A ferry in the distance shuttled tourists. He was wary of the smaller boats that offered visitors tours of famous residences. He credited his publicist and a great deal of money with helping him keep it a secret that he owned a magnificent villa on Lake Como.

Soon it wouldn't matter. Who would want to try to catch a glimpse of a former great *calcio* star? Perhaps he should sell it instead of rattling around such an extensive property. But where would he go next? Though he stubbornly tried not to feel sorry for himself, he couldn't overcome the suffocating depression that loomed just on the edge of his mind. Turning, he strolled across the wide stone balcony, past inviting seating areas featuring luxurious outdoor furniture. Opening the French doors, he entered the villa.

Silence struck him, making almost a sense of loneliness wash over him. It was of his own doing, having cleared the enormous house of staff when he had returned last month. Not wanting prying eyes, he limited his staff, mostly to Armando, who had been with him for a while and whom he trusted. Alfonso counted on Armando to manage most of his personal life, from stocking the refrigerator with fresh food to overseeing Concetta, his housekeeper who now only came once a week to clean discreetly. Armando cooked for them some nights, but more often, he sailed over to other towns and picked up cuisine from local chefs, trying to entice Alfonso's appetite. Despite the delicious meals, Alfonso lost weight. Muscle would be next if he was not diligent about his daily workouts. In fact, glancing at his watch, he saw it was time to change and visit his elaborate exercise facility on the lower level.

As he walked toward his bedroom, Alfonso startled at a thundering crash. *Dio*, had someone crashed on the lake? He ran outside toward the stone railing again and glanced around. His stone jetty lay below. Filled with cobblestones, the blooming hydrangeas were surrounded by black lanterns that hung from low posts. It appeared calm and unharmed. Armando shouted at him from the wooden pier below on his left, and Alfonso finally saw the small boat. It had not only crashed into his larger vessel but also splintered part of his dock. Now it lay tipped on its port side.

Running quickly down the white stone stairs, Alfonso lithely jumped down to his private dock and ran past Armando. Seeing the extensive damage, his heart beat faster, concerned for the boat's occupants. Armando was right on his heels. Despite being in his early seventies, the older man was in phenomenal shape.

Peering into the unoccupied boat, Alfonso's gaze then darted around the area. Had the occupants been thrust into the lake? It was only Armando's shouts in rapid-fire Italian that drew his attention to his right, where a small figure was lying prone on a piece of the splintered dock. *Dio*, was she dead?

Dropping to his knees, he quickly assessed her. The woman looked to be near his own age and was wearing jeans and a yellow T-shirt. A life vest was twisted around her, with the straps dangling beside her. Blood matted her brown hair, which fell in a messy tangle to her chin. Her eyes were closed. He shook her shoulder, calling to her and then swearing in Italian. She didn't move. Behind him, Armando shouted that he was calling for an ambulance.

Nodding, Alfonso gripped the woman's hand. It was warm, and it brought him comfort, as he hoped it was a good sign. Soon he was aware of the sirens of the lake's patrol ambulance, and he frantically looked for it. Glancing back at her face, he was shocked to see a pair of gray eyes staring back at him. Heavily fringed with dark lashes, her beautiful eyes studied him.

He spoke to her in Italian, inquiring her name. She continued to stare back at him, her face calm and almost serene. A small smile came to her lips, and then she closed her lovely eyes once again with a sigh.

Alfonso's heart simply stopped at that moment. He shook her shoulder and shouted again for her to open her eyes. He checked her long neck for a pulse and was relieved when he found one. Aware of the ambulance arriving, he brushed a hand over his tousled curly hair. He shivered, either from the shock of the accident or simply the weather; the wind was picking up, and he could feel drops of rain on his exposed arms.

Medical personnel jumped onto his dock, carrying their equipment. They examined her quickly before carefully scooping her onto a backboard and carrying her onto the medical marine boat.

A medic ran back and inquired about her identity. Alfonso shook his head and told him he did not know. Perhaps it was his expression that caused the medic to ask him if he wanted to go with her. He nodded yes for no legitimate reason. He did not even know this woman, yet he leaped into the ambulance, calling out his intent to Armando. Armando stared at him, clearly confused. "Why are you going with this stranger?"

Alfonso looked down at the unknown woman lying still on the backboard, then back at Armando. "Because right now, I am all she has," he replied, returning his gaze to her. Over his shoulder, he called to Armando to pick him up at the hospital.

Without another word, the boat sped off, quickly cutting through the water. Spray lashed his face, but Alfonso's eyes never left the unconscious woman. His chest ached with the weight of an unspoken promise.

# *author's note to the reader*

Dear Reader:

Verona! My smile couldn't have been any bigger than when I arrived in this beautiful city. I'll admit it, I've seen *Letters to Juliet* a thousand times. And if you haven't, run to watch it!

Verona is a magical city, preserved in time and I enjoyed every minute—especially those cappuccinos and *cornettos* (yes, that coffee shop is real!).

Thank you to my daughters, who have also watched that movie with me and engaged in my obsession with Verona. Special thanks to my daughter, Delanie, who traveled to Verona with me in search of an amazing adventure. I learned if I faced any challenges, I definitely want her by my side.

If you want more...there is! Tour through more regions of Italy in this series: *From Italy with Love*. We travel all over, but we'll always swing by the Amalfi Coast to say hi to the family.

Grab some delicious pasta or a gelato and enjoy more from Italia! Remember to sign up for my newsletter at Tessrini.com/newsletter to read a bonus chapter from *My Secret Positano*.

Cin Cin!
XO, Tess

Tess Rini has spent her professional life focused on non-fiction writing, from her journalism degree to her editing and writing magazine articles and content for local government. She has published one non-fiction book under a different name.

Tess was raised on a self-induced steady diet of Harlequin romances and so it was inevitable that she should try her hand at romance writing. The idea took off when she combined her love of Italy with her love for romance novels.

When not writing, she can be found relaxing in her Oregon home, traveling or cooking Italian cuisine (her specialty!) for her husband, four daughters and son-in-law. Keeping her company while writing or watching Hallmark movies is her adorable, but anxious, golden retriever.

Sign up for her newsletter at Tessrini.com/newsletter to read a bonus chapter from *My Secret Positano* and stay up on all the latest Italy news.

Website: tessrini.com
Or follow her on social
Facebook @tessriniauthor
Instagram @tessrininauthor